PRETTY HOSTAGE

JULIA SYKES

Copyright © 2019 by Julia Sykes

All rights reserved.

No part of this book may be reproduced in any form or by any electronic or mechanical means, including information storage and retrieval systems, without written permission from the author, except for the use of brief quotations in a book review.

Cover design: PopKitty Design

Editing: Edits in Blue, Editing by Rebecca

For my readers,
and for the wonderful women in the Romance industry.

I owe you everything.

Thank you for your love and support.

CHAPTER 1

MATEO

"Tie her up," Adrián ordered, his voice clipped with impatience. My boss hovered on the brink of madness, but I would protect Sofia from him at any cost. If he tried to harm her, I'd attack him, no matter if he was my best friend.

Maneuvering her willowy body with care, I set her down on one of his straight-backed, wooden dining chairs. A length of rope lay on the table, waiting to bind her.

I gritted my teeth and reminded myself that Valentina's life was on the line. I'd help Adrián put on a little show in order to save the woman he loved.

A show. That's all this is.

He won't hurt Sofia.

My friend was ruthless, sadistic. And his obsessive

love for Valentina had only exacerbated those qualities rather than soothing them. As long as his love was in danger, Adrián would be volatile. His capacity for brutality eclipsed even my own.

He passed me the rope, pressing it insistently into my hands. Steeling my resolve, I quickly bound Sofia's wrists behind her back, tying her in place with expert speed. Rope came in handy in my line of work.

And in my darker sexual predilections.

Innocent, sweet Sofia didn't deserve any of this. I'd shielded her from my crueler impulses for years. I would shield her from Adrián's cruelty, too.

A low groan left her chest as she stirred back to consciousness. Instantly, I was on my knees before her. She sagged forward, her glossy, mahogany curls falling over her delicate features. I cupped her cheek in my hand, supporting the lolling weight of her head. Her skin was softer than I'd imagined in my fantasies. My fingers stroked her cheekbone before exploring the gently sloping line of her jaw.

"Do it properly," Adrián snapped.

I shot a glower at him over my shoulder, not breaking contact with Sofia. Now that I was finally touching her after long years of denial, I couldn't pull away.

My friend's pale green eyes glowed with fevered desperation that bordered on insanity.

"You do it, or I will," he threatened softly.

No fucking way. He wouldn't touch Sofia. Not when I could be the one to bind her.

Fuck.

How many times had I come in my hand thinking about having her at my mercy? I'd sworn I wouldn't defile her with my deviant desires, but now that I had her trapped and vulnerable...

My perversions were too deeply ingrained to deny. I liked how helpless she was.

My blood heated with a fiery cocktail of desire and anger. I was furious with Adrián for forcing me into this dark scenario that I'd always craved but had firmly suppressed for Sofia's sake. She was all lightness and purity, and as much as I coveted her, I'd never wanted to despoil that sweet innocence with my depraved urges.

I have to do this, I reasoned. Valentina's life depended on it.

Sofia's father, Caesar Hernández, had kidnapped Valentina in a power play to usurp Adrián. For a decade, Caesar had been a reluctant associate, helping my boss expand his cocaine empire throughout the west coast. Now, he'd chosen to ally himself with Adrián's enemy, Hugo Sánchez, and orchestrate a coup. Caesar planned to ingratiate himself with Hugo by offering Valentina to him as a gift.

Adrián wouldn't let Hugo have the woman he

loved, not even over his dead body. War was brewing in our organization, and we had to end it before it began.

Sofia was the key to our victory. Caesar might be a dirty, oily son of a bitch, but he doted on Sofia, his only child. Once he understood that we had her, I was certain he'd do anything to get her back, including throwing Hugo to the wolves and surrendering Valentina to Adrián.

Caesar was well aware of my brutal nature, as well as my perverted tendencies. The threat of sexual violence against his precious daughter would bring him back in line.

I retrieved a second coil of rope from where it lay on the dining table. When I drew it around her chest, my fingers skimmed beneath her breasts. I could feel her body heat through her thin purple dress, and I wondered if her skin hidden by the cotton garment was as soft as her cheek.

I fell into a methodical headspace, losing myself in the familiar tie as I drew the rope back over her breasts. Her faint, rosy scent permeated my senses, intoxicating me. All my focus honed on her: the unique, feminine way she smelled; her gentle warmth; the smooth bronze skin that peeked above the neckline of her dress.

My touch lingered there, trailing over the tempting swells of her breasts.

Sofia was bound. Completely vulnerable. At my mercy.

And my dick was getting hard.

When I drew the rope taut, her lashes fluttered, and she let out a husky moan that sounded almost like desire.

I swallowed a grunt, struggling to get my own desire under control. I tied the rope off behind her back, binding her breasts in a lewd display. A hungry growl rumbled from my chest, and I caressed her cheek again, utterly entranced.

I was dimly aware that Adrián was placing the video call to Caesar, his phone ringing loudly through the speaker.

The conflict between the two drug lords receded to the back of my mind. I couldn't stop touching Sofia. My fingers sank into her hair, testing the weight of her voluminous, perfect curls for the first time. They spilled over my fingers, their silky texture enthralling.

"*Princesa*," Caesar rasped, the endearment heavy with horror. "Get away from my daughter!" His shout echoed through the dining room, but it barely penetrated my awareness; my full focus was on Sofia.

She blinked slowly, the sparkling emerald of her lovely eyes peeking through her thick, dark lashes. "Daddy?" she slurred.

Possessive anger washed through me in a red

wave. *I* was touching her. She shouldn't be thinking of anyone else, not even her panic-stricken father.

My fingers tightened in her hair, commanding her attention. Her eyes lifted to mine, focusing on my face. A little shocked yelp left her pouty lips, and she tried to shrink away from me.

I wouldn't allow that. I couldn't.

My hand fisted in the curls at her nape, ruthlessly tugging her head back, so she was trapped under my stare. She trembled, her breaths coming faster as her pupils dilated. The rapid rise and fall of her chest made her breasts strain against my ropes. Savage hunger knifed through my gut, my arousal almost painful.

"What are you doing?" she asked breathily. She tried to twist away, her eyes widening when she realized I'd tied her up. Her struggles further incited my lust, and when she gasped my name, I almost lost control.

"Mateo."

Fuck, that little fearful hitch in her voice made my blood run hot in my veins. This was everything I'd ever wanted from her, and the fulfillment of my darkest fantasies awoke desire so keen, it set my teeth on edge.

A low, animal sound clawed from my chest, the primal need to conquer and claim overtaking my mind. My hand left her cheek to trail down her throat. I pressed my palm against her neck, my fingers coming to rest on her artery. It pulsed beneath my touch, so susceptible to the lightest pressure.

Her lips parted on a sharp intake of breath, and her gorgeous eyes remained trapped under my gaze. There was nowhere for her to run, no way to escape me. She was completely powerless under my hands and in my ropes.

Despite my raging desire, a strange sense of calm settled over me. After years of self-imposed, tormented denial, I finally had her thoroughly under my control. Half a decade of pent-up frustration melted away, and I indulged in the first physical contact with Sofia I'd ever permitted myself.

"As you can see, we have your daughter." Adrián's cold voice floated over my shoulder.

He was speaking to Caesar. Their conversation was none of my concern, and I hardly bothered to listen to the exchange. All that mattered was the woman bound before me, her breath coming in sharp little panting gasps and her lithe body trembling for me.

"Let her go," Caesar demanded.

Not fucking happening. My fist tightened in her hair, and her head dropped back farther. Her lips were offered up to me. I'd always wondered how lush and plump they'd feel.

I didn't hesitate to continue exploring her,

rubbing my thumb across her pretty mouth, tracing the soft *O* of her parted lips. The thought of sliding my cock over her tongue tormented me, but I would content myself with learning her body with my hands first. I wanted to take my time with her, to savor her. To worship her, even as I craved to see her kneeling at my feet and worshipping *me*.

"Don't hurt Sofia," Caesar begged. "She's innocent."

Innocent. The word threaded through my mind, penetrating the lustful haze.

Yes, Sofia was innocent. I'd wanted to keep her that way. I'd coveted her, but I'd always kept my distance.

My touch faltered on her face.

"So is Valentina," Adrián shot back at Caesar. "If you want your daughter to live, you'll welcome me into your home and allow me to kill Hugo. You've made a mistake, but it's one I'm willing to forgive. You're loyal to me from now on, or Sofia will suffer."

Oh, there were so many ways I wanted to make her suffer, and none of them involved my usual, bloody forms of torture. Forcing her to orgasm again and again until she wept for mercy would be a good start.

"Whatever you want," Caesar agreed desperately. "Just give her back to me. Don't hurt my little girl."

"I'll be at your house in twenty minutes," Adrián

told him. "Open your gate for me. And if you try to betray me again, Mateo will deal with Sofia. Don't tell Hugo what's happening. I won't risk him running back to Bogotá. He dies today."

"Yes," Caesar agreed quickly. "Just don't let that animal touch Sofia."

Animal. I certainly felt more like a beast than a man. My base desires for Sofia were savage, primal.

"I'm on my way." Adrián ended the call. "Stay with her," he ordered me.

I kept stroking her trembling body. "What am I supposed to do with her?" I asked absently. I had plenty of ideas, but ingrained loyalty to my boss pulled the question from my lips.

"Keep her," he replied, his footsteps retreating as he rushed off to rescue Valentina. "She's yours now."

Mine.

"Mateo," Sofia whimpered. "What's happening?"

I realized I'd fisted both hands in her hair, yanking her head back to expose her throat. I eased my hold, massaging her scalp in little circular motions. Her long lashes fluttered, her eyes sliding out of focus as her fear faded, and the tension eased from her neck and shoulders.

Seeing her bound and trembling was my most fevered fantasy come to life. But having her relax into my hands was something I'd never dared to imagine.

My dark thoughts about possessing her had always been strictly sexual in nature.

Now, she melted under my touch. Even though I knew she was sleepy from the drugs, it felt like trust.

Something strange and warm pulsed in my chest, completely foreign and immediately addicting. Sofia was far more precious than I'd ever realized. I craved more of this softness from her, a deeper surrender.

For years, I'd held myself back in the interest of preserving the innocence I found so appealing about her. I'd seen very few pure, sweet things during the course of my brutal life. Usually, I took what I wanted on greedy impulse if it was within my grasp; a toxic trait I'd internalized growing up in poverty.

Sparing Sofia had been the one selfless thing I'd ever done. She'd been within my reach—I'd even caught her regarding me with interest in the past—but I'd resisted corrupting her.

Now that I felt her softening and sighing under my touch, a new possibility opened before me. Maybe I could have everything I wanted: Sofia's sweet nature preserved and caged just for me. I could make her mine, ensure she submitted to even my most depraved demands. And she would do it all eagerly, serving me out of utter devotion.

This would require more finesse than forced seduction, but I found the outcome far more appealing. I could slowly condition Sofia to welcome my touch, to associate my hands on her body with pleasure and security.

By the time I was finished with her, she would beg to be mine.

My ruthless hands—so accustomed to bloody brutality—stroked her with tenderness that would have shocked me if I weren't so entranced by her.

"Don't be afraid," I murmured. "Go back to sleep. I won't let anything bad happen to you, *florecita*."

Sofia was as soft as a flower's petals, and as delicate. I could feel her fragile bone structure and the slender lines of her body beneath my gentle exploration. I was aware that she was musically inclined in her studies, and while she appeared physically fit, she obviously didn't occupy her time toning her muscles.

With my massive frame, I could easily overpower her without breaking a sweat. My sexual tastes had always been rough and demanding, but I'd have to handle this little flower with care if I didn't want to damage her. I could crush her with the slightest flex of my fingers, but I would be gentle for her.

Sofia was my hostage now, and although it was within my power to use her however I wanted, I still had enough humanity in me that the idea of rape disgusted me. Her father didn't know that, but his ignorance of my true nature worked in our favor.

Caesar Hernández knew me only as Adrián's brutal enforcer. He'd seen other men suffer and die at my hands, and I hadn't batted an eye as I carried out my violent tasks. Maiming and killing didn't bother me in the slightest, as long as the men I was dispatching deserved it. And in our criminal world, all of them did. Anyone who provoked Adrián was fair game. He might be my boss, but I loved him like a brother.

No one was permitted to hurt the people I loved. If they tried, they'd signed their own death warrant as far as I was concerned.

I had no other ambitions in life, no desire to gain power or influence; I was more than happy to take a supporting role and protect Adrián. I'd do anything asked of me.

Including holding Sofia hostage. That wouldn't be a hardship.

I hadn't stopped caressing and petting her, allowing myself to indulge in the heady pleasure of her softness beneath my hands while I had her bound and helpless.

Her lovely eyes closed, and she let out a long sigh as she slipped back into unconsciousness. Her fear had roused her for a time, but now that she felt safe, she succumbed to the drugs I'd administered.

Sofia didn't fear me. After I'd abducted her this afternoon, she had every reason to be terrified of me. She was either incredibly naïve, or she understood my protective instincts when it came to her. Probably the former, considering her father had shielded her from most of the ugly truths about our criminal activities.

But I preferred to think that she trusted me implicitly. I'd find out soon enough when she woke up in my home.

I freed her from the ropes that bound her to the chair, unable to stop myself from tracing the pretty indentations the braided pattern had left in her skin. I wished I could see the marks on other parts of her body: around her breasts, between her legs.

I took a breath and struggled to suppress my lust. I wouldn't be binding Sofia again. Not for a while, at least. Not until she submitted to it willingly. This had been purely for show to intimidate her father into cooperating.

Maybe keeping Sofia would be more of a hardship than I'd like to think. Having her in my home, watching her at all times without handling her as I wished, was going to be torture. I wasn't certain if I'd be able to survive the constant arousal that she incited within me, especially now that our relationship had taken a darker turn.

Keep her. She's yours now. Adrián's words played through my mind. He'd issued an order, but he'd also given me a gift.

Mine.

I'd tried to save her from myself, unwilling to taint her purity with my bloody hands. With a few words, Adrián had given me permission to take what I'd longed for.

I wrapped my arms around her, scooping her up and holding her against my chest. I was cautious not to grip her too hard, cradling my precious possession with aching care.

I barely watched where I was walking as I carried her out of the house and to my waiting car; I couldn't take my eyes off her angelic face. She appeared relaxed and peaceful in my arms. The hunger I'd always felt for her sharpened, becoming so keen it was almost painful.

Yes, I craved more of this: more of her beauty and light in my ugly, dark world.

I shifted my hold on her, so I could open the passenger door on my bright yellow Ferrari. Usually, I paid more reverence to my flashy vehicles, my hands lingering over the elegant lines of my expensive possessions. Working for Adrián meant I was able to afford all the fast toys I could possibly want, and I wasn't ashamed of my ostentatious choices. I treated my cars with care, but the Ferrari was far less treasurable than the woman in my arms.

I arranged her body on the black leather seat and buckled her in. When I was certain she was secure, I paused to stare down at her.

Her tight curls were in disarray. They'd always appeared to have a life of their own, falling around her face in voluminous waves. Now, they'd been broken by my fingers and were far more unruly than I'd ever seen them. I decided that I liked the wildness of it. Sofia was always perfectly polished and poised, but this was her more natural state. I felt like a voyeur seeing her like this, which only added another layer to her sexual appeal.

I traced her lush lips with my thumb, imagining them swollen from my kiss and her hair mussed after sex.

That erotic image was enough to make me clench my hand into a fist and withdraw from her on a frustrated growl. I couldn't use her like that anytime soon. Coaxing out her willing, eager submission would take patience.

I wasn't a patient man, but I would try. For her, I'd temper my impulse for instant gratification. She might be mine, but I still wanted her to choose to give herself to me. Anything else would be twisted and hollow.

On a deeper level, I knew that violating her while I held her as my captive would blacken what was left of my soul. I might be a monster, but I'd never forgive myself if I were the one to snuff out Sofia's innocence.

I intended to keep her for myself, just as she was now: vibrant and giving, quick to share her smile.

I would settle for nothing less. From now on, no

one would be more determined to protect sweet Sofia than me.

I got into the driver's seat and started my Ferrari, the car's snarl echoing my own savage feelings. I took a breath and inhaled her intoxicating, rosy scent. My dick stiffened, and I ground my teeth.

Controlling my impulses when it came to Sofia was going to take every ounce of strength that I possessed.

CHAPTER 2

SOFIA

I let out a grumpy groan and rolled onto my side, tugging the sheets over my head to wrap myself in a little cocoon. My mouth was dry, but lethargy sapped my muscles. I would drag my ass out of bed and get a glass of water in a little while. For now, I wanted to go back to sleep until the effects of last night's party wore off.

My mind churned, my thoughts sliding through my brain like slow, thick molasses. I didn't remember partying last night. The last thing I remembered was watching YouTube clips from *The Voice* on the big screen TV in my apartment.

Dark eyes flashed through my memories, and I felt the phantom touch of big, masculine hands on my body.

I threw the covers off with a gasp, jolting upright

as instinctive fear shredded my sleepy confusion. The world spun around me, and I clutched my head to stave off a wave of dizziness.

"Stay calm. You're okay."

I yelped, shocked at the male voice in such close proximity. I jerked my head around, trying to search for the threat. Everything blurred, and I lost all sense of balance. I felt myself falling back, but a corded arm braced around my shoulders to support me.

"You're safe, Sofia." I recognized the deep, rumbling voice: Mateo Ignazio.

A little thrill buzzed through my system, despite my confusion. I always responded this way when Mateo was near.

"Mateo?" I rasped, my tongue feeling too thick in my mouth. I blinked, trying to get the world to settle into place around me. "I don't...feel good."

I felt hungover and beyond disoriented. I squeezed my eyes shut and breathed through my nose to center myself as I took note of my surroundings as best I could. I was definitely in bed. But the sheets felt silkier than those on my own bed, and they didn't caress my body. I was fully clothed, but I usually slept naked.

I took another breath. Mateo was in bed with me, and he was close enough for me to smell his unique, masculine scent. He'd never been this close before. I inhaled deeply, savoring him.

The fleeting pleasure I found at his nearness dissipated into fear. He *had* been this close before. The last time his scent had permeated my senses, he'd been holding his hand over my mouth and sliding a needle into my neck.

Disjointed images flooded my mind: Mateo pinning me against the wall of my apartment; Mateo's hands tugging sharply at my hair; Mateo's fingers wrapped around my throat. I hadn't been able to move, even though I'd struggled to get away from him.

Adrián had been there, too. And my father...

"Daddy," I gasped, still half-blind.

Mateo's arm firmed around me, his powerful muscles flexing. "Adrián is dealing with your father," he said roughly.

"What do you mean?" I asked, desperate. My hand found the front of Mateo's shirt, fisting in the soft cotton material. I had a terrible feeling I knew what he meant. On some level, I'd always known Adrián Rodríguez was a dangerous man. He was my dad's sort-of boss. More of a business associate, really. Adrián came to meet with Daddy at our house sometimes, and I'd briefly interacted with him at social events hosted by my father.

Adrián was gorgeous in a scary kind of way. Definitely male model material, but his pale green eyes were cold as ice. I would have avoided him altogether if it hadn't been for the fact that Mateo was always close by his side. I'd been drawn to Mateo ever since I'd met him when I was fifteen years old. He had a dangerous aura about him, as well. But in that delicious, tattooed bad-boy kind of way that made my belly flutter.

"Don't let Adrián hurt my dad," I beseeched, my eyes finally focusing on Mateo's rugged features. His lips thinned, obscured by his thick black beard. His displeasure was clear. "You won't, will you?" I continued. "You wouldn't let Adrián hurt Daddy."

"Your father should be fine," Mateo replied tightly. "As long as he cooperates."

My head pounded as I struggled to sift through hazy memories. I remembered a conversation between Adrián and my father.

You're loyal to me from now on, or Sofia will suffer. Adrián's cold threat surfaced in my mind. I jerked against Mateo's hold. He pulled me closer to his stone chest, his arm an iron band around my shoulders.

"What are you going to do to me?" I asked on a horrified whisper. My heart twisted in my chest. I never would have imagined that the man I'd secretly pined for was capable of hurting me. But Adrián had definitely told my father that Mateo would hurt me if he didn't *cooperate.*

Mateo's restraining hold on my body remained

firm, but his free hand cupped my cheek. "I'm not going to hurt you, *florecita*," he promised, his tone smoothing to a gentler cadence. "Don't be afraid."

I pressed my palm against my pounding forehead, trying to alleviate my headache. "I don't understand what's happening."

"Here. You need to drink some water." His hand left my cheek, and suddenly, smooth glass touched my lips. I parted them automatically, grateful for the cooling liquid on my parched throat. After a few gulps, I tried to turn my face away.

"Finish it," he commanded sternly. "Then, I'll explain what's going on."

I didn't like that he was withholding information to ensure my compliance, but I was thirsty enough that I ignored my irritation.

As he tipped the glass all the way up so I could swallow the last sip, a trickle of water slipped past my lips and spilled onto my chest. Mateo's arm tensed around me again. When I finally peered up into his black eyes with full clarity, I realized his dark gaze was fixed on the little droplets that glistened on my cleavage.

I shifted in his hold, my skin heating and unease stirring in my belly. I quickly swiped the water away.

"Please," I begged when he didn't start explaining immediately. "Talk to me."

His eyes snapped back up to my face. "Your father abducted Valentina."

"What? He wouldn't do that!" I insisted, denial instantaneous and vehement. I'd met Valentina for the first time earlier today. She'd just moved to LA to be with Adrián, whom she obviously loved deeply. We'd met up at my favorite café to discuss her interest in enrolling at UCLA. She'd wanted to ask me questions about the university, and we'd made plans to go shopping together this weekend. I'd assumed we would become friends.

There was no way Daddy would hurt Valentina.

Mateo's eyes narrowed, searching my features. "How much do you know about your father's business?"

"He..." I swallowed, suddenly uncomfortable with my own naivete. "He works with Adrián. They... import and export stuff. Right? Daddy never discusses business with Mom and me. He says he wants to provide for us, and we don't need to be bored with the details."

Mateo's head canted to the side. "You really don't know, do you?"

"I would know what's going on if you would tell me," I snapped, losing my patience. Panic was taking hold in my chest, making it difficult to draw breath. Adrián had threatened my father. He'd threatened my safety. And now, I was in a strange bed with Mateo.

This definitely wasn't the fantasy scenario I'd imagined sharing with him when I touched myself late at night, indulging in my secret desires beneath the protection of my duvet.

"Your father is in the employ of the Rodríguez cartel," Mateo informed me bluntly. "He traffics cocaine from Colombia into the States. Adrián's family controls the product at the source from their base in Bogotá, and he oversees distribution on the west coast. Your father has worked for the cartel since well before you were born. Obviously, he's hidden the harsher realities of this world from you, but you're involved now." He scowled. "If Caesar had remained loyal to Adrián, you could have been saved from all this."

"No," I insisted, still deep in denial. "You're lying. Daddy's not like that. He wouldn't hurt anybody. If Adrián thinks he kidnapped Valentina, he's mistaken. That's just not true."

The harsh lines of Mateo's features softened slightly, his eyes warming with something like pity. "I'm sure Caesar only wanted to shield you from ugly truths. That's what I wanted for you, too. But that time is over now. Your father ordered his men to abduct Valentina in a power play against Adrián. He intends to give her back to her husband, Hugo Sánchez, in return for backup usurping control of California from Adrián." Grim lines appeared around his mouth. "Hugo is not a good man. Adrián will do whatever it takes to keep Valentina safe from him. That's why I had to... Well, that's why you're here with me."

"But I don't have anything to do with all that. Even if it is true." I still didn't believe it, but I would set aside my denial for a few minutes, so I could gather more information to assess my situation.

"No, you don't," Mateo agreed. "But your father loves you. And Adrián loves Valentina. You're leverage, so he can get her back."

"Leverage?"

He nodded. "You're going to stay here at my house. Caesar won't defy Adrián again as long as you're with me."

"I can't stay here!" I burst out. "I have my own apartment. I have my classes. And my friends."

"You aren't going back to your apartment," he said, as though it was a done deal. "Maybe you can attend your classes again at some point. We'll see."

"But I have finals coming up," I protested, as though that was the most pressing issue at the moment. Everything else was just too much to contemplate, so my mind stuck on this fact.

"I'm sorry, but that doesn't matter anymore. Not right now, at least."

"It doesn't matter?" I shouted, slapping his rock-hard chest. "My grades are on the line. My future.

You're talking about fucking up my whole life plan. Because...what? There's a misunderstanding between Daddy and Adrián."

Mateo's thick black brows drew together, casting forbidding shadows over his eyes. "This isn't a *misunderstanding*. Your father has challenged Adrián. He's threatened the woman he loves. Caesar brought this upon himself."

"But I didn't," I protested. "I haven't done anything."

He traced the line of my jaw, his feather-light touch in shocking contrast to his iron grip on my shoulders. "No, you haven't done anything wrong, *belleza*. And you don't need to be afraid. Your father will fall in line because he thinks I'm a threat to you. But I will never hurt you. I swear."

"Then you can't stop me from leaving." I tried to push away from him.

His gentle touch on my cheek shifted, his hand coming to rest on my throat. He didn't apply pressure, but my breath stuttered.

"I can, and I will," he warned calmly. "I don't need to harm you to keep you here with me."

I licked my lips, a small shudder racing through my body. Mateo stroked the column of my neck with his thumb, but he didn't release my throat. His dark eyes burned into me, staring with an intensity that I didn't fully understand. My skin pebbled, even though heat flashed through my body.

"I want to talk to my father." I intended to make a demand, but the words came out as a meek request.

Mateo continued to brush his thumb up and down my neck. I realized he was tracing the line of my artery. I could feel it pulsing beneath his touch, and I became hyperaware of the threat he posed. I should fear my vulnerability in his powerful arms, but a strange sense of calm settled over me. My lashes fluttered, my thoughts drifting away. Maybe the drugs Mateo had given me hadn't fully left my system. I felt weak and achy in ways I wasn't at all familiar with.

"What did you give me?" I whispered.

"Give you?" he asked, his voice deeper than I'd ever heard it. His eyes were hooded, and he appeared as though he might be drugged, too.

"The drugs," I murmured.

He blinked, shaking off whatever was affecting him. His hand left my throat, and I drew in a shuddering breath.

"Nothing that will have long-term consequences," he reassured me. "Now that you're hydrated, it'll fully wear off soon."

His eyes were intent on mine, as though he'd be able to detect whether or not the drugs lingered in my system just by studying me. When he continued to stare and didn't say anything else, I decided to press for my request again.

"I want to talk to my father. Please, let me call him."

He blew out a short sigh and reached into his pocket. Keeping me secured against his chest with one strong arm, he retrieved his phone with his free hand. He didn't say anything to me as he selected a contact and connected the call.

"Adrián," he said into the receiver. "Is it done?"

I tensed. Mateo wasn't calling Daddy for me. He was calling his terrifying boss. The man who had ordered him to kidnap me and hold me hostage.

Mateo idly stroked his thumb up and down my arm, as though he was seeking to soothe my tension without really thinking about what he was doing. Despite the frightening, confusing things that had happened to me today, I believed him when he promised he wouldn't hurt me.

I don't need to harm you to keep you here with me.

A small shiver raced over my skin at the memory of his stern declaration. His thumb rubbed the goose bumps that suddenly pebbled my flesh. I blinked up at him, finding myself trapped by his intense, rapt stare once again.

He jerked his head to the side. "Yes, boss," he said to Adrián, refocusing his attention on their conversation. "I have her at my house. I assume you want me to hold onto her for a while?"

I scowled and strained against his hold. He didn't even seem to register my small struggle. He simply continued stroking my arm as he talked to Adrián about me. Discussing my abduction as though it was totally normal.

This couldn't be real. It certainly wasn't *my* normal. Maybe I never had been really aware of what Daddy's business entailed. But surely, he wasn't actually capable of trying to hurt Valentina? The vibrant, sweet woman I'd met earlier this afternoon wasn't a threat to anyone. Some of the men Daddy worked with—like Adrián—were scary, but there was nothing dangerous about Valentina.

Was my dad secretly just as scary as Adrián Rodríguez? I couldn't reconcile my doting father with a man like Adrián, whose cruelty was evident in each of his perfect features, somehow enhanced by his physical beauty. With his panther's eyes and sleek demeanor, his predatory nature was impossible to miss.

"I'm glad Valentina is safe," Mateo said. "And Hugo?"

Adrián's reply elicited a chilling reaction. Suddenly, Mateo's jaw set, and his dark eyes glinted with a savage, terrifying light I'd never seen before. His lips curved with sadistic satisfaction. "I'll leave you to it, then," he told Adrián smoothly before ending the call.

As soon as Mateo's gaze focused on me, the cruel expression faded. Even though his features softened, my fear lingered. The man holding me wasn't the sexy bad boy I'd fantasized about for years. He was just as dangerous as Adrián.

He reached out and touched his fingertips to my furrowed brow, and I flinched.

His mouth pressed to a tight slash, and his muscles bulged and flexed around me as he slowly withdrew his hand.

"It's over," he announced coolly. "Valentina is safe with Adrián. You can talk to your father now."

Before I could begin to formulate a response, he retrieved my rose gold phone from where it rested on the nightstand. I gabbed at it like the familiar object was my lifeline, but he snatched it back, holding it out of my reach with a warning frown.

"What's your passcode?" he asked.

"I'm not telling you." My defiance came out more breathlessly than I would have liked. I swallowed and tried again. "Give me my phone."

"I don't think so, *florecita*. You're in my house, and you'll play by my rules." His voice dropped deeper with the ring of command, but there was no menace in his tone. Nothing he'd said to me so far had been issued as a threat, but his unyielding authority was clear.

I wasn't truly scared of him—not like I probably should be—but I was undeniably intimidated.

"Your passcode," he prompted.

"I don't want to tell you," I protested weakly. "That's private."

"Not from me," he countered. "You don't have automatic phone privileges anymore. You'll have to earn them."

"What?" I should have sounded more indignant, but I couldn't seem to eliminate that breathless quality to my query.

"You want to go back to your classes? You want to return to your normal routine? I'll allow it, but only after you've proven that I can trust you to behave. I have to know that you will obey me unquestioningly."

"Obey you?" This time, I did sound indignant.

He simply nodded, ignoring my outburst. "I can't have you running back to Daddy at the first opportunity. Until you convince me that you'll be my good girl, you're not leaving this house." His words turned rougher, his eyes taking on that strange, almost drugged appearance again. His countenance made a light tremor race through my body, but the reaction wasn't entirely one of fear.

"And you don't get your phone privileges back until you promise not to try to call anyone for help. I will know if your promise is insincere. You don't get to lie to me, Sofia. If you try, there will be consequences."

My breaths turned shallower with each calmly-spoken sentence that left his lips.

"Consequences?" I couldn't seem to manage more than stilted questions; just a word or two leaving me on a little puff of air.

A single black brow lifted, and the dark promise hung between us. He didn't give me any details, and that set me even more off-balance. If I didn't know what he might have in store for me, I couldn't mentally prepare for it. That made the idea of challenging him all the more unnerving.

"Your passcode," he drawled. It wasn't a question; it was an edict.

The four digits slipped from me on a meek whisper.

One corner of his lips tilted in a lopsided, arrogant smile. His eyes remained locked on mine for the space of several heartbeats.

"Good girl." The two words were issued slowly, as though he was savoring them on his tongue. His deep, rumbling voice made them settle over me and weigh on me like a heavy blanket.

He'd told me that I would have to learn to behave as *his good girl*. That I would learn to obey him. The words of praise were both positive reinforcement for my acquiescence and a statement of his first, small victory. As though he was taming me, training me like he would a new pet.

I didn't like it.

I *shouldn't* like it.

But something stirred low in my belly, warming my insides.

Before I could sort through the confusing sensations, he found my father's number in my contact list and connected the call, ensuring it was on speaker. It seemed I wouldn't be allowed a private conversation.

The phone barely finished its first ring before my father's voice rasped across the line. "Sofia?"

"Daddy!" His name hitched in my throat.

"Where are you?" he asked, frantic. "What has he done to you, *princesa*? If that animal touched you—"

"I haven't," Mateo said coldly, letting my father know he was listening to every word. "Much," he added with menace.

I stared up at him with alarm. He'd never used that tone with me, and I felt a jolt of true fear for the first time.

He placed the phone in my hand and rubbed his thumb over my chilled skin. He held one finger up to his lips, warning me not to contradict him. A tiny bit of my fear ebbed. I didn't like that he was scaring my father, but he was silently communicating that the menace wasn't directed at me.

I responded with a shaky nod, quick to demonstrate my compliance. He might be stroking me gently, but I became keenly aware of just how big he was. His huge muscles surrounded me, his corded arm around my shoulders and his granite chest pressed against my side. A firm flex could bruise me.

"Please," Daddy begged. "Don't hurt her. Give her back to me."

"No," Mateo said, a clipped refusal. "Sofia's staying right here with me. She's not coming home. You betrayed Adrián. You caused the woman he loved to be hurt and terrorized. You don't want me to hurt your innocent daughter? Why don't you tell her what you did to Valentina? She's innocent, too. Why don't you tell Sofia what kind of monster her husband, Hugo, was? He beat and raped his wife, and you were going to send her back to that hell just to gain power." Barely-suppressed rage roughened the nauseating accusations.

Shock made my fingers go numb around my phone. Despite the renewed tension in his body, Mateo gently cupped his hand around mine, helping me maintain my grip.

"That's not true," I whispered. "Daddy, tell me that's not true!" The desperate demand issued from my constricted throat on a horrified squeak.

"*Mi niña...*" The pleading edge to the endearment was nearly as damning as a detailed admission.

My eyes began to burn, my chest tightening. My head swung back and forth, physically denying the awful revelations about my father, even as the truth began to sink into my mind.

"Sofia, please," he begged, beseeching me to instantly forgive and forget his terrible sin. "*Princesa*, I—"

I abruptly hung up on him and tossed my phone across the bed, as though flinging away a poisonous snake. I couldn't hear any more. I couldn't bear to hear my sweet Daddy's voice after all I'd just learned about his capacity for ruthless cruelty.

I buried my face in my hands, pressing my palms against my eyes in an effort to hold in my tears. How could I have been so blind?

You knew, an insidious little voice whispered in my mind. *Some part of you always suspected.*

I began to shake, my limbs trembling violently.

Oh, god. I'd willfully kept myself in blissful ignorance for my entire life. Of course I realized my father's associates were dangerous. Of course I understood that Daddy wouldn't have been so vague about his *business* if it hadn't been distasteful.

But I'd been so starved for love. My mother had always been cold and distant, a true narcissist incapable of caring about anyone else. Not even her own daughter. I was simply a way to keep Daddy tied to her, a tool to ensure her own financial security and cushy lifestyle.

I couldn't believe how pathetic I'd been, clinging to a little girl's naivete because I was too desperate for affection from at least one parent.

Cold seeped into my bones, and my teeth began to chatter. My entire falsely cheery world was crumbling around me.

Daddy was a vicious drug lord.

The man holding me so tenderly was, too.

How could I have secretly pined for Mateo all these years, indulging in girlish fantasies about his bad boy vibe?

What did I think? That he was some brooding hottie that I could redeem with my love?

God, I was so stupid.

My criminal captor ran his big hands all over my body. I wanted to resist him, but his steady warmth seeped into me despite my desire to pretend that he didn't have an effect on my body.

So fucking stupid. Years of idealized longing had obviously warped me, rendering me helpless to control my physical responses to him.

I should hate Mateo. I should fear him.

"Please," I begged. "Leave me alone."

His only response was to gently shush me. His warm grip and persistent stroking silently communicated that he wasn't going anywhere.

I didn't have any control over my life anymore. My entire reality had been shattered in the course of a day.

I was a hostage, a pawn in a dangerous game between brutal men.

And yet, as exhaustion rolled over me, I couldn't help relaxing in Mateo's arms. His long fingers slid into my hair, applying gentle pressure to direct my face against him. I stiffened for the space of a second, but he began to massage my scalp in little soothing circles. I turned my cheek into his chest, seeking more reassuring contact. My tears wet his shirt, but he didn't seem to mind.

When his fingers rubbed lightly against little pressure points behind my ear and at the base of my jaw, I slid deeper into relaxation. I melted against him, sinking into his heat.

"Good girl." His murmured praise followed me down into mercifully peaceful sleep.

CHAPTER 3

MATEO

I stirred toward wakefulness, enjoying the soft warmth of my bed for a few minutes longer. My alarm hadn't gone off yet, so I had time to rest.

And deal with my morning wood.

I skimmed my palm over my abs, pausing when I registered the worn cotton of my t-shirt.

I didn't usually sleep in my shirt.

Or my jeans, for that matter.

Fuck, they were way too tight against my erection. Acting on instinct, I shifted to ease the discomfort.

A sleepy little grumble accompanied a huff of warm air across my neck.

My eyes snapped open, my brain jolting to full awareness. I wasn't in my own bed.

The last thing I remembered was settling down

beside Sofia in my guest bedroom. I'd indulged myself for too long, and I must have fallen asleep while I was petting her.

She nuzzled her cheek into my chest, her irritation at my movement melting away as she slipped back into a deeper sleep.

My breath stuck in my lungs, and for a moment, I was scared to breathe. What if I woke her? She might have cuddled up to me in her sleep, but that didn't mean she wouldn't scream and scramble away if she opened her eyes to see the evidence of my arousal.

I'd resolved that I would coax out her willing surrender, but the thought of her trembling and staring wide-eyed at my cock made perverse lust pulse through me.

I bit back a curse and ran my hand over my face.

Fantasizing about her looking at me with an intoxicating mixture of fear and desire was dangerously tempting. My brain chose to fixate on that image, and my erection throbbed, straining against my jeans.

If I'd come hard in the past just imagining fucking her, having her soft body pressed up against me while these wicked images ran through my mind threatened to make me lose control.

I gritted my teeth, mustering my resolve. I wouldn't come in my pants like some horny teenager.

I pressed my palm against my eyes, as though I could push the filthy thoughts out of my brain.

But I'd obsessed over her too often over the last five years. I must have conditioned my body to associate Sofia with this surge of arousal.

What would it be like if she opened her pretty emerald eyes and gave me a sleepy smile before sliding down my body? What if she wanted to help ease my discomfort? What would it feel like to have those lush lips caressing my dick, worshipping me?

Jesus fucking Christ!

When Adrián had given her to me yesterday, I'd worried that having her in my home but waiting to fuck her would be torture. I never would have imagined that blue balls could be more agonizing than taking a beating.

Right now, I'd welcome a fist to the face. That might knock some sense into me. Because there was no way the sweet, innocent woman tucked against my side would enjoy the prospect of giving me a morning blowjob on her first day in captivity.

She's my fucking hostage, not my girlfriend.

Unfortunately, my dick didn't care about the differentiation. If anything, the idea of having her completely under my power, obeying my every command, intensified my desire.

Instinct urged me to tear my body away from hers to escape her painful allure. But that would definitely rouse her. Instead, I took a breath and slowly extricated myself from her loose embrace.

Her cheek slid from my chest as I shifted, and I moved with care until she rested on the pillow instead. I placed my feet on the carpeted floor and eased off the mattress, wincing when it jostled slightly.

I blew out a small sigh of relief when she didn't stir.

A flash of shame heated my cheeks. As the biggest motherfucker in almost every room I walked into, I wasn't accustomed to tiptoeing around anyone. And if I wanted something—a flashy car, a rough fuck—I procured it for myself without hesitation or compunction.

My caution when it came to Sofia suddenly grated on my pride a little. Why should I have to sneak around my own home for the sake of not alarming my captive?

I stared down at her, uncertain if I clenched my fists at my sides out of irritation or to prevent myself from succumbing to the urge to touch her.

With her high cheekbones, long lashes, and lush lips, Sofia had always appeared sensual. The wide-eyed innocence that belied her sinful beauty only made me crave her all the more. Her effervescent personality was so at odds with the way I functioned. Sofia was quick to share her bright smile, and she wanted to be friends with everyone she met.

As Adrián's personal bodyguard, it was my job to scare the shit out of everyone close to him. No grins or giggles for me.

I might get off on the idea of Sofia trembling under my hands, but I didn't want her to truly fear me. I didn't want to be the one to erase her smile.

Which meant I had to deal with my hard-on before she woke up and freaked the fuck out.

I softly padded across the guest room on bare feet, all concerns over my bruised pride gone. It was my job to intimidate the men who might threaten my boss, but scaring Sofia wasn't one of my assigned duties. There was no shame in protecting the fragile beauty who had snuggled up to me as she slept, trusting me even though I didn't deserve it.

I wanted her to feel safe around me. No matter how I taunted her father with threats to her wellbeing, I would never allow any harm to come to Sofia.

I would shelter her from any threat, and that included suppressing my own twisted desires until she was ready to accept them. Because if I treated her the way I'd imagined obsessively for years, I would mark her perfect skin with my hands, my teeth, my ropes...

I slipped out into the hallway, my footsteps falling faster as I rushed into my own bedroom. By the time

I reached the shower, I'd hastily stripped out of my clothes. I stepped directly under the cold spray before the water had time to heat. The chill on my skin made me suck in a sharp breath through my teeth, but it didn't do much to alleviate my erection. As the water warmed, I gripped my shaft and thought about all the depraved things I wanted to do to my helpless hostage.

If I hadn't been so desperate for release, I might have been embarrassed at how quickly I finished. As it was, I moved on and rushed through my morning routine. I had to get back to Sofia. She might wake up at any moment, and I wasn't there to guard her.

I didn't intend to allow her enough time to find her way outside my house and escape, but if she tried, I would have to enforce some consequences. I didn't think she'd like the punishment I had in mind for her if she misbehaved.

I would definitely like punishing her far too much. I'd managed to rein in my more savage instincts so far, but I'd only had her in my possession for a few hours. And she'd been asleep for most of them.

I wasn't at all certain if I could continue to leash those instincts if she defied me.

Best not give her a chance to try.

As soon as I finished my quick shower and brushed my teeth, I tugged on the first clean clothes I could find and hastened back to the guest room.

The slight tension that had gripped my muscles eased. Sofia hadn't moved an inch from where I'd left her tucked under the covers. She was still soundly asleep, so I wouldn't have to worry about punishing her for any naughty behavior this morning.

Just thinking about it made my dick stiffen, even though I'd come only a few minutes ago.

I cleared my throat to distract myself as much as to wake her.

She grumbled and pulled the covers over her head.

One corner of my lips twitched. It seemed Sofia wasn't a morning person. She'd reacted like this last night when the drugs I'd given her had finally worn off. I'd thought her grogginess was a symptom of what I'd dosed her with, but it was becoming apparent that she was simply a heavy sleeper.

"Sofia." I smiled around her name, remembering how she'd huffed at me this morning when I'd shifted beneath her.

She burrowed deeper under the duvet, as though she could block me out. I'd never realized a little growl could sound so cute.

I considered leaving her to sleep in, but she needed to get up and eat breakfast. I'd abducted her early yesterday evening, and it had been too long since she'd had a proper meal.

Sofia might be my hostage, but that didn't mean

she would be mistreated. Quite the opposite. I would never condition her devotion if I was cruel to her.

Casual cruelty wasn't part of my nature, anyway. I might do terrible things for Adrián, but that was just business. I took care of the people who mattered to me.

Although there were only two people in the world that I really gave a shit about—my mom and Adrián—protecting them was my top priority. Now, Sofia had been added to that very short list. She was my responsibility, so it was my job to see to her wellbeing. Regardless of how grumpy she might be.

Besides, she was cute when she was like this. Her grumbling and hiding under the covers reminded me of how innocent she was. Her life had been untainted by worry or fear, and she had the luxury of stubbornly sleeping the day away in peace.

At this point, she should have woken up on instinct. Even if she was a heavy sleeper, the fact that a man was looming over her bed and calling her name should have set off alarm bells in her mind. And yet, she seemed mildly irritated rather than terrified.

I would preserve that sweet innocence, despite the circumstances that had brought her into my home.

Her father had changed her world when he'd decided to abduct Valentina. The blame for ripping

Sofia out of her easy routine lay entirely with him. Not me.

I never would have claimed her for myself if Caesar hadn't forced my hand. As long as I kept her safe and well cared for, I didn't have anything to feel guilty about.

"Sofia," I said, more loudly.

"Go away," she groaned.

Definitely not afraid, I noted with amusement.

"I'm not going anywhere. It's time to wake up, *florecita.*"

Suddenly, she flung the covers off with a gasp. Her wide, luminous green eyes met mine. For a moment, she simply stared at me, her lips parted in shock.

I decided to give her sluggish brain a minute to wake up and process her situation.

"What are you doing here, Mateo?" she demanded with surprising vehemence.

My brows lifted. "You're at my house. Don't you remember what happened yesterday?"

Before I could worry over whether or not the drugs I'd given her had messed with her mind, she snapped at me.

"Of course I remember!" She crossed her arms over her chest, her eyes narrowing. "I mean, what are you doing *in* here? I was sleeping. And you just barged in without knocking."

My lips curved, the small smile surprising me. I

supposed she wasn't aware that I'd slept beside her all night. My presence hadn't disturbed her at all. I found her easy trust charming.

"I don't think it would have made a difference if I'd knocked," I remarked. "You wouldn't have woken up. Do you always sleep this heavily?"

She shook her head, her curls swaying in wild disarray around her lovely face. "It doesn't matter if I wouldn't have woken up. You don't just come into a girl's room without an invitation. No invitation means no boys allowed."

An involuntary chuckle rumbled from my chest. She pouted in response.

Fucking adorable.

"I'm not a *boy*," I informed her. "And this is my house. I don't have to wait for permission to enter any room."

"Don't you understand anything about privacy?" she spluttered. "Get out!"

"We talked about this last night, *belleza*. You have to earn the right to privacy. Did you really think I was just going to let you wander around unsupervised? Until I know you'll behave, I can't let you out of my sight. I won't give you a chance to try to escape. And if you do try, I don't think you'll like what will happen when I catch you."

She threw up her hands in exasperation. "I wasn't trying to escape. I was *sleeping*. You don't have to watch me when I'm asleep. Obviously, I wasn't trying to go anywhere."

"Obviously." I smirked at her. "Now, get out of bed, Sleeping Beauty. You need to eat breakfast."

"What are you, my warden?" she demanded, displaying far more fire than she had last night. Apparently, I'd poked the hibernating bear, and she was not at all pleased about it.

I shrugged, unapologetic. There was no point lying to her. "Kind of."

Her mouth opened and closed a few times, and her tanned cheeks took on an angry flush. "Are you saying I'm your prisoner? Seriously, Mateo?"

She sounded as though she truly didn't believe I was capable of holding her hostage. I found her reaction...kind of sweet. Most grown men were terrified of me. Then again, they were fully aware of my capacity for violence. Despite her changed circumstances, Sofia was still cocooned in her falsely safe worldview. This delicate little flower was speaking to me with more raw ire than anyone had dared in a long time.

My smirk widened to a grin.

"Is this funny to you?" she railed.

"Yeah," I admitted. "Surprisingly, it is. I assumed you'd be skittish this morning. Maybe crying. Instead, you're yelling at me."

Her cheeks colored a deeper shade of red. "I'm

not yelling!" she insisted, her voice elevated to a much louder volume than usual.

"All right, then. You're not yelling. Maybe you're yowling at me. Like an angry little kitten. Kittens are usually angriest when they're hungry, you know. You should get out of bed and have breakfast with me."

She slapped her palms down on the mattress, fuming. "I'm not having breakfast with you!" she declared hotly. "You know what? I'm not doing anything with you." She got to her feet and stormed toward me, every line of her willowy body drawn with defiance. "I'm going home."

My smile dropped to a stern frown, and I stepped to the side to block her path out of the bedroom. My fingers curved around her shoulders, holding her in place with little effort.

She shoved at my chest; a tiny bird beating its wings against the confines of its cage.

I slid one hand to her nape, cradling her slender neck in a careful grip. I didn't bother trying to restrain her flailing arms. She wasn't hurting me, and she'd tire herself out long before I so much as broke a sweat.

"Settle down," I commanded.

"Let me go," she seethed, slapping my chest with what I was sure was her full strength. It did sting a little.

"If you continue acting like a brat, I'll treat you

like a brat," I warned, remaining calm but firm. "And if you're trying to push my boundaries, you'll find that I push back."

The furious tension didn't ease from her body, but she didn't slap me again.

"Are you done?" I asked, testing her just like she was testing me.

She slammed her fists against my chest. "No!" she challenged. "I'm not done. But you are. Let me go right now."

My hold firmed around her neck, a slight flex of my fingers. She stilled instantly, her fists unfurling until her palms pressed flat against my chest. She wasn't pushing me away anymore, and her body softened.

"I'll let you go when you promise to behave." I kept her locked in my steady stare.

Her head tipped back slightly, an unconscious sign of capitulation. Like any weaker animal cornered by a predator, she instinctively offered me clear access to her vulnerable throat, demonstrating her submission.

Keeping my grip on her nape, I lifted my free hand so I could stroke her exposed throat, letting her know that I was satisfied with her surrender. A small shiver raced through her body, and I curled two fingers beneath her chin, guiding her to tilt her head back farther to grant me even better access. She didn't resist, and the angry sparks left her eyes. Her lashes fluttered as she gazed up at me, the last of her anger easing from her features.

"I want to go home, Mateo." The harsh ring of demand had bled from her tone, and the words came out as a meek request.

"That can't happen, *florecita*," I told her gently as I resumed stroking her neck, tracing the line of her pulsing artery. It seemed to calm her, and her reaction satisfied me. The strange, new warmth I'd experienced yesterday unfurled in my chest.

"I can't return you to your father."

She flinched and cut her eyes away. "I didn't mean... I don't want to see Daddy." She peeked up at me, imploring. "I just want to go back to my apartment. I want to go to class and be normal."

"I wanted that for you too, *belleza*," I admitted. "But you can't go back to your apartment. Even if I were willing to return you there, your father could have men watching for you. If I leave you exposed, Caesar will take you back. I can't allow that. I won't." The final declaration came out rougher than I'd intended.

She swallowed, and her eyes began to shine. "I won't go home with him," she promised. "I don't want to talk to Daddy right now. I need time to process all this."

Fuck, she was still so naïve.

"He's not going to give you a choice, Sofia." I

tried to deliver the blow softly. "If he gets you back, he will betray Adrián again. As long as you're free, you can be used against him at any time. He won't expose himself to that weakness, not after last night."

"Daddy...wouldn't hurt me." The assertion hitched in her throat, her pale complexion suggesting that the very idea was so horrific that she could barely force the words out.

"No, I don't believe he would. But he wouldn't let you return to your classes, either. You're either confined to my home or to his for the foreseeable future. And I'm afraid that surrendering you to him isn't an option. If I did, things would get very bloody for Adrián and me."

Her jaw went slack with shock, as though the prospect of violence had never occurred to her.

"I don't want that," she whispered. "I don't want any of this."

I finally released her nape to ease my fingers into her hair. I began to massage her scalp without really thinking about what I was doing. She cuddled up to me so sweetly when I soothed her, and I craved more of that.

I only applied the slightest pressure to the back of her head before she tucked her face against me. The warmth in my chest expanded, pulsing outward through the rest of my body.

I indulged in the strange new peace I experienced

when she turned to me for comfort. I'd spent my adult life building my body to be as massive and strong as possible. But I'd never felt more powerful than I did when she pressed herself close to me, seeking my protection.

I couldn't put the broken pieces of her blissfully ignorant reality back together, but I would protect her and provide for her. Once she eased into acceptance, she would be happy to belong to me.

"You're going to be okay," I murmured against her tangled curls. "You're safe with me."

CHAPTER 4

SOFIA

I sniffled against Mateo's chest, clinging to him despite the fact that he was essentially my captor. Confusion and distress muddled my ability to sort through my feelings about him.

On a rational level, I should hate him. I should still be yelling at him and hitting his granite body with all my strength.

But Mateo hadn't hurt me, even though he'd had plenty of opportunities to do so since he'd abducted me. He could have acted on the chilling threats he'd made to my father. If he wanted to *touch* me, my lack of consent wouldn't prevent him from doing whatever he pleased.

His massive arms surrounding me should incite fear; his sheer, overwhelming size was a reminder of his strength and my physical vulnerability.

But so far, he'd only used his big hands to comfort me, stroking my body with tenderness. I knew he could bruise my flesh with minimal effort, but he touched me as carefully as one might handle a small kitten.

I shivered against him. He'd teased me for acting like an angry kitten while I'd been yelling at him. It had pissed me off at the time, but now, I was grateful for his gentle attention. My miserable new reality was setting in, and Mateo's steady heat was undeniably reassuring.

I didn't want to be his hostage. But I didn't want to go home, either. The idea of being held against my will by my father was somehow worse than being Mateo's captive. I was sure Daddy wouldn't hurt me, but the revelations about his ruthlessness and cruelty were far more painful than anything Mateo had done to me so far.

In fact, Mateo hadn't caused me any pain at all. Ever since I'd woken up in his house, he'd tried to ease my distress.

I felt the phantom touch of his hand firming on my neck, remembering when he'd rebuked me for hitting him. My brain seemed to stall out whenever he handled me like that. But it wasn't unpleasant or scary.

He'd issued vague warnings about *consequences* if I

tried to escape. That made me uneasy, but I shrugged off my budding concern.

If leaving his house meant I would be forcibly taken back to my father and imprisoned in my childhood home, I didn't have much desire to escape from Mateo. As long as I was here with him, I didn't have to fully face the awful truth about what Daddy was really like when he wasn't around me. The indulgent father who'd joined me for childhood tea parties with my dolls couldn't possibly be capable of condemning Valentina to rape and abuse. It was too painful to even contemplate.

Staying with Mateo would allow me to avoid that pain. Especially if he offered hugs like this one.

My stomach rumbled, and I realized I hadn't eaten anything since I'd met with Valentina at the café yesterday afternoon.

That meeting felt like it had taken place weeks ago, even though I knew it had been less than twenty-four hours ago. My entire world had changed, and recalling my easy joy at befriending Valentina seemed surreal. Had I really been gushing about the curriculum at UCLA and giggling about a girls' shopping trip this weekend just before she'd been taken and terrorized on my father's orders?

"You need to eat, *florecita*," Mateo murmured, pulling me out of my churning thoughts.

"Okay," I agreed, my voice small. I really was

hungry, and I didn't feel like arguing with Mateo anymore. My morning outburst and subsequent tears had left me feeling wrung-out and weak. I didn't have any reason to fight him, anyway. Not after he'd just explained the bleak alternative to staying here with him.

He released me from his warm embrace. I swayed toward him as he stepped away, reluctant to lose his reassuring heat. He grasped my shoulders, steadying me.

"There's a new toothbrush under the bathroom sink," he supplied. "Why don't you freshen up a little, and then we can have breakfast. You'll feel better after."

Now that he mentioned it, I realized that I did feel kind of gross. I was still wearing yesterday's dress, and I knew my hair must be a crazy mess.

"I need to shower," I said softly. Maybe I could cleanse more than just my skin. Hot showers usually helped me clear my head, and I could definitely use some clarity right now.

"There are fresh towels in there, too," he said. "Use whatever you need."

I tugged at my dress. "But I don't have any clothes to change into."

He traced the line of my jaw, his dark eyes focusing on my features with the strange intensity that made my stomach do funny flips.

"You can wear my clothes." The offer sounded more like a rumbling decree.

"Your clothes won't fit me." I glanced down his huge body. Before my gaze could linger on his powerful muscles, he touched two fingers beneath my chin to redirect my attention to his face.

"We'll find something that works." He continued to stare at me with that disconcerting, unwavering intensity.

I shifted on my feet, suddenly hot and off-balance. "But I don't have any fresh underwear," I protested just before my cheeks burned with mortification.

Had I really just said that out loud?

One corner of his mouth tilted in a wicked smirk, and he brushed his thumb over my lower lip. "That's too bad. I guess you'll just have to make do without."

His darkly pleased expression and dismissive words should have sent a chill of fear through my system. Although my skin pebbled, heat licked along my veins.

"But I need my stuff," I countered weakly. "I don't have my haircare products or anything."

He touched a particularly unruly curl, tucking it behind my ear. "You don't need any makeup or hair products."

I shook my head slightly. Mateo clearly didn't understand the importance of a strict regimen to keep my curls in order. I loved my hair and made every effort to ensure it looked glossy and polished.

When I was little, my mother had despised dealing with my hair. She'd told me it was a frizzy mess, and she'd insisted on taking a flat iron to my curls every day. Of course, she'd assigned a nanny to manage the boring task. She might have hated the idea of her daughter looking untidy, but it didn't bother her enough that she would see to fixing it herself.

I'd finally rebelled at the age of fifteen. I threw the straighteners in the garbage and bought every product I could find for curly hair until I discovered the perfect daily routine.

"Yes, I do need my products." My argumentative spark returned, and I straightened my spine. "My hair will be a mess without them."

Mateo shrugged. "There's no one here you need to impress."

I stiffened and took a step back, pulling away from the heat of his hands. I didn't care about impressing anyone. My hair was a point of personal pride, a symbol of my decision to take control over my own life. His dismissiveness was a cruel reminder that I no longer had any control. My choices, my freedom, had been taken away.

I turned sharply and stalked into the bathroom

without another word, making sure to slam the door as a warning not to follow me.

I needed some space from Mateo. I couldn't think straight when he was touching me. Just because he was being gentle didn't mean I had to roll over and meekly accept my fate as his hostage. I didn't have to cling to him when I cried, like a stupid little girl who was desperate for reassurance and affection.

Shoving down my roiling emotions, I focused on freshening up. I might not have any of my usual supplies for my morning routine, but I could at least brush my teeth and take a shower.

I found the toothbrush in the cabinet under the sink, just as Mateo had promised. For a fleeting moment, I wondered why he had a spare, new toothbrush stocked and ready to go.

Idiot, I scolded myself. There was a very obvious reason why a man might keep extra toiletries in his house: to have a supply on hand in case a woman spent the night unexpectedly.

Of course Mateo was prepared for female *overnight guests*. Women probably swooned for him all the time. He was jacked and gorgeous and insanely sexy with his broody, bad boy vibe.

I rolled my eyes as I brushed my teeth. I had to get that girlish fantasy out of my head. Mateo might not be cruel, but he was definitely a dangerous man.

I wondered if the other women he brought to his

house knew he was a criminal. Was he sweet to them too? Did he hold them as tenderly as he'd held me?

Frustrated with my wayward thoughts, I slapped the toothbrush down onto the sink and stomped the short distance to the shower. The water warmed within seconds, and I jerked the curtain closed with a bit more force than necessary as I stepped under the hot spray.

What did it matter to me if Mateo was nice to the women he fucked? I might have harbored a stupid crush on him for far too long, but that was over now. Sure, I liked when he comforted me. I'd been through some traumatic events since yesterday afternoon. Of course it felt good to be comforted by a friend.

Well, Mateo had never really been a *friend*, necessarily. He'd kept himself at a distance, and I never saw him unless he was with Adrián. It wasn't like we'd ever had any time alone together.

But I'd known him for years. He wasn't some stranger who'd kidnapped me off the street. So, it was only natural that I accept the solace he offered.

Just because I liked it when he hugged me did *not* mean I was jealous at the thought of some other woman sleeping in his bed and utilizing his supply of fresh toiletries.

I yelped when I heard the bathroom door open.

"Relax." Mateo's voice drifted through the steam-filled bathroom. "I can't see anything through that shower curtain. I'm just setting some clothes on the sink for you. Finish up so we can have breakfast. You need to eat."

I huffed my irritation at his high-handedness, but the bathroom door thumped shut again before I could consider a retort.

Thankfully, he exited the bathroom right before my stomach rumbled loudly. I didn't need my traitorous body to prove his point and validate his overbearing behavior.

But I *was* hungry.

I turned off the water and stepped out of the shower, grabbing a towel to dry off quickly. I'd mostly managed to keep my hair out of the spray. Although I longed to wash and style it, I was worried that I'd only make it worse by dousing it in the shower without my usual products to set the curls properly.

Careful to avoid my reflection in the fogged mirror—I didn't want to see my beloved curls in such disarray—I reached for the clothes Mateo had set out for me. My eyes widened when I unfolded his black, cotton t-shirt. I'd seen him wear shirts like this plenty of times, and I always thought of them as almost indecently tight. But without the massive man to fill it out, the garment appeared to be made with more fabric than one of my sundresses.

I tugged it over my head, and the soft material slid down my body, falling all the way to my knees.

Holy shit. Given my silly infatuation, I'd always been very aware that Mateo was big and brawny. But wearing his enormous shirt really put his size into perspective.

I eyed the sweatpants that were folded on the counter. The notion that they might somehow stay on my hips was utterly ridiculous.

Sighing, I glanced down at my body. The baggy t-shirt didn't expose an inch of my thighs, which I always kept carefully hidden. It actually covered me far more modestly than some of the cocktail dresses I owned.

I usually wear underwear beneath even my most daring cocktail dresses, though.

My cheeks heated at the thought of walking around without underwear. Even if there was no one here to see me but Mateo, it was still a discomfiting prospect.

I swallowed hard. Actually, being alone with Mateo without wearing panties was probably worse than going commando at a party. No one at a party would know. The man waiting for me in the bedroom was fully aware that I didn't have anything covering my sex.

"Come on out, Sofia," Mateo prompted, his impossibly deep voice penetrating the door. "I'm hungry, too."

I took a breath and braced myself to face him. He

might be bossy, but he'd been kind to me so far. It would be inconsiderate of me to delay his breakfast if he was hungry. I hated the circumstances that had brought me into his house, but I didn't hate Mateo. He hadn't given me cause to be cruel to him.

When I opened the door and stepped into the bedroom, Mateo made a strange sound, almost like a growl. I froze, finding myself trapped in his dark stare again. How could he make me feel shivery and hot at the same time?

"What happened to the sweatpants?" he asked on a rasp. His eyes trailed over my body, fixing on my bare legs before pausing somewhere around my navel.

I tried not to squirm, but I felt like I might as well be standing naked before him. Heat flashed through my body, and my skin pebbled.

Mateo's eyes lifted to my chest, and another odd, strangled sound rumbled from him.

I peeked down at myself, mortified to realize that my nipples were hard buds, and they were all too visible against the soft material of Mateo's shirt. My arms flew to my chest, crossing over my breasts to hide the embarrassing display.

"The sweatpants won't fit me," I mumbled, my cheeks flaming.

He ran a hand over his face and drew in a shuddering breath. At least he wasn't looking at my nipples anymore.

"I'll figure out a way to get you some clothes that fit properly," he said, his voice more strained that I'd ever heard before.

"Thanks." I shifted on my feet, feeling very awkward and still far too hot.

He jerked his head to the side, breaking eye contact as he started walking out of the bedroom and into the hall.

"Come on," he urged. "I'll make you breakfast."

I heard him mutter something under his breath as I followed after him. It sounded suspiciously like a curse word.

Clearly, I wasn't the only one bothered by my state of undress.

CHAPTER 5

MATEO

"What are you doing?" Sofia asked as I retrieved a mixing bowl and frying pan from the kitchen cabinet.

"I figured I'd make scrambled eggs," I replied. "Do you like eggs? I have bacon, too."

I glanced over to where she was sitting at my kitchen island. Thankfully, I couldn't see her bare legs anymore. But she leaned forward on her elbows, watching me with open curiosity. The position made the neckline of my t-shirt gape open, offering me a tantalizing glimpse at her chest.

Jesus fucking Christ.

I tore my eyes away before I could start staring again. Rationally, I knew I wouldn't be able to see her breasts if I kept looking; the shirt wasn't at all low-cut. But somehow, it seemed more indecent than some of the flirty dresses I'd seen her wear at her father's parties.

When I'd offered for her to wear my clothes, I'd liked the idea of her swaddled in my shirt and sweatpants. I hadn't bothered to puzzle out exactly why it appealed to me, other than the fact that clothing her was part of caring for her.

But then she'd stepped out of the bathroom wearing nothing but my t-shirt, and I'd almost choked on my own tongue. The baggy garment completely obscured her curves, but knowing that she was only hidden from me by the thin barrier of cotton made my cock jerk to attention.

Had I really thought that not allowing her underwear was a good idea? It had seemed enticing at first.

Now, I realized that was a big fucking mistake. Was I intentionally *trying* to tempt and torture myself?

"I like scrambled eggs and bacon," she assured me, completely oblivious to my sexual frustration. "I just figured you meant you'd pour some cereal or something when you mentioned you were going to make breakfast."

"Despite all appearances, I'm not a total caveman," I informed her, keeping my eyes trained on my task. "I'm fully capable of making scrambled eggs."

"I don't think you're a caveman," she said, sounding far too sweet for my own good. "I'm just surprised that you're cooking. Does your chef have the day off or something?"

I paused, setting the egg carton on the counter so I could turn to meet her eye. She was still regarding me with open curiosity. Considering my actions yesterday, she should be watching me warily, perhaps even fearfully. Instead, I felt like some sort of exotic animal she was studying, as though I was a strange, interesting new species she'd never seen before.

I shifted, suddenly off-balance. How long had it been since anyone other than Adrián had looked at me without a flash of wariness? My boss and best friend wasn't afraid of me because it was my job to watch his back. He knew I'd be loyal to him forever, no matter what.

As far as everyone else was concerned, I was a potential threat. Given that I served as Adrián's personal bodyguard, my entire purpose was to threaten, to intimidate.

Even the women I fucked from time to time were wary of me. They were drawn to me because they liked the little thrill of fear they experienced in my presence. That suited my tastes, so it had never bothered me before.

But now that Sofia was looking at me with fascination rather than trepidation, I realized that I liked her innocent attention. It didn't even seem to occur to her not to trust me, despite the fact that I'd drugged her and imprisoned her in my home.

She was watching me expectantly, waiting for an answer to her question.

"I don't have a chef," I said, knowing that I'd taken a few seconds too long to reply.

Being with Sofia was far more confusing than I ever could have anticipated. For years, I'd lusted after her. I'd wanted her body, her sweetness, her beauty. When I'd imagined having her for myself, I'd never thought about what it might be like to simply talk to her.

She rested her chin on her palm, leaning toward me. "You don't have a chef? Why not?"

I cocked a brow at her, wondering exactly how cosseted her life had been. "Do you think it's normal for everyone to have a personal chef at their disposal?"

"Of course not." She waved her hand, gesturing at my expansive kitchen. "But with a house like this, I figured you would."

I nodded, accepting her reasoning. A lot of people with my kind of money would hire a chef. Sofia had grown up in an obscenely wealthy home, so it was only natural for her to assume that I might keep a similar lifestyle.

"I like to cook," I told her as I turned back to my task.

Before I could finish cracking the first egg on the side of the bowl, she continued her enquiry. "Really? What do you like about it? I always feel like cooking is kind of boring. I'd prefer to be doing something else with my time. Then again, I can't manage much in the kitchen other than using a microwave."

I shrugged. "I didn't have a house like this growing up. My mom cooked all our meals, and I wanted to help. So, she taught me."

"Huh," Sofia mused. "I've never really thought about a man liking to cook. I mean, I guess that's just my biased view of gender norms based on my personal experience. No one in my family cooks, but I especially can't imagine my dad in the kitchen. What did your dad think about you helping your mom out?"

"He didn't think about it at all." I kept my attention on beating the eggs. "He wasn't in the picture."

"Oh. I didn't know. Sorry, that was an insensitive question."

"It's okay," I reassured her in a familiar rote tone. "It's a good thing that he wasn't around."

It would have been better if no men had been around at all.

I shook off the dark line of thinking before I got caught up in an old cycle of rage and guilt. If Sofia was distraught after only a peek at the ugly truth about human nature, she'd be deeply disturbed by my mother's life story.

"But it was hard on my mom raising a kid on her own," I continued, trying to sound casually conversational. "She didn't exactly arrive in the States legally, and she barely spoke any English when she got to California. She risked everything to give me a good life, so I've always done everything I can to make her life easier. When I was little, that meant helping with cooking and cleaning."

"You clean this big house too?" Sofia asked, incredulous.

Her shock at the prospect of me doing chores allayed my sour mood. I'd come from nothing, but now that I worked for Adrián, I had more than I could possibly ever need. I'd been raised in poverty, and it was an undeniable stroke to my ego that Sofia couldn't discern that fact immediately.

Her father—like many others in our organization—considered me barbaric, at best. Their fear of my lack of civility served my purposes in protecting Adrián; no one harbored any illusions that I possessed a shred of gentlemanly restraint.

Sofia didn't seem to understand this about me. Perhaps it hadn't even occurred to her to feel disdain for my background.

The ghost of a smile flitted around my mouth as I poured the beaten eggs into the hot pan. "No, I have a housekeeping service. I wouldn't have the time to keep this place spotless, even if I wanted to. I enjoy cooking, but I'm happy to hire someone to clean. If you think cooking is boring, imagine spending your free time mopping and vacuuming four thousand square feet."

"Wow. Daddy hired a maid just to clean my apartment once a week." She sighed. "I've never really thought about it before, but I guess I've been pretty spoiled. No wonder I can barely operate a toaster."

"What do you usually do for your meals, then?" It felt a little odd having such an inane conversation, but I suddenly found that I was just as curious about Sofia as she was about me. "Surely, you don't have a chef come to your apartment."

"I mostly eat on campus or go out to dinner with friends. God, I feel so useless sitting over here watching you cook for me. I would offer to help, but I'd probably ruin whatever you're doing."

I chuckled. It was strange to hear the sound fill my kitchen. "It's just scrambled eggs and bacon," I reassured her. "They're hard to ruin. Come here. I'll show you."

"I don't want to mess it up." Despite voicing her concern, she hopped off the stool where she'd been sitting and skirted around the kitchen island to join me by the stove.

"You can't possibly mess it up," I promised, trying to keep my gaze focused on her face.

She shot me a wry smile, seemingly unaware of my struggle not to devour her with my eyes. "I think you're overestimating my capabilities."

"I'm sure you're more than capable of doing anything you put your mind to." Her cheeks flushed before I added, "And you don't have to handle the pan unless you want to. I'm going to teach you how to scramble an egg. Watch and learn."

She peeked around me and sniffed delicately. "Is it supposed to smell like that?"

I bit out a curse. I'd been so distracted by her that I'd forgotten about the eggs. I hastily lifted them off the heat and scraped the charred mess off the pan.

She giggled. "Are you sure you should be offering me cooking lessons?"

"Hmmm," I mused. "Maybe not. But only because you're too distracting, not because I'm a bad cook."

"Oh. If I'm distracting you, I can sit down again and give you space." Her smile faltered slightly as she made the offer. It seemed she'd missed the lust in my words entirely. She thought she was inconveniencing me, not making my brain go stupid because of the intoxicating sound of her laughter.

My hand shot out to prevent her from pulling away. "Stay right here." I hadn't intended to sound so commanding.

She froze, her gaze fixing on my fingers where they encircled her slender wrist. Without thinking, I rubbed my thumb across the delicate veins at the base of her palm. Her plump lips parted slightly, and her eyes lifted to mine. They were dark with unmistakable desire, her pupils dilated.

This attraction wasn't one-sided.

I could fuck her right now.

If she wanted me, too, why did I have to hold myself back? With a little more seduction, her body would accept me easily. Judging by the way she was looking at me, my advances would be welcomed.

Later. I shut down that line of thinking for the time being.

Taking Sofia's virginity deserved more time and finesse than a quickie in my kitchen. I was well aware of her virginal status, because her father had used it as a bargaining chip to sweeten a lucrative business deal. Caesar had arranged her marriage to Pedro Ronaldo, the head of one of the Mexican cartels that helped traffic our cocaine from Colombia to the US. The marriage was meant to solidify the alliance between our organizations, and it further enriched Caesar.

As a dutiful daughter, Sofia might have agreed to the loveless match—I doubted she'd ever even met Ronaldo—but that didn't mean I would allow her to go through with it. She was mine now, so the deal with Ronaldo was dead. He didn't matter anymore.

I would fuck Sofia soon, but not before breakfast on her first day as my hostage. I needed to at least give her a little time to acclimate to the changes in her life, and I would put in the effort to learn all of her personal pleasure points before I took her virginity. I wanted her to love every second of surrendering herself to me for the first time.

Now that I'd experienced the heady sensation of her leaning into my touch without fear or reservations, I wouldn't risk that. No matter how my body burned for her.

I forced myself to loosen my grip on her wrist. To make an excuse for my possessive touch, I lifted her hand and pressed the spatula into her palm.

"I promised to teach you how to scramble an egg," I said, my voice rougher than I would have liked. "Let's try this again."

She beamed at me, her perfect smile hitting me square in the chest. "Okay. You've shown me how to burn an egg, so I know to avoid that in the future. What's your next pro tip?"

Fuck, that sassy mouth made me want to bend her over the counter and take a wooden spoon to her ass. Then, she could use those lush lips to make amends for teasing me.

I cleared away the fantasy before I did something

I'd regret. Sofia was attracted to me, but I was sure the innocent girl I'd obsessed over since we were teenagers wasn't remotely prepared for that kind of play. I would have to take this slowly, even after I took her virginity.

Her effortless, easy trust was precious to me, and I didn't want to lose it by pushing her too hard, too fast.

I'd waited five years for Sofia. I could wait a little while longer if it meant she would truly be mine.

CHAPTER 6

SOFIA

This whole situation was too bizarre. Cooking with Mateo was actually *fun*.

Before this morning, I'd rarely seen him smile. He'd always been aloof, mysterious, and broodingly gorgeous.

Now, he smiled whenever I teased him, a sexy, indulgent smile. Although he was clearly amused, there was something darker in his eyes when he looked at me like that. He didn't appear angry or cruel. Maybe...*hungry* was a better word to describe it.

Whatever it was, it made me feel all hot and shivery at the same time. I'd never experienced anything like it before, but around Mateo, it seemed to happen often. The sensation was new and foreign, but I liked it *a lot*.

"Finish your eggs," he commanded, tipping his chin in the direction of my mostly-empty plate.

"I'm full," I replied. "I don't usually eat this much for breakfast. I'm more of a mocha latte and pastry to-go kind of girl."

"Two more bites."

I smirked at him. "Are you really negotiating with me about two bites of eggs?"

His smile was a touch more twisted than my own. "It's not a negotiation. Go on. You didn't eat enough yesterday. You need more calories this morning."

I rolled my eyes, but I took a single bite to placate him. When I set down my fork, he fixed me with a hard stare. He wasn't smiling anymore, but his eyes were still glinting with the strange intensity that made my blood heat.

"Fine," I scoffed, polishing off the eggs as though I was somehow challenging him with my flippancy. I let my fork clatter onto the empty plate. "Are you happy now?"

"Yes." His mouth quirked up at the corners. "I'm very happy you did as you were told. Good girl."

I attempted to huff in irritation, but I had to press my lips together to suppress my own smile. "Not this again," I complained.

"What? You don't like being my *good girl?*"

God, why did his voice have to sound like pure sex when he said those two words? They were all deep and slow and rumbly. I could practically feel them caress my skin as palpably as his big hands had stroked me when he'd held me this morning.

"I don't like how bossy you are." My accusation came out far too breathily, and I couldn't look directly at him.

"I thought I warned you about lying to me," he drawled.

Suddenly, his warm breath fanned across my neck, and his tone dropped lower as he leaned in close. "You do like when I'm bossy. And that makes me happy. Do you want to know why?"

"Why?" I whispered, an automatic response to his low prompting. I didn't register that my eyes closed. My other senses were far too overwhelmed to compete. His scent surrounded me; his heat licked at my skin; his deep voice filled my mind like a warm, heavy fog.

"Because I like when you obey me, Sofia." I could practically hear his dark smile. "I like it because I want to protect you, and I'll issue commands with your best interests in mind. But sometimes..." He paused, and I felt his lips ghost over the shell of my ear. "Sometimes, I'll order you to do things for my pleasure. You'll want to obey just because you know it will please me. Because you do like being my good girl. And I promise you'll be rewarded for your obedience."

His forefinger touched my neck, brushing along the line of my artery. A needy little whimper eased up my throat.

He made a satisfied humming sound that I felt deep in my body, as though he'd plucked a bass string somewhere low in my belly.

A blaring ringtone jolted me out of the moment, and my eyes snapped open. Mateo's heat withdrew from me, and he muttered a curse.

"I have to get this," he told me, not waiting for me to respond before he answered the call. "Adrián," he said into the receiver, suddenly clipped and business-like. "Yes, she's fine." His eyes remained fixed on me, even though I wasn't actually included in the conversation. "I'm not sure yet. We'll see."

I frowned and crossed my arms over my chest. Mateo was talking to Adrián about me again, and I didn't appreciate not being invited to voice my own opinion. I might not hate Mateo, but I also wasn't thrilled about this arrangement. Being with him was better than being imprisoned in my childhood home, but it still wasn't what I would have chosen.

It didn't seem that anyone actually cared about my choices.

While I'd been having fun with Mateo over breakfast, I'd managed to forget my anguish at utterly losing control over my own life. It was easier to allow myself to be distracted by him than to dwell on my awful new reality. I'd struggled with control issues in the past, and I'd worked hard to overcome my negative coping mechanisms.

Finding out that my father was a drug lord and being held hostage by my long-time crush was a hell of a lot more to deal with than my mom trying to dictate my teenage hairstyle.

I took a deep breath and blew it out slowly, purposefully releasing the tension that was beginning to build in my chest. The last thing I needed right now was to fall back into old, addictive habits that I'd kicked years ago.

"Yes, boss," Mateo said. "I'll keep you updated."

He ended the call and slipped his phone back into his pocket, only to withdraw my own rose gold phone a second later.

Automatically, I reached for it. He pulled back slightly and fixed me with a warning frown.

"Oh, come on," I complained. "You're seriously not going to give me my freaking phone?"

"I don't know what you might do if I give you access to call for help," Mateo countered. "So for now, I am the only one who handles your phone."

I threw up my hands, exasperated. "I'm not exactly being a difficult prisoner here," I pointed out. "I'm not fighting you or trying to run away. We just made scrambled eggs together, for god's sake. Believe me, I don't want to go home and see my dad anytime soon."

He studied me for a long moment, his eyes scanning my face as though he could look right into my thoughts and read my sincerity.

"All right," he allowed. "If that's true, then this won't be a problem. Tell me which of your friends I should text so they don't worry about why you're not in class. And I'll need the names of your professors, so I can email them to make an excuse for you."

"But you don't have to do that," I insisted. "You said I could go back to my classes if I behaved. I'm not fighting you."

His head canted to the side, considering. "I said you *might* be able to go back to your classes, once I can trust you to obey me, no matter what."

"Ugh, enough with all this *obedience* bullshit," I insisted hotly. "You know what? No. I'm not going to tell you who to text and email."

"*No?*" I heard the danger in his soft tone, but I ignored it. I was too righteously pissed off.

"That's right: *no*. If you're so worried that people at UCLA might notice my absence and get concerned about where I am, then I'm not going to help you resolve this little issue. But you could just make this easier on both of us and let me attend my classes. I won't go to my dad's house, and I won't go to my apartment, either." I remembered Mateo's bleak warning of what might happen if I went back to my apartment. I couldn't bear the thought of being forcibly dragged back to Daddy.

"I'll just go to class, and I'll come right back here after," I continued. "I promise."

His black eyes narrowed. "You think this is a negotiation?"

"I think it's a compromise," I countered.

"Well, you're wrong," he said bluntly. "In my house, there are no compromises and definitely no negotiations. You do as I say, or you face consequences."

"*Consequences.*" I made sure to put the word in air quotes. "Yeah, you mentioned them last night. Like what? What are you going to do if I don't help you hold me hostage?"

His eyes sparked. "Punish you."

My mouth went dry, and my little tirade ended abruptly. "Wait. What?"

"You heard me."

"But..." I licked my lips, struggling to weigh up my options. "But what does that mean, exactly?"

His brows rose. "Keep testing me, and you'll find out."

"You said I could go back to my classes when you know you can trust me." I tried to change tactics. "You can trust me now. I promise I won't try to run away from you or get help from anyone."

He shook his head. "I don't know that with one hundred percent certainty. Not yet. I'm sure you think you're being sincere right now, but you could change your mind once you're out in public. I won't let you leave this house until I know you'll do whatever I say without question."

"That's not fair," I argued. "I'm telling you the truth, and you don't want to believe me. I shouldn't be confined to your house just because you have trust issues."

"And I suppose you think I should be more like you and trust everyone?" he shot back. "You don't live in that world anymore, Sofia. Your pretty little life was a lie. Most people aren't good. They aren't kind. I would be a fool to blindly trust everyone I meet."

His barbed comments cut to my core. I was still trying to avoid thinking about how my cushy, safe reality had been cruelly shattered. I was fully aware that I'd been foolish and perhaps even willfully ignorant to believe Daddy's lies, so I could keep living in my normal little bubble.

And I'd definitely been acting like an idiot to enjoy cooking breakfast with Mateo, my unbending jailor.

"You're right," I seethed. "I have been foolish. I was stupid to think I could ever trust *you*. But you aren't good. You aren't kind. You're a criminal. Just like Adrián. Just like my dad. You think I'm going to help a criminal keep me captive? You think I'm going to be a compliant little hostage? Fuck you, Mateo."

His face turned stonier with each accusation I hurled at him. When I spat my final insult, he remained silent for several of my racing heartbeats.

"Go to your room," he ground out.

"Excuse me?" I choked. He couldn't be serious.

"I warned you before: if you act like a brat, you get treated like a brat. Now, go to your room." He enunciated each word.

A crazed laugh burst from my chest, booming through the kitchen. This was all too insane. He honestly thought he could put me in time-out like a naughty child?

I had one second to note the hard resolve that turned his features to granite before my world turned upside down.

"Hey!" I exclaimed, shocked to find myself slung over his shoulder. "What are you doing?"

His fingers bit into my thigh, silencing me as effectively as a palm against my mouth.

Oh, god. His big hand was braced right beneath my ass. The thin cotton barrier of his t-shirt did little to protect my vulnerable flesh from his iron hold. The heat of his hand branded me, and I became very aware of the fact that he was only an inch away from touching my sex.

I went limp against him, too overwhelmed to

consider struggling. Not that I would have any chance against his strength, anyway.

Had I thought that being sent to my room seemed childish and silly only moments ago?

Mateo definitely wasn't joking around. And I'd never been more aware of the womanly parts of my body. Something pulsed between my legs, and my nipples pebbled.

He made that low, growly noise again.

I nearly moaned in mortification. Did he somehow know what was happening to me?

I shouldn't feel turned on right now. Being carried off by big, sexy Mateo had been a particularly favorite fantasy of mine for several years, but not like this. Not when he was holding me against my will and *punishing* me for refusing to obey him.

The world spun again, and my feet touched soft carpet. Mateo's hands remained on my hips just long enough to steady me before he pulled away.

He stared down at me, and I suddenly felt very small in his huge shadow.

"You're going to stay in here and think about your behavior," he ground out. His muscles bulged and flexed, as though he was physically restraining himself from doing more to me. "You get to come out when you agree to cooperate. For now, I'll answer any texts or emails as they come through to your phone.

But until you decide to be good for me, you're not leaving this room."

He turned toward the door.

"Wait, you're not staying in here with me?" God, why did I have to sound so pathetic?

The idea of being sent to my room had seemed preposterous, but now that it was actually happening, I found that I didn't like it at all. As an extrovert, I didn't enjoy much alone-time in general, and enforced isolation was a painful trigger point for me. Daddy used to confine me to my room when I'd disappointed him. The withdrawal of affection was more devastating than if he'd belted me for bad behavior.

Being left alone with my thoughts the day after my entire world had crumbled would be awful.

"No, I'm not staying," Mateo said, his eyes softening slightly in response to my flash of distress.

"But I don't want to be in here by myself."

One corner of his lips quirked in a small smile, but he seemed more regretful that amused. "That's how punishments work, *belleza*."

For a moment, he lingered, and I thought he might change his mind. Then, he walked away and shut the door behind him. I heard the lock click into place.

It seemed Mateo had been completely serious when he'd warned me that there would be consequences for disobedience.

I realized I was hugging my arms around my chest, and I quickly dropped them to my sides. Just because Mateo was choosing to treat me like a naughty child didn't mean I had to act like one.

There was a TV in the room, for god's sake. It wasn't like I was locked in a dark dungeon.

If Mateo thought I'd cave to his demands just because I had no choice but to watch TV all day, he was mistaken. Plenty of people binge watched TV. I didn't often make a habit of it, but it wasn't as though it would be a hardship.

I found the remote and settled back onto the bed, arranging the pillows in a comfortable pile.

If Mateo didn't trust me when I promised him that I could go to my classes but not try to run away from him, then that was his problem. I wouldn't just roll over and help him keep me away from school. My knowledge of who to contact in order to avoid an emergency alert being sent out for me was my only tiny bit of leverage in this situation.

This is going to be easy, I told myself as I tuned in to HGTV.

IT WASN'T EASY.

It was every bit as awful as I'd feared.

There were only so many different shows I could

watch about home renovation before they all started blending into one another, but I managed to keep myself distracted for the first few hours. I barely even thought about the heavy weight of guilt pressing down on my heart.

On a rational level, I knew feeling guilty was completely unwarranted in this situation. I hadn't done anything wrong. Mateo was the one committing a crime against me. I was just standing up to him and advocating for myself.

But the emotional response to this kind of punishment was too deeply ingrained in my psyche. Daddy had isolated me like this when I failed at something important.

If I was rude or even insensitive toward an important guest: *Go to your room.*

If I didn't get an A on a test: *Go to your room.*

I'd even been punished like this when I was in kindergarten and didn't get a gold star for playing well with others.

I hated the crushing guilt associated with disappointing the only parent who showed me any affection. It wasn't as though Mom cared enough to comfort me or offer reassurance.

By the time Mateo brought me a sandwich for lunch, it was all I could do to not apologize like a desperate little girl to try to win back his approval.

But the only thing I hated more than being

isolated was losing control over my choices. When I was younger, Mom had kept me on a strict regimen to enhance my physical appearance, controlling everything from my hairstyle to the clothes I was allowed to wear. Having a pretty daughter reflected well on her, and her standards were exacting.

The guilt of disappointing Daddy was awful, but being deprived of my autonomy had broken me once before.

I would never let that happen again.

But the day in isolation went by painfully slowly. Mateo's lunchtime check-in had been ages ago. The sun was beginning to set behind the trees that lined what I assumed was his back lawn. I didn't really have an understanding of the layout of his house and property, but the swath of green grass visible outside my window was obviously a lawn. The turf ended at a thick tree line, and I couldn't see anything beyond that.

I thought I was still somewhere near LA, but I had no idea which neighborhood I was in, and I didn't have any means to get my bearings.

It didn't really matter where I was located, anyway. I might as well have been on the moon for all the difference it would make.

There was nowhere for me to go if I left Mateo's house. Not really.

I refused to go back to my childhood home and

face Daddy. But according to Mateo, returning to my apartment wasn't an option, either. If I went there, I might as well just drive straight to Daddy and save myself from being forcibly abducted again.

Where else was I going to go?

I supposed I could crash with one of my friends, but I didn't want to bring this shitstorm into any of their lives. If Daddy was ruthless enough to hurt Valentina in exchange for power, what might he do to my friends if he wanted me to come home, and they stood in his way?

Going on the run was an option, but not one that appealed to me. I didn't want to abandon everyone and everything I knew. Even if the remnants of the life I was cleaving to had always been a lie, I didn't want to leave them.

Everything was spiraling out of my control.

I pressed my palms against my closed eyes, as though I could stop my cyclical thoughts if I applied enough pressure.

I inhaled deeply, practicing the breathing exercises I'd learned in therapy. They'd served me well over the last five years, and I hadn't had a single incident since I was fifteen.

I also started styling my curls at fifteen, I recalled. That little act of asserting my independence and individuality had saved me from myself.

Well, my curls, my music, and a lot of expensive therapy.

Against my better judgment, I ran my hands over my hair. My chest tightened when I felt the frizzy mess.

I took another breath and forced my arms to my sides, pushing my palms flat against the mattress.

I'm not going to lose my shit just because I can't style my hair. That's insane behavior.

I forced myself to focus on whatever inane sitcom was playing out on the TV, pretending I didn't notice how tight my skin felt. How much I itched to move, to scream, to run. To do *something* that I could control.

My gaze drifted toward the bathroom, but I quickly snapped my attention back to the TV.

Not that, I told myself firmly. *I'm not doing that.*

I heard the soft *click* of the lock disengaging, but I didn't bother to turn to look at Mateo. He was going to ask me if I was ready to comply with his demands. And I wasn't going to.

If I couldn't control anything else, I could control this: I didn't have to cave and help him smooth over my sudden absence from school.

He could keep me in miserable isolation, but now that I'd found the only tiny thing that I *could* control, I wouldn't surrender it for any reason. It was the only thing tying me to sanity.

"You didn't eat your lunch," he noted, his voice heavy with disapproval.

I simply shrugged, choosing not to respond. I'd moved from guilt to numbness at this point, and I no longer felt the stupid impulse to apologize.

He sighed. "Well, you *will* eat your dinner."

The rich scent of lasagna hit my nose, and I finally turned to face him. "And what happens if I don't?" I asked, all bitterness and no fire. "Will there be more *consequences*?"

He took a moment to consider his answer, his eyes studying my face. Whatever he saw in my expression, he didn't like it.

His mouth pressed to a thin slash, and he nodded curtly. "Yes, there will," he confirmed. "So, you'd better eat every bite."

"Whatever you say, warden," I mumbled, but there was no force behind my antagonistic comment.

This morning, I'd felt playful with Mateo. Even when I'd been mad at him, I'd felt like I could express my feelings. Yelling at him might not have been very nice, but at least I'd been engaging with him on an emotional level.

Whatever I'd felt for him then was gone now. I felt hollowed out, and all I had left was my grim determination to cling on to my one last shred of control with a death grip.

I took the plate he offered me without really

looking at him. He watched me eat in silence, which I would have found weird if I weren't so focused on not telling him anything about my contacts at school. If I kept him locked out completely, he couldn't manipulate me into surrendering.

He took the plate back when I finished the final bite.

"I'm guessing you're not ready to cooperate with me," he said, his resigned tone telling me he already knew my answer.

I simply shook my head and laid back on my little nest of pillows, turning my attention to the TV.

"Sofia." He said my name slowly, his tone tense with uncharacteristic uncertainty. "I don't like how you're reacting to this, but I can't just change the consequences. I have to be consistent."

"No one's asking you to change anything," I said dully, refusing to engage.

"I'll stay in here with you," he announced, as though he'd arrived at a solution. "See? I can compromise."

"I don't want you in here. Just go away, Mateo."

If I let him stay, he might put his tender hands all over my body and break down my resistance. I refused to let that happen.

He hesitated, so I rolled over onto my side, facing away from him; the physical equivalent of *fuck off*.

"We'll talk more tomorrow," he said. It sounded like a command.

If he thought I'd get all melty if he bossed me around and called me his *good girl*, he was mistaken.

When he'd invaded my space and my senses with those dark words this morning, I'd felt far happier than I should have, given my circumstances. I could see now that I'd just been allowing him to distract me from my miserable situation. As soon as Mateo reminded me that he was part of that misery, I severed any emotional bonds I'd been forming.

I might have harbored an intense crush for years, but now, I didn't feel anything for Mateo. Not anymore.

CHAPTER 7

MATEO

Fuck. I tossed my Xbox controller aside, giving up. Had I really thought that playing a mindless video game could distract me from the disturbing image of Sofia's hollow stare?

When she'd ignored me at lunchtime, I'd assessed that she was just sulking. But by the time I took her dinner, the giggling girl I'd played with this morning had been replaced by a cold, emotionless woman.

I'd thought confining her to the bedroom was the mildest punishment I could impose on her. When she'd accused me of being an untrustworthy criminal, it had been all I could do to cling on to control. The stinging insults were too venomous coming from my sweet Sofia.

My immediate impulse had been to take her over

my knee and give her a sound spanking until she agreed to obey me.

But the shred of conscience I possessed acknowledged that I would be acting in anger. That impulse had more to do with my feelings about losing her trust than it did about her disobedience.

And if she thought I was a bad man for demanding her phone contacts, she'd think I was a complete monster if I spanked her for upsetting me with her pointed accusations.

Sending her to her room had seemed like the most restrained option available to me. I'd chosen that punishment because I thought I was being cautious with her.

Maybe that had been a mistake. She'd responded so well to my touch this morning; she obviously thrived on physical contact. I'd thought depriving her would be an effective way to drive home the lesson I was trying to teach her.

Instead, simply a day in isolation seemed to have broken her spirit far more thoroughly than I could have managed with a sound thrashing.

I ran a hand over my face, frustrated. If I didn't actually care what Sofia thought of me, this wouldn't be so difficult. Spanking her until she submitted would have been the obvious course of action. But I'd decided that she wasn't ready for me to push her that far. I'd decided I wanted her to obey me because she trusted me, not because she feared me.

Despite everything I'd done to her so far—drugging her, abducting her, and imprisoning her in my home—she hadn't looked at me with true fear. I never wanted that to change.

My fists clenched at my sides as my indecision tore at me. She'd told me to leave her alone, but she was my captive. I didn't have to honor her wishes. I could do whatever I wanted.

And I wanted to hold her and pet her until she snuggled into me and smiled again.

Forcing myself on her wouldn't earn her smile.

My phone pinged, and my stomach dropped. That tiny little sound was my unique alert that someone had set off my security system. I quickly opened my app and determined that the breach was located at the back of my property. Someone had made it over the walled barrier I'd hidden in the tree line behind the house.

There was only one person who would be desperate enough to dare to assault my home: Caesar Hernández. Sofia's father had sent men to retrieve her.

Possessive rage ripped through my body in a torrent I'd never experienced before, driving me to action before I fully considered a plan or assessed the risks. If I'd been thinking clearly, I would have sent a message to Adrián for backup, and I would have stationed myself as close to Sofia as possible to shelter her from a defensive position.

As it was, mind-numbing fury propelled me toward my enemies, my muscles straining with the imperative to rip apart anyone who was foolish enough to try to take her from me.

I could have grabbed one the many Glocks I kept stashed around my home as I dashed to the back door. But using a gun to dispatch the men who threatened what was mine wouldn't satisfy me. Vicious, primal instinct urged me to mutilate them with my bare hands.

Based on the heat signatures provided by my security system, there were three of them.

An easy number to handle on my own. Caesar had opted for a stealthy extraction rather than a full-on assault. I almost wished there were more attackers for me to punish. Only three might not be enough for me to vent my rage.

I pressed the button on my app that activated the floodlights behind my house just before I dropped my phone onto the grass. I wanted full use of my hands for this.

The assailants cursed when the sudden wash of light seared their eyes. Their seconds of blindness provided all the time I needed to launch my attack.

I put one man down with a punch to the throat.

The second man's jaw shattered beneath my fist. The third tried to aim an assault rifle at me, but I ripped it from his hands before he could get his bearings.

Satisfied that the other two were incapacitated for a few minutes, I decided to take more time with this one. I whipped the rifle around and slammed the butt of the gun into his ribs, hard enough to ensure they cracked, but not hard enough to puncture his lung.

None of them would be allowed to die for several more hours, at least. Once my rage was sated by their blood, I could dump whatever was left of them at Caesar's doorstep as a warning to never fuck with me again.

"Sofia is *mine*," I snarled into the man's face as I tackled him to the ground, pinning him with my hand around his throat.

"Wait," he choked, his fingernails scrabbling at my wrist.

I squeezed, cutting off his air supply. His eyes bulged, and his face turned purple. Just as he started to go limp beneath me, I eased off.

"You don't get to die yet," I seethed. "Did you really think you could come into *my* home and take her from me? I'll send you all back to Caesar in pieces."

"We didn't come...to take her." The man struggled to speak through heaving breaths. "Just a message."

I flexed my fingers around his throat. "You expect me to believe that you broke into my property armed with assault rifles just to deliver a message?"

The man held his hands up, desperate to placate me. "Precautions. Caesar knows..." He coughed and gasped. "Attacking you will mean war. He wants to make a deal."

"And why couldn't he just call me?"

"Would you have listened?" he rasped.

I growled down at the man, because I knew he was right. "I don't have to make a deal with Caesar," I ground out. "I have Sofia. He has to prove his loyalty to Adrián if he ever wants to see his daughter again."

"He knows this. But he wants... She's engaged. The alliance with Pedro Ronaldo. Caesar can't back out. It will upset the balance of power with the Mexican cartels."

My hand tightened around his throat, and I barely retained the presence of mind to prevent myself from crushing his windpipe. "I don't give a fuck about the Mexican cartels. If Caesar thinks I'll give Sofia to Ronaldo, then he doesn't understand what I'm really capable of."

The man's mouth opened and closed. I loosened my grip enough to allow him to breathe. I wasn't nearly finished with him.

"You might not...care. But Adrián Rodríguez

does," he persisted. "Ronaldo expects to marry a virgin, and if you—"

Bone and cartilage crunched beneath my hand, and the man's face went slack.

I threw my head back and roared out my fury. He wasn't supposed to be dead yet.

The other two were still alive, though. I could hear them groaning behind me.

I pushed to my feet, stalking toward them. They cowered in my shadow.

I could kill them so easily. I *wanted* to kill them. They'd tried to take Sofia away from me.

We didn't come to take her. Just a message. I recalled the dead man's words. *You might not care. But Adrián Rodríguez does.*

I jerked my hand through my hair. I couldn't do something that might start a war. Not without talking to Adrián first. I wouldn't make a rash decision that would drag him into bloodshed and mortal danger.

"Get up," I snarled at the two assailants who were still breathing.

Barely.

"Take your dead friend and get the fuck off my property."

They struggled to their feet, and the man with the broken jaw swayed before dropping back to his knees.

"You can walk out of here, or I can throw your corpse over the wall," I threatened.

The prospect of a gory death provided the man with enough adrenaline to get moving. I followed them the short distance through the tree line to the defensive wall, watching to ensure that they actually left. They struggled to scale it with the ropes they'd used when they'd broken in. But my silent menace gave them the strength they needed to coordinate climbing over and dragging the dead man with them. They didn't even hiss in pain when the barbed wire they'd cut to access my property sliced at their skin. Fear was a powerful drug.

Once I was sure that they were in full retreat, I walked back through the trees and retrieved my phone from where I'd dropped it on my lawn. My fingers shook slightly from residual rage, but I managed to put in the call to Adrián.

"What's wrong?" he asked immediately, knowing I wouldn't call at this hour unless there was a problem.

"Caesar sent men to break into my house." My words were so roughened with unspent fury that they were barely intelligible.

Adrián seemed to understand. "They came for Sofia?"

I recognized his deadly calm tone all too well. My sadistic boss was prepared to mete out some punishment of his own for this threat to his control of the territory. Caesar had always been a reluctant associate. He'd been in charge of the Rodríguez cartel's west coast operation before Adrián's father had exiled him from Colombia and posted him here in California. Adrián had ruthlessly wrested power away from Caesar years ago, subjugating him.

"They said they came to deliver a message," I said, managing to regulate my voice to something slightly more civilized. "Caesar thinks the arranged marriage between Sofia and Pedro Ronaldo still stands. He wanted to make sure I don't..." I gnashed my teeth, too enraged by Caesar's demands to say them out loud.

"I see," Adrián replied coolly. He was already aware of Sofia's engagement to Ronaldo, and he understood what a promise like that entailed in our world.

Ronaldo would be expecting a virginal bride.

"I won't give her to him, Adrián," I vowed. "I *can't* give her to him."

"I know," my friend said heavily.

If I were simply another lackey in his employ, Adrián wouldn't permit any rebellious shit from me. He would expect me to fall in line and do what was best for our organization, or I could take a bullet to the brain instead.

But we were as close as brothers, even if he was my boss. I worked for him because I was happy to get paid obscene amounts of money to watch his back. Protecting him didn't feel like a job.

"I'm going to call Caesar and smooth things over," Adrián promised. "But under no circumstances are you to fuck Sofia. I'm going to have to give him my word that she will remain a virgin for as long as you have her as your hostage."

"You're going to let Caesar keep his deal with Ronaldo?" I demanded, incredulous.

Before I could snap at my friend that I wouldn't comply with his order, he continued on. "Yes, I'm going to let Caesar keep his deal with Ronaldo. For as long as Ronaldo is alive, and he won't be for much longer. I owe Stefano Duarte a favor, anyway. I'm sure he'll be eager to help me take out his main rival for trafficking our product through Mexico."

"You'll support Duarte over Ronaldo?" I knew all too well that Adrián owed Stefano Duarte a huge favor—the brutal drug lord who liked to style himself as a gentleman criminal had helped us rescue Valentina from her abusive husband and smuggle her safely back to California.

Duarte and Ronaldo both profited off their *friendship* with the Rodríguez cartel as they trafficked our Colombian cocaine through Mexico and into the States. But Duarte had decided to bet on Adrián, while Ronaldo had cozied up to Caesar.

The uneasy peace we'd brokered since Adrián had

stolen Valentina for himself was about as stable as a house of cards. And mishandling the situation with Sofia could bring the whole thing crashing down.

"I can't openly support Stefano Duarte," Adrián said. "Things are tense enough without me assisting him with a full-on assault on Ronaldo. But I can start working with Duarte to support his efforts to choke off Ronaldo's business and bleed him dry. Someone will kill him soon enough if he's not bringing in money. A wedding date hasn't been set yet, and Sofia has another year before she finishes college. Ronaldo won't be a problem by then.

"In the meantime," he continued, his tone sharpening, "Sofia's virginity has to remain intact. If I'm going to give my word to Caesar, you will have to honor it."

"I know," I agreed. Adrián's word was everything. His power and his control of this territory relied on pervasive fear, but also stability. If Adrián made a promise, he had to keep it. Otherwise, he'd get a knife in the back quickly.

I wouldn't be the one to put his safety at risk by making a liar out of him.

A year. I could last a year without taking Sofia's virginity. There were other ways to take my pleasure from her that didn't involve breaking her hymen.

"I mean it, Mateo," Adrián warned. "You can do whatever you want with her, as long as she remains a virgin. But keep your cock in your pants. No penetration of any kind. No *loopholes*."

"Don't talk about her like that," I snapped, knowing full well what he was referring to. I might have fantasized about claiming every one of Sofia's holes for myself, but I wouldn't tolerate anyone else talking about her so crassly, not even my best friend.

"Don't get shitty with me," he said coldly. "I know you were already considering it."

I bit out a curse. "Okay," I allowed. "I agree to your terms. Sofia will remain a virgin until Ronaldo is dead. But she's mine, Adrián. I won't touch her, but this doesn't change anything. She still belongs to me."

"I didn't say you couldn't touch her," he replied drily.

I heard a car engine rev, and my stomach dropped. The sound was far too close to be coming from the road. Someone else was on my property, and I'd left Sofia unguarded.

I ended the call and sprinted toward the sound. If the intruder wasn't bothering to mask their escape, they must already have Sofia in their possession.

It seemed I would get the chance to kill another man before the night was through.

CHAPTER 8

SOFIA

My heart hammered against my ribcage, and my stomach churned.

He's a criminal. Mateo is a violent criminal. Oh, god...

My throat convulsed, and I swallowed hard against the urge to vomit.

The floodlights that had suddenly shined through my window only seconds ago now illuminated a nightmare scene.

Mateo's massive body was a darker shadow against the tree line at the back of the property. I couldn't see his face, but I recognized his brawny frame.

He moved brutally and faster than I could have imagined, given his size. I scarcely had time to draw in a horrified breath before two men were dropped by Mateo's meaty fists.

A third man shifted something that was slung across his shoulder. Was that...*an assault rifle?*

In the second it took me to slap my hand over my mouth to stifle a scream, Mateo had ripped the gun out of the man's hands and jammed the weapon into his ribs. Mateo launched himself at the injured man, and they both went down.

All four men were on the ground. The floodlights made the grassy lawn glow an eerie neon green, casting the tree line into deeper shadow. I couldn't make out what was happening anymore, and for a moment, I feared for Mateo. At least one of those men had a freaking assault rifle.

But no shots rang out.

I pressed my face close to the window, straining to see if he was okay.

Then, a feral roar echoed through the night, sending a chill racing up my spine. Surely, that was a wild animal. It couldn't be human. It couldn't be Mateo.

That animal. It was what my father always called Mateo. I'd thought he was being mean and judging Mateo for his less-than-tailored appearance.

I'd liked how wild Mateo looked. I liked his thick black beard and indecently tight t-shirts. I'd never swooned for a clean-cut man in a suit the way I did for Mateo in jeans and a leather jacket.

But Daddy hadn't been making snide remarks about Mateo's style.

He knew something about Mateo that I didn't. He knew that the rough-around-the-edges man I had a crush on was actually a vicious criminal capable of brutal violence.

The shadowy form of Mateo's huge body stood tall once again. I could make out two other men struggling to their feet. I didn't see the fourth man, the one who had held the rifle.

A few seconds later, they all disappeared into the trees.

How long until he comes back?

Because Mateo was definitely coming back for me. He had made it clear that he was holding me hostage, and he didn't intend to let me go. I'd put a silly spin on the situation, pretending like being at Mateo's house wouldn't be all that bad. Even when I'd been emotionally hollowed out by the isolation punishment he'd imposed upon me, I'd still been completely delusional about Mateo's true nature.

Why did I keep doing this? It was as though I'd hardwired my brain for denial and willful ignorance my entire life, and I couldn't break the habit. Every time Mateo revealed something awful, I somehow managed to minimize it or distract myself from thinking about it altogether.

But I couldn't minimize the horrific shock of

violence I'd just witnessed. I couldn't distract myself from the memory of his beastly roar.

He would come back out of the trees soon. He'd come back into the house. There was nothing to stop him from coming into this room.

And I was trapped, locked in.

I pressed my hands against the window, and touching the cool glass jolted my brain to register the fact that it was a possible means of escape. There was hardly any drop from the windowsill to the ground outside. If the window wasn't sealed, I could easily leave this room.

It seemed utterly ridiculous that this had never occurred to me throughout the course of the day.

Then again, I hadn't really wanted to leave until now. I'd thought the alternatives were being forcibly taken to Daddy or going on the run.

I'd take my chances anywhere, as long as I could get away from Mateo. Sitting docilely in one monster's lair because I was scared of others was beyond stupid behavior.

If I was going to escape, it was now or never. Mateo could walk back into the yard at any moment, and I had to start running.

I reached for the window latch, silently berating myself when it opened without resistance. God, I'd been such an idiot to not try this sooner. Instead, I'd sat in a locked room like a miserable, scolded child all day.

I pushed the window open and sat on the sill, swinging my legs outside. The night air kissed my bare legs, and I realized that I was only wearing Mateo's huge shirt. For the space of a second, I considered going back for my dress and flats, but I couldn't waste any precious time.

I pushed off the sill, dropping only a few feet before my toes hit the grass. Uncertain of where I was going, I took off running. I knew I had to get out of this overly-bright yard before Mateo came back, so I raced along the exterior of the brick house. I took the first left turn I could find, tucking myself into shadows.

I paused to assess my surroundings. Although it wasn't nearly as bright as the yard, soft golden lights illuminated the area. Judging by the large, white-columned porch, I appeared to be at the front of Mateo's house. The driveway had been designed around a central fountain, the pavement encircling the water feature. The golden light wasn't bright enough to reveal the entire driveway, and the asphalt disappeared into darkness. I couldn't tell how far I was from the nearest road. And even if I got to a road, I didn't know how far I was from Mateo's nearest neighbors.

I had to get as far away as I could, as fast as possible. Mateo would come after me the moment he realized I was gone.

There was a large structure on the opposite side of the porch. I'd initially assumed it was a wing of the house, but at second glance, I registered garage doors. I'd never seen a garage that large, but I didn't waste any time pondering it. If I could get a car and drive away from here, that was all that mattered.

I jolted to action, sprinting to the structure. The huge doors wouldn't open from the outside, but I quickly discovered a smaller entryway. When I darted inside, overhead lights automatically came on.

Holy shit.

Mateo had a lot of fancy cars. And motorcycles. And some strange vehicles I didn't have a name for. I was pretty sure one of them was the Batmobile.

Before I could despair that I had no idea how to hotwire a car, I noticed the neat rows of keys hanging on the wall to my right.

I grabbed the closest one and pressed the unlock button. A black BMW flashed its lights, but it was two rows back, and I wouldn't be able to get it out of the garage without moving other cars out of the way.

Frantic, I started pressing random unlock buttons on different keys until one of the cars closest to the door made a cheery little beeping noise.

The last thing I needed if I wanted to remain

inconspicuous was a bright yellow Ferrari, but I was running out of time and options.

I found a switch near the big garage doors, and they slowly began to open. Hoping that they would somehow lift more quickly, I flung myself back toward the car and wrenched open the door before dropping into the driver's seat. It took a few tries for me to steady my shaking hands, but I managed to get the key into the ignition.

The car roared to life, making me jump.

Shit!

Too loud. I was making too much noise.

Acting on muscle memory, I put the car in drive and slammed down on the accelerator. The Ferrari snarled, but it didn't move an inch.

My heart leapt into my throat, and I anxiously searched the car for the source of the problem.

"Oh, no," I groaned. "No!"

Mateo drove stick shift. I'd only learned how to drive an automatic.

Panicking, I started slamming my feet down on the pedals and moving the stick shift in random patterns. The Ferrari growled at me, angry that I was fucking with its expensive mechanics.

Mateo appeared in the open doorway, his huge body seeming somehow even larger when illuminated by the car's headlamps at close range.

A strange yelp leapt from my throat, and I scrambled to lock the doors.

His muscles tensed and bulged, his dark eyes searching for something I couldn't see. His teeth were half-bared, and I knew if the car weren't snarling so loudly, I'd hear a similar noise rumbling from his chest.

His gaze met mine through the windshield, his furious expression dropping to one of concern. "Who else is here?" he demanded. "Who are you running from?"

"You!" I shrieked, pressing down on the gas pedal.

The Ferrari hissed and spit, but it didn't move.

"Stop that," Mateo ordered. "You're ruining the transmission."

His features pinched with irritation, but the terrifying beast of a man was gone.

That didn't mean he wouldn't come back.

"Get out of the car." The command took on a more coaxing lilt, but I wasn't falling for his softer side. Not again.

I shook my head in wild denial.

He sighed and walked toward the Ferrari, approaching me on the driver's side. He peered down at me through the window.

"I know I made a mistake today," he said, his deep voice rich and soothing. "I didn't think sending you to your room would upset you so much. I shouldn't have left you alone. I'm sorry." He crooked his finger at me, beckoning. "Now, come on out of there."

"No," I choked.

He cocked his head to the side, considering me. "I know you're mad at me, but—"

"I'm not mad!" I burst out, hysterical. "I'm scared. You scare me. I want to leave."

Hot tears tracked down my cheeks, blurring my vision.

He pressed his hand against the glass, as though he could reach through it and touch me. "Sofia..."

The pain in his rough tone ripped me apart. I wanted to believe in *this* Mateo. The man who was tender with me and comforted me.

This man wasn't the one I'd just witnessed unleashing shocking violence.

A sob wracked my chest, and I buried my face in my hands.

"I'm going to unlock the door now, Sofia," he said gently. "Don't be afraid."

The longing rasp in his voice tore at my heart more viciously. He didn't want me to be afraid of him.

I didn't want to be afraid of him.

But I was.

He must have a spare key, because I heard the locks disengaging. I didn't bother trying to stop him from opening the door. What was the point? I couldn't drive this car. I wasn't going anywhere.

He dropped down on one knee, getting on eye level with me. He regarded me cautiously, the tension in his body suggesting that he was restraining himself from reaching for me.

Part of me wanted him to. I wanted to feel him stroking my body, reassuring me that everything was going to be okay.

"I saw you," I admitted on a strangled whisper.

"What did you see?" he prompted, sounding more strained than ever.

"I saw you...beat those men." The words didn't seem nearly strong enough to capture the horror of Mateo in violent motion.

"And what else?" he pressed.

"They... They got up and you all went into the woods."

He blew out a breath, and his shoulders relaxed slightly. "I'm sorry you saw that. I know it must have been upsetting for you."

A tiny, maddened laugh bubbled from my chest and died in my throat.

Upsetting was the understatement of the century.

"This isn't my life," I lamented, wishing that speaking the words aloud would make them true. "My life isn't like this. I don't want it to be like this."

"I'm sorry, *florecita*, but this is reality." He delivered the blow quietly, but it still made me flinch. "Your father sent those men. I thought they had come to take you from me. I couldn't let them do that."

"Because I'm your hostage," I said miserably.

"Because you're—" He ended on a low grunt, holding in whatever he'd intended to say.

"Because I care about you, and I don't want to leave you exposed and vulnerable. I'll protect you, Sofia. I know it's confusing for you right now. But I swear, I'll protect you with my life. I will never hurt you."

"I want to leave," I whispered, although I tasted the lie on my tongue.

"Do you?" he challenged softly. "If you're not here with me, your father will find you and take you back home with him. Is that what you want?"

"You know I don't," I said brokenly.

"Then stay here and let me take care of you. I won't let anyone hurt you, Sofia. And you don't have anything to fear from me. I fought those men because they were a threat to you. I'm sorry you had to see me like that, but I'm not sorry for what I did. I would do that and worse a thousand times over to keep you safe."

I sniffled, but I didn't have a verbal response to such an overwhelming statement. I was still deeply shaken by witnessing the reality of Mateo's violent capabilities.

But he hadn't been violent with me. He could

have unlocked the door right away and ripped me out of the car by force. Instead, he'd spoken to me quietly and was giving me the chance to absorb what was happening in my life. He was waiting for me to trust him to keep me safe.

I definitely wasn't ready to trust him implicitly, as I'd mistakenly done this morning. But I did believe that he wouldn't hurt me.

"Are you ready to go back inside?" he asked, allowing me time to make a decision.

I managed a jerky nod.

"You're shaking," he murmured. "I'm going to carry you."

He reached for me, and I cringed.

"Easy," he cajoled, not pulling away. He braced one brawny arm behind my shoulders and another beneath my thighs.

He carefully extracted me from the car, pulling me close to his chest.

I closed my eyes and allowed my cheek to rest against his shoulder. My entire world was falling apart, and although Mateo had a hand in its destruction, he was the only solid thing I had to lean on.

"That's better," he soothed me. "Good girl."

CHAPTER 9

MATEO

I didn't allow myself to sleep beside Sofia after pulling her out of my Ferrari, even though I was tempted to. I'd held her and let her cry in my arms until she'd exhausted herself. Then, I'd tucked her into bed and made sure she was asleep before retiring to my own bedroom for the night.

As a gesture of goodwill, I didn't lock the door to the guest room. I didn't want her to wake up feeling trapped and frightened. Not after last night.

Recalling her abject terror at the sight of me made my stomach knot.

Never again. I would never give her cause to look at me like that again: like I was a monster out of her worst nightmare.

I was choosing to give her space this morning, but I set an early alarm for myself as a precaution. I didn't intend to give Sofia time alone to think about sneaking out again. I owed her a punishment for that already, and it would be tricky enough to administer without adding to her transgressions.

She was still soundly asleep when I went in to check on her. Deciding to let her rest, I went down to my basement home gym and put in a short workout. As long as I kept my phone nearby, I would be alerted to any disturbances to my security system. No one could get onto my property without my knowledge.

And Sofia couldn't get out, either.

Judging by the open window in the guest room when I'd put her to bed, she'd snuck out that way in her mad dash to my Ferrari. This morning, I made sure to activate the security alert associated with window breaches on my home, something I obviously should have done sooner. I hadn't thought Sofia would actually want to leave desperately enough to make a break for it, but I also hadn't anticipated her witnessing me brutalizing the men who'd tried to infiltrate my property.

Thank fuck she hadn't seen me crush the dead guy's throat. If she was so distraught over shadowy violence from a distance, I shuddered to think how she would react to that kind of gore up close.

I limited my workout to the bare minimum, resolving to put in more reps later in the day. Now that I had Sofia to protect, it was more important than ever that I keep my body in peak physical condition.

After half an hour of weights, I wiped down my equipment and took the stairs to up to the ground floor two at a time, eager to get back to her before it got too late in the day.

I checked the guest room on my way down the hall. The bed was empty, but the bathroom door was closed, and I heard the shower running.

I set out another one of my clean shirts for her to wear, leaving it on the bed and shutting the bedroom door behind me to grant her some privacy.

After a quick shower of my own, I returned to her room. My hand was on the doorknob before I stopped myself from barging right in. I didn't like having barriers between me and Sofia, but I hated the terror in her eyes even more. I would prove to her that she didn't need to fear me.

She would come around soon enough. Our chemistry was undeniable, and she'd definitely been attracted to me at breakfast yesterday morning. I had to convince her that I was every bit as much that man as I was the vicious protector she'd seen last night. She would adjust to the darker part of me over time, once she understood that I didn't act in violence because I derived twisted enjoyment from it.

Even though brutality didn't faze me, I wasn't inherently sadistic like Adrián.

Resisting my impulse to simply open the door and remove the barrier separating me from Sofia, I chose to knock.

A few seconds later, the door opened a crack, revealing an inch of her lovely face. "You knock now?" she asked dully.

I missed the fiery challenge in her tone. She'd acted up yesterday morning, and I'd enjoyed the push and pull with her.

Now, she sounded tired, even though she'd only just woken up. Her luminous skin was pale, the usual sparkle gone from her emerald eyes. Even her mahogany curls seemed to have lost their luster.

I'd been the one to break her like this, but I would fix her. I'd figured out what she needed.

Depriving her of touch and connection yesterday had been a terrible mistake. Sofia needed tactile stimulation, physical affection. Even when she'd been shaking and sobbing after her terror last night, she'd leaned into me when I offered comfort. She craved my reassuring touch.

"Yes," I said. "I knock now." I held out my hand, waiting for her to choose to take it. "Come on. It's time for breakfast."

Her gaze lowered to my hand, her lips plumping in a small pout. The little flash of emotional reaction confirmed that I was taking the right approach with her. I could coax her back into my arms with a little patience on my part.

"And what if I don't come out for breakfast? Will there be more *consequences*?" She sounded more petulant than bitter, and the door eased open another inch. Her gaze was still fixed on my hand, as though it was a shiny object that she was tempted to take.

"Definitely," I informed her, keeping my tone calm rather than forbidding. "But they won't involve me leaving you alone in your room."

She peeked up at me, a little spark of curiosity flashing in her lovely eyes. "What would they involve?"

I quirked my brow at her. "Do you want to find out?"

After only two seconds of indecision, she huffed, "Fine." She opened the door wide and snatched my hand. "I'm hungry, anyway."

I hadn't stipulated that she had to hold my hand to avoid facing consequences; I'd simply told her that she had to eat breakfast.

But she clung on to me, her slender fingers firm around my palm. I was fairly certain she thought she was displaying some form of defiance by squeezing so hard, but it didn't hurt me in the slightest.

She stalked down the hall, and I allowed her to pretend she was pulling me along to the kitchen with her. We both knew that I didn't have to go anywhere I didn't want to. It would be physically impossible for her to force me to move.

But I much preferred this spirited version of Sofia to the sad, spiteful woman I'd left in solitary confinement yesterday. So, I indulged her. Besides, she was kind of adorable when she was fuming. My angry little kitten.

I intended to cuddle her close and make her purr.

When we reached the kitchen, I extricated myself from her hold and picked up one of the stools at the kitchen island, moving it next to the stove. I patted the plush black velvet seat.

"This is where you sit," I informed her. "Optimal viewing position for a chef-in-training."

She crossed her arms over her chest, making me wonder if she was hiding her peaked nipples.

That was probably best for both of us, given my newly-imposed rules. Resisting the urge to fuck Sofia was already giving me blue balls, and I was making things even harder on myself by depriving her of underwear.

That issue would be resolved in a few hours, thank god.

I patted the chair again. "Up you get," I prompted. "I cook, you watch."

She hesitated for a second longer before she

rolled her eyes and hopped up onto the stool with an exaggerated huff.

"Are Drama classes part of your Music degree?" I teased.

She pursed her lips, narrowing her eyes at me.

I chuckled and started getting out the ingredients I would need to make breakfast. She didn't manage to stew in silence for even a full minute.

"I'm a Theater minor, I'll have you know," she said in an accusatory tone.

I shot her a smirk. "That doesn't surprise me. You do have a knack for the dramatic. Are you sure you don't want to double major?"

"You're infuriating," she said on a soft growl. "It should be illegal to be so annoying before breakfast."

"You're just hangry. Don't worry, little kitten. I'll feed you soon."

"Oh my *god*." She threw up her hands in exasperation, but her cheeks flushed pink. "I didn't know they let hardened criminals use silly words like *hangry*." She tried for spite, but now that she'd moved her arms, I had a clear view of her hard nipples against the gray cotton of my t-shirt.

I shrugged, forcing my gaze to her face. "Everyone gets angry when they're hungry. But you seem particularly susceptible to it. Are you always this grumpy in the morning?"

She quickly crossed her arms over her chest again,

her lashes flying wide as she realized that she'd given me a clear view of her nipples.

"I don't usually see this time of morning at all," she grumbled. "I made sure I wasn't scheduled for any classes before ten AM this semester."

"Poor *florecita*," I said with exaggerated pity. "Don't you know little flowers need morning sunshine? No wonder you're so grouchy. You're not getting enough vitamin D."

"I'm *not* grouchy," she insisted.

"You are right now," I countered. "Here, nibble on this while I cook." I offered her a chunk of cheddar cheese from the block I'd grated to fold into the eggs.

She snatched the morsel out of my hand and popped it into her mouth, glaring at me as though she'd somehow challenged me.

I grinned and turned my attention to finishing my task. I didn't intend to get distracted by her and burn breakfast again. I wanted her to enjoy every aspect of her meal this morning.

As I went through the motions of making omelets, Sofia's posture gradually relaxed. I wasn't sure if it was the little nugget of cheese that had improved her mood or if she was simply forgetting to be annoyed with me.

Despite her swings of emotional upheaval over the last two days, Sofia was remarkably resilient. Her default demeanor was cheery, and nothing seemed to keep her down for long. Even when she'd argued with me, I'd never seen her in a true rage. Given the circumstances, she had every right to be angry, and I admired that she'd advocated for herself rather than cowering from me.

She asked a few questions about my technique while I was cooking, her natural curiosity soothing her irritation further. By the time I plated the omelets and set them down on the kitchen island, all of her grumpiness had melted away.

She tried to pick up the stool she'd been sitting on to return it to its usual place.

"Leave it there," I ordered before she could lift it.

"But where will I sit?"

I patted my thigh. "Right here."

Her eyes widened, and her lips parted slightly. She stared at me, her gaze flicking from my face to my lap and back again.

"Mateo." She said my name breathlessly. "I don't know..."

I tapped two fingers against my knee, silently coaxing her. I didn't have to issue a verbal command. She would choose to come to me. She wanted the contact, craved it just as keenly as I did.

She took a hesitant step toward me, her eyes searching mine. "Won't it be weird if I sit on your lap?"

"No, *florecita*," I promised her as she took another

step closer. "It won't be weird. You'll like it. And so will I."

Slowly, she closed the distance between us. Just before she was close enough to touch, she stalled. Her teeth sank into her lower lip, and a little furrow appeared between her brows. She clasped her hands together, her fingers knotting.

"I should be afraid of you," she whispered.

"No," I reassured her. "You shouldn't. I will never hurt you, Sofia. I just want to take care of you. Let me."

She inched closer, as though she couldn't hold herself back.

"I'm going to help you up." I lifted my hands to her hips, moving slowly enough that she had time to stop me if she wanted to.

She didn't stop me. Her eyes closed as soon as I gripped her waist, and she blew out a long sigh. Even this simple touch seemed to ease her anxiety in a way my words couldn't.

By the time I shifted her body and had her curled up on my lap, she'd completely relaxed into my hold.

"Does this feel weird?" I asked, my voice coming out rougher than I intended. Sofia wasn't the only one affected by our connection.

"No," she admitted, tilting her head into the crook of my neck. "You smell good." She took a deep inhale. "God, you're like weed or something."

"What?" I tried to smother a laugh. "I smell like weed? I'm pretty sure I should be offended."

"No, I mean..." She breathed deeply, and I felt her melt against me. "You smell like pine and...I don't know. *Man*. You smell like *man*. It makes me feel good. Like, really chilled out and relaxed."

"Does it make you feel safe?" I asked quietly.

"Yeah," she admitted on a sigh. "I feel safe with you, Mateo. I probably shouldn't, but I do."

"Trust your instincts. You're safer in my arms than anywhere else on Earth. I swear."

She snuggled in closer, and that addicting warmth she elicited unfurled in the center of my chest.

Sofia might still feel conflicted about what she'd seen me do to those men last night, but her body recognized me as her protector. Somewhere deep in her psyche, her primal brain trusted me, even though she questioned that on a rational level.

I just needed to allay her justifiable concerns. Proving that I could provide for her and care for her was a good place to start.

Keeping one arm braced around her shoulders, I reached forward with my free hand and picked up a fork. She shifted to do the same, but I flexed my hold on her a bit tighter, directing her to stay put. She responded instantly, settling back against me and dropping her hand into her lap.

I speared a bite-sized portion of the omelet on

the fork and lifted it to her lips. She blinked up at me, the little wrinkle appearing between her brows again.

"What are you doing?" she asked.

"Taking care of you."

"I'm perfectly capable of eating breakfast without your help." The assertion came out on a soft, questioning tone rather than being issued as a hard challenge. Sofia was interested in what I was offering, but she didn't understand it. I knew she wasn't anywhere near ready for me to explain the complexities of what I wanted from her.

Submission. Devotion. Trust.

And a power exchange that involved sexual deviancy that would shock my innocent little flower to her core.

For now, I would work on trust, and I would test her submissive tendencies soon.

"I know you're capable of eating your own breakfast, but I *want* to help."

When she continued to study me as if I was a particularly difficult puzzle, I pressed her. "It will make me happy, Sofia."

"Okay," she breathed, agreeing instantly. My good girl wanted to please me.

I swallowed a hungry growl and tamped down my answering arousal. A hard-on pressing into her ass wouldn't do wonders for my cause at the moment. I wouldn't risk spooking her.

She continued watching me when she parted her lips to accept the first bite, searching my features. My mouth curved in a genuine smile when she accepted what I offered, my expression of pleasure untainted by mockery or dark amusement.

She swallowed and offered a shy smile of her own in return. "I still think this is kind of weird," she admitted.

"But you like it, don't you?"

"Yeah." Her smile took on a wry twist. "You were right. I do like it."

I didn't feel the slightest impulse to gloat over being proven right. This wasn't a game with a winner and a loser. As long as Sofia enjoyed exploring this dynamic with me, we would both win. I intended to introduce her to my more perverted needs in a way that ensured she became just as addicted to me as I was to her. By the time she accepted that she was mine, she would submit to my every deviant demand and beg for more.

"Good," I declared, fighting back my arousal by focusing on her sweetness. "I like it, too."

When I lifted the second forkful to her lips, she protested. "What about you? Aren't you going to eat?"

"I take care of you first," I replied. "Always."

Her cheeks flushed a delicate shade of pink, and she accepted the nourishment I offered. She didn't hesitate or protest again; she simply surrendered to what was happening between us, adapting to my control beautifully.

After she'd eaten every bite of her omelet and finished her glass of orange juice, I tucked into my own portion. The eggs had cooled slightly while I was feeding her, but I didn't care. It was the best fucking breakfast of my life.

She rested her cheek on my shoulder as I ate, quiet and content. We'd made remarkable progress in the space of a couple hours. Not long ago, she'd been peeking at me through a cracked bedroom door, hurt and wary. Now, she was all sweetness and softness, relaxing against me with no thought of spite or bitterness.

When I'd cleaned my plate, I glanced down and noted her eyes were closed, her features serene.

Over the years, I'd imagined her writhing and begging for orgasmic release, or screaming out my name when she came. My filthy, crude brain hadn't been capable of conjuring up a purer, equally satisfying fantasy where she drifted off into bliss in my arms.

The warmth in my chest expanded, washing outward through my body in a slow wave. I brushed my fingertips over her cheek, marveling at how soft and delicate she was.

She made a little humming noise and leaned into my touch.

My breath stuttered. I didn't deserve this level of trust. I'd craved to possess it, but I hadn't done enough to earn it. And yet, Sofia offered it freely, so easily that I suspected she'd been fighting her nature when she'd expressed doubt in me.

Yesterday, I'd accused her of being foolish for trusting anyone and everyone. The world was a dangerous place, and I hadn't been lying when I'd told her most people weren't good or kind.

But Sofia was good to her core.

That goodness made her vulnerable. It had made her susceptible to her father's lies, and he'd hurt her deeply with his deception. It made her susceptible to *me*.

When I'd entered her apartment, stalked her into a corner, and slipped a needle in her neck, she'd seemed confused by my actions rather than horrified. As though she truly couldn't imagine a world in which I was a person to be feared.

I was surer of my decision to keep her for myself than ever. Sofia needed to be protected, and no one would be more devoted to preserving her sweet nature than me. She might have been dragged out of her falsely safe bubble and into the cruel reality of our criminal underworld, but I would shelter her from the darkest parts of it.

We had established trust. It was time to work on her submission.

"Sofia," I murmured, stroking the column of her neck with a feather-light touch. "It's time to talk about your punishment."

CHAPTER 10

SOFIA

"What?" I asked, his statement not quite penetrating the warm fog that blanketed my thoughts.

"You tried to run away last night." His deep voice rolled through my mind like slow thunder, soft and rumbly. "I warned you that there would be consequences if you tried to escape."

Consequences. Unease stirred as a flash of my feelings from my period of isolation disrupted my happy place. I pressed myself closer to him, my fingers curling in his shirt.

"I don't want you to shut me in the bedroom by myself again," I said, my voice small. "I don't like being alone."

"I know you don't." He soothed me, massaging my scalp with his long fingers. "I won't punish you like that ever again. I thought I was going easy on you, but I was mistaken. You need to be touched."

I nodded my agreement, loving the feel of his huge hands stroking my body with such tender care. I definitely didn't want him to stop touching me.

"I'm sorry I tried to leave," I said with complete honesty. "I was just scared. I won't do it again."

"I know you won't, *dulzura*. That doesn't change the fact that you've earned a punishment."

I peeked up at him. His features were relaxed, his dark eyes hooded with the drugged appearance I'd first noted on the night he abducted me. He didn't appear threatening at all.

But he was saying he wanted to punish me.

"I don't understand why you're talking about punishing me if you know I won't try to leave again," I said, more curious than argumentative. "You don't seem to be mad at me. Are you mad at me?"

"No, *florecita*. I'm not mad. And if I were, I wouldn't discipline you until I cooled off. I will never punish you because I'm angry with you."

"Then why?"

"Because you disobeyed me, Sofia. I warned you there would be consequences if you did. I'm going to discipline you for that."

"I still don't get it. If I don't want to escape, why is this necessary?"

"Because the transgression isn't erased just

because you've changed your mind since then. When you're with me, I'm in charge. That means I take care of you."

"But you just took care of me by making me breakfast," I protested.

"Sometimes, taking care of you means discipline."

I huffed, a little tinge of annoyance souring my blissful peace. "This is very high-handed. I don't think I like this part."

He chuckled. "You will, and you won't. I'm sure you won't be accustomed to the sting for your first spanking. But you might like the sting. I guess we'll find that out soon."

Spanking? He couldn't be serious.

But he'd been dead serious about sending me to my room yesterday. He might like to tease and laugh with me, but Mateo didn't joke about doling out consequences.

I had a sneaking suspicion it wouldn't work, but I tried pouting, anyway. "I don't want you to spank me."

He grinned. "You really don't understand how punishments work, do you, *belleza*? If you wanted me to spank you, it wouldn't be a punishment." His smile twisted slightly. "But if we discover that you do enjoy it, I'll have to come up with cleverer ways to discipline you in the future."

My mouth went dry. His dark eyes were sharp with hunger, and something tugged low in my belly.

"What if I don't do anything to deserve a punishment in the future?" I challenged, not realizing that I was implicitly accepting this arrangement by engaging in a conversation about hypothetical future scenarios.

"You will. You might love being my good girl, but you like testing my boundaries almost as much."

He got to his feet, keeping me in his arms.

"Where are we going?" I asked as he started walking through the open-plan kitchen and into what appeared to be his living room. With the L-shaped, brown leather couch and massive TV mounted above the slate fireplace, the space had a man-cave vibe.

"This will be more comfortable on the couch," he explained as he sat down, taking me with him. "Well, more comfortable for me, at least. You, on the other hand..."

He shifted his grip on my body, maneuvering me as effortlessly as a doll. Suddenly, I found myself staring at the hardwood floor, my hips folded over his knees.

"Hey!" I tried to push myself up, but he grasped my wrists and pinned them at the small of my back. His grip was as careful with me as ever, but his hand might as well have been an iron shackle for all the chance I had of breaking free.

"What are you doing?" I objected, squirming over his lap.

His other hand rested on my thigh, his huge palm pressing just beneath my ass. His t-shirt provided a flimsy barrier, but I felt his thick thumb push down on my tender flesh. If he shifted half an inch, he'd penetrate the juncture between my legs. His fingers flexed, and I stilled on a gasp.

"I'm going to spank you now," he told me, his voice calm and deep.

"But you promised you wouldn't hurt me," I protested weakly.

"This won't hurt you," he assured me. "It will sting, and you'll ache after, but it won't hurt you."

His hand shifted on my thigh, his fingertips teasing beneath the hem of his shirt. In this position, it fell to the backs of my knees, but when he started easing the fabric upward, I stiffened.

He paused his progress, stroking the few inches of flesh he'd exposed. "I'm not going to do anything other than spank you. I won't touch you in any other way. Not unless you ask me to."

I bit my lip, torn. I didn't want him to see my thighs. I didn't want him to ask about the scars.

But I didn't want to stop him, either. If I tried, he would definitely ask more questions, and then he'd find out about my scars, anyway.

As I wrestled with what to say, he continued to

pet me. Something long and hard jerked against my belly.

I bucked on his lap, gasping in shock. I'd felt boys' erections before. I might be a virgin, but I enjoyed making out.

None of those *boys* had felt remotely like Mateo.

He was big *everywhere*.

"You don't need to worry about that," he said, his voice rougher than it had been a few seconds ago. "I'm not going to try anything. I want you, Sofia, but I'm in control of my actions. I swear I won't force myself on you."

I licked my suddenly dry lips. How many times had I fantasized about Mateo being the one to take my virginity?

But this was different. In my fantasies, I didn't have scars. I didn't have shameful marks on my body.

My mind churned, searching for a way to get through this without Mateo finding out about the scars.

They're just on the front, I reasoned. If he lifted the hem of the shirt farther, he would only see the backs of my legs. And if I kept them pressed together, there was no way he'd see the mark on the inside of my left thigh.

"Okay," I whispered, giving him my consent to continue.

He worked slowly, easing the soft cotton over my

skin. The cool air on my bare flesh made me shiver. Or maybe that was just Mateo. I felt all hot and shivery at the same time again. It made me a little lightheaded, my thoughts going fuzzy until all I could focus on was the sensation of his hands on my body.

By the time the fabric bunched at my lower back, my skin was pebbled, and I was practically quivering.

He trailed his fingertips beneath my bare bottom, exploring the shape of my curves. His hard cock pressed into my belly: a stark contrast to his gentle, reverent touch.

The warmth in my body pooled between my legs, creating liquid heat. A strange, musky scent I'd never smelled before teased through the air. Whatever it was, it made him groan and shift his cock against me.

"You are so fucking perfect," he said, his voice rough with desire and awe. "More perfect than I could have ever imagined."

My cheeks flamed, and I squeezed my legs together, hiding my glaring imperfections from him. I never wanted him to see the ugly marks, not when he spoke to me as though I was the most breathtaking thing he'd ever seen.

He started petting me, rubbing his palm over my ass. "Relax," he soothed me.

Despite my worries about him seeing my scars, the tension eased from my body as he continued to stroke me. The liquid heat between my legs grew slicker, and my sex began to pulse in time with my heartbeat. My back arched without conscious thought, offering myself into his hands.

I wanted more. I reveled in the heady pleasure elicited by his fingers on my flesh, but somehow, the delicious sensation made me even needier. I didn't understand what was happening to my body, but I craved...more.

Smack!

The sound of his huge hand slapping my bottom cracked through the room, registering just before the shocking sting. I sucked in a gasp, and he spanked me again before I had a chance to release it on a sharp cry. I squirmed over his lap, seeking to move away from the impact of his palm.

"Mateo!" I protested, tugging against his iron hold.

Judging by his body's reaction, he liked when I cried out his name. His cock was a hard rod beneath my belly, straining against the confines of his jeans. His grip firmed around my wrists, keeping me pinned as he continued to pepper stinging blows all over my tender flesh.

My skin was on fire, and he made sure to evenly distribute the heat all over my bottom and upper thighs, leaving no sensitive spot unpunished.

Something strange was happening to me. Although the spanking stung fiercely, the heat of his unrelenting, punitive hand sank beneath the surface of my skin. It permeated my body in my most vulnerable places, joining with the warmth between my legs and stoking it to a conflagration. My labia became swollen and achy, and my clit pulsed.

My struggles to get away slowly shifted into needy writhing, and I tried to seek relief by stimulating myself on his thigh.

A harder blow crashed down on my bottom, a shocking rebuke.

"Naughty girl." His chastisement was gravelly with his own desire. He delivered another stinging slap. "You can have your reward if you ask nicely when we're done."

"Please," I whimpered. I wasn't sure if I was begging for the spanking to stop or for more delicious, hot contact.

He released my wrists, and his fingers sank into my hair, tugging my head back. The position forced me to arch into his hand, rendering me helpless to do anything but accept his discipline.

"Tell me what you did wrong," he commanded. His tone was deep and rough, but not with anger.

"I tried to leave," I squeaked, quivering in his immobilizing hold.

He switched tactics, stroking my enflamed skin with his fingertips. I shuddered at the sudden contrasting sensation. My nerve endings jumped beneath his touch, more sensitive than I ever could have imagined. The slickness between my legs slipped down my inner thighs, and I barely had the presence of mind to keep them pressed together.

Another hard smack. "Are you sorry for disobeying me?"

"Yes." I'd already been sorry before he'd started the spanking, but somehow, this scenario eased the guilt I'd been feeling. He wasn't punishing me with emotional pain. He was exacting his discipline on my flesh, and I found that I much preferred this tactile method of correction.

He resumed stroking me, and I trembled under his hands. The tender touch alternating with the punitive slaps pulled me deeper into his thrall. Despite the fact that this was a punishment, it felt like a form of affection. Like he cared enough to see the lesson through rather than leaving me alone to simmer in guilt and anguish.

Suddenly, his short fingernails raked over my abused flesh, drawing a strangled cry from my chest.

"Promise me you won't do it again."

"I promise!" I swore, the last of my guilt leaving me in a rush, seared away by the heat of his hands. "I promise I won't try to leave."

I didn't want to go anywhere. I wanted Mateo to keep touching me, and I didn't care how. The intensity of his attention was so gratifying that it was almost overwhelming. I was greedy for more.

He rested his palm against my heated skin, his grip on my hair easing. He no longer tugged on the curled strands, but he didn't release me from his hold. My cheek rested on his knee, and warmth leaked from my eyes to wet his jeans.

Was I crying? I wasn't sad, and I wasn't in pain.

He started petting me again, trailing his fingers all over the area he'd spanked. "Good girl."

A shuddering sigh left my chest on a long exhale, and my eyes drifted closed as more tears fell. I floated in blissful peace, basking in Mateo's praise and affection.

As he continued to touch my hypersensitive skin, I sank deeper, losing myself to the sweet sensation. All I could think about was how good it felt to have his hands on me. I became keenly aware of the pulsing between my legs, the throb so powerful that it caused desperate discomfort.

"I promised I wouldn't hurt you. That didn't hurt you, did it?" he asked, his voice rich and deep. He sounded as though he was at peace, too. Although I could still feel his insistent erection pressing into my belly, he wasn't tense or frustrated.

"No, but..." I bit my lip, uncertain how to express what I was feeling. "I ache."

I pushed back against his hand, seeking more.

His touch shifted, his fingers teasing between my closed legs. My clit was a hard, aching bud, my lower lips swollen and puffy. My thighs parted slightly, welcoming more without conscious thought.

He didn't explore farther; he continued to tease and stroke, whipping my need to a fever pitch.

"Does my good girl want her reward?"

I whined and nodded, desperate.

"You have to ask, Sofia. You have to beg if you want me to play with your pretty pussy."

"Please," I whimpered, opening wider to urge him on. "Please, Mateo."

Two of his thick fingers slid through the wetness on my labia, and I cried out at the foreign, delicious contact. No man had ever touched me like this before. And while I'd harbored fantasies about what it might be like for Mateo to touch me here, I never could have prepared myself for the shock of pure pleasure elicited by the barest brush of his fingers against my sex.

He explored farther, pushing forward in a slow glide. The first feather-light touch to my clit rocked my body with a hit of bliss, drawing a gasp from my chest.

"Are you always this sensitive, *dulzura*?" he asked, his voice impossibly deep. "Or is this just for me?"

He brushed my clit again, and I let out a wanton moan.

"I don't..." I struggled for words, for breath. "I've never..."

A harsh growl rumbled from him, and his palm suddenly pressed against my soaked lips, gripping my entire sex in his huge hand.

"All mine," he snarled.

I shuddered, pleasure washing through me. I wasn't frightened of the animal sounds he was making. Not anymore. I craved this primal possessiveness, this savage intensity. His obsessive hold reassured me that he didn't want to let me go. He wouldn't abandon me and leave me bereft.

"Come for me, *florecita*," he commanded, grinding his palm against my pussy lips. His fingers pressed down directly on my clit, rubbing in a firm, demanding rhythm.

"Mateo!" I screamed out his name as a tidal wave of ecstasy slammed through my body. Pleasure swept me up in a ruthless torrent, claiming my entire being. My body shook with the overwhelming force that wracked my system, and my fingers and toes curled as the pleasure rushed outward from my sex to flood every inch of my flesh.

"Good girl," he praised while I continued to whimper and writhe over his lap.

His approval pushed me higher, prolonging my ecstatic release. My world glowed with incandescent, white light, blinding me until all I could sense was the sound of his approval, the bliss of his hands, and his intoxicating, masculine scent. It mingled with the new, strange scent I'd noticed earlier. It smelled forbidden and decadent, and I heard Mateo inhale just before his cock jerked beneath me.

"Fuck, *belleza*," he groaned. "You're going to kill me."

I didn't quite understand what he meant, but he didn't sound upset. I reveled in his admiration, enthralled by the silky feel of his fingertips sliding through the wetness on my inner thighs.

Suddenly, his touch faltered, and I felt him tense beneath me.

"What's this?" he asked, his tone less warm than it had been moments ago.

He rubbed my thigh, and I felt his fingers running along the line of my scar. It was a neat, perfectly vertical cut, precise and deep. He traced the entire length of the mark; four and a quarter inches carved into my thigh.

Panic slammed through me, obliterating my bliss. I tried to close my legs, to hide my shame.

His huge hands wrapped around my thighs, spreading me wide so he could get a better look. I twisted against his hold, desperate to escape his judgmental stare. If he managed to turn me over, he'd see the revolting mess of neat, straight cuts that had mutilated the rest of me.

"Stop," I begged, completely helpless against his strength.

He didn't ease up. Instead, his fingers flexed around my legs, his entire body tightening beneath me.

"Did someone do this to you?" The disgust that roughened his tone was unmistakable.

The cathartic tears that wet my face were washed away by tears of anguish. He'd told me I was perfect, but now, he was staring at the evidence that I was damaged beyond repair.

"Let me go," I beseeched, ragged and frightened.

His hands held firm, his incredible strength pinning me in place for his horrific inspection.

"Who did this?" he demanded.

I shook my head wildly. The answer to that would disgust him even more. Shame twisted my stomach, bile burning at the back of my throat.

"You promised," I choked out. "You promised you wouldn't touch me if I didn't ask you to. Please, let me go."

He released me instantly, and I shoved myself off his lap, stumbling away. He stood, reaching out as though to steady me.

I shrank back, grateful for the tears that blurred my vision. The sight of his revulsion would break me.

My fingers fisted in his massive t-shirt, tugging it down to ensure it hid my ruined body.

"Sofia..."

He took a step toward me. I dodged back.

"Do you want some space?" he asked, his tone soft and sad.

Of course, he was disappointed that I wasn't perfect like he'd thought.

I nodded, swallowing a sob. I hated being alone, but facing Mateo's disgust was far worse.

"You can go to your room." It was a suggestion, but it held an authoritative ring that indicated he desired my compliance. "I won't lock you in, and I'll be right out here."

He didn't have to lock me in to keep me in his home. There was nowhere else for me to go, and I was imprisoned with him by circumstance even more effectively than if he'd kept me in shackles. If I were chained up, I would try to fight my way free. But given the opportunity to choose my jailor—Mateo or Daddy—I chose Mateo.

Even if he didn't want me anymore, staying with him was slightly less painful than facing my father's lies.

I turned from Mateo and trudged to the bedroom, utterly miserable without the warmth of his embrace to reassure me.

CHAPTER 11

MATEO

"You look like shit," Adrián drawled when I opened my front door to admit him.

"Adrián," Valentina scolded softly, pressing closer against his side to bump his body with her petite frame.

His arm tightened around her waist, his fingers biting into her hip to hold her with more force than was strictly necessary. She tilted her head against his chest, welcoming the harsh affection.

When I'd first seen my friend with his beloved Valentina, I'd worried he would hurt her accidentally because he was maddened by possessive rage. Over the last few weeks, I'd realized that she liked when he hurt her. Adrián would never truly harm Valentina, but he marked her obsessively. She seemed to enjoy bearing his marks just as much as he enjoyed inflicting them. She was the perfect match for my sadistic friend.

"Sofia's bags are in the car," Adrián informed me, tossing me the keys to his black Jaguar. "Valentina and I will show ourselves in."

He pushed past me, walking into my house as though he owned the place.

Essentially, he had bought it for me. If I weren't in Adrián's employ, I never would have earned the kind of money necessary to buy this house. And I knew he paid me far better than anyone else who worked for him. He claimed it was because I was his most valuable asset, but I suspected he simply didn't mind giving me plenty of money to buy the stuff I wanted.

Having a billionaire drug lord as a best friend had its perks.

"I'll be right behind you," I said to his retreating back. "Don't scare Sofia in the two minutes it takes me to unload."

"I won't let him," Valentina promised, shooting me a reassuring smile over her shoulder.

Adrián definitely did not deserve that sweet woman, but I was pleased that he had her. If she chose to love him, I was happy for them.

Besides, he might thrive on subjugating her, but Valentina held far more control over Adrián than anyone else I'd ever seen. Even in our friendship, I was definitely the one who took orders, not the other way around. On the surface, Valentina was submissive to Adrián. But he would do anything to make her happy, and that tipped the balance of power in her favor.

If Valentina promised me that she wouldn't let Adrián scare Sofia, I was confident that I didn't have to worry about it.

For the two minutes it took for me to grab Sofia's bags, at least.

I popped the trunk on the Jaguar and loaded up her stuff, a bit taken aback at how much they'd brought. When Valentina had offered to go to Sofia's apartment and pick up some of her things, I'd been expecting a small duffel bag.

Valentina appeared to think that Sofia was about to take a month-long cruise and would need at least three changes of clothes every day.

I hustled everything into the house, finding that Valentina and Adrián had made themselves comfortable on my couch. Sofia was still taking some time and space for herself in the bedroom, so Adrián spooking her wasn't an immediate issue. I doubted he would actually try to scare her, but he terrified most people innately.

"How much stuff do you think Sofia could possibly need?" I asked Valentina as I set down three large duffel bags and slung another two off my shoulders.

"You're welcome," Adrián said pointedly.

Valentina placed a calming hand on his forearm. "Sofia will want her full range of clothing options, as well as all of her makeup and haircare products," she explained.

"Sofia doesn't need any makeup," I declared. She hadn't worn any since I'd taken her as my hostage, and she was as lovely as ever.

Valentina rolled her eyes. "Women can choose to wear makeup just for themselves, not for men. Sofia's sole purpose is not to look pleasing for your benefit. You want her to be comfortable here, don't you? Trust me, she'll feel much more at home if she has access to all of her things."

At home. The two words took me by surprise, sticking in my brain. I'd decided to claim Sofia as mine, but I hadn't really thought about her making a home here. But if I didn't intend to allow her to leave me, it only made sense to move all of her stuff to my house.

"Yeah, I want her to be comfortable here," I agreed. "Thanks, Valentina."

Adrián cleared his throat, and Valentina shot him a wry smile.

"I think Adrián wants you to thank *him*. He's actually the one who went to pack up all of Sofia's stuff. He wouldn't let me go to her apartment in case Caesar had men watching the place. So, we did the whole thing over video call to make sure he knew what was most important."

I stared at my boss, the vicious kingpin who was notoriously feared by even the most ruthless criminals. The concept of him running an errand like this was preposterous.

"You did that for Sofia?" I asked, incredulous.

His pale green eyes glinted, and the hard planes of his face turned to granite; a silent warning that I shouldn't make a big deal out of his uncharacteristically helpful behavior.

"I did it for Valentina," he said coolly.

I offered a small nod, deferring to his desire to save face. I recognized that cold stare all too well, and it meant *don't fuck with me*.

"And I'm very grateful," Valentina told him, tucking herself close to his side and clasping his hand in hers.

He didn't take his eyes off me, but as soon as she cuddled up close to him, his dangerous aura dissipated slightly.

"I did it for you too, Mateo," he informed me, shockingly genial. "I figured you don't want Sofia to hate you. I thought this might help." His gaze swept over me, assessing. "And judging by the look of you, you need all the help you can get."

I ran my hand though my hair, attempting to smooth it into a more civilized style. I'd mussed it all to shit while I stewed in my frustration over the last three hours since Sofia had disappeared into the bedroom.

"Thanks," I said, genuinely grateful for his help, even if I was baffled by it. "For packing Sofia's clothes, I mean. Not for telling me I look like shit."

Adrián shrugged. "Someone had to tell you. This tortured caveman appearance isn't going to help your case if you want to attract Sofia's interest."

He turned his attention to Valentina, giving her shoulder a tight squeeze to reprimand her before she had the chance to admonish him. "And don't tell me that I should be nicer to Mateo," he warned her. "He's already freaked out enough over the fact that I ran this little errand. If I'm any nicer, it'll ruin my reputation."

"You're still a cold, cruel bastard, as far as I'm concerned," I reassured him, trying and failing to hide my smile.

"Asshole," he shot back, keeping his expression completely neutral. Coming from him, that was the equivalent of a teasing smirk.

Banter with Adrián was weird from an outsider's perspective, but I knew him well enough to understand that he was being positively playful at the moment.

Valentina glanced from him to me and back again before waving her hand through the air, dismissing whatever was puzzling her. "I'm not going to pretend I understand the dynamics of this friendship between the two of you. I'll leave you to insult each other, or whatever you usually do for fun when I'm not around. I want to talk to Sofia. Do you think she'll want to see me?" she directed the question at me.

Her soft features were pinched, the fine lines around her chocolate eyes drawn with anxiety. Valentina was worried for Sofia's emotional wellbeing. Adrián had convinced her that I wouldn't harm Sofia, but Valentina was still obviously troubled by the idea that my hostage might be distressed.

"I don't know," I replied truthfully. "She was feeling okay this morning, but I... She wasn't doing great, last time we spoke. She's in the guest room." I gestured in the direction of the hall.

Valentina extricated herself from beneath Adrián's proprietary arm. "I'll go see if she wants company. I'm sure this is confusing for her. She's a sweet girl."

"Yeah," I agreed, my stomach knotting at the memory of how I'd damaged that sweet trust. "She is."

If Valentina detected the strain in my tone, she didn't linger to ask me about it.

Adrián, on the other hand, pounced as soon as she disappeared down the hallway. "So, you fucked up," he surmised. "How bad is it?"

I winced. "Pretty bad."

"Stop hovering over there," he ordered, irritated. "Offer me a drink like a decent host, and then come sit down."

"You are such a dick," I informed him. "I'm not on the clock right now. You don't have to bark orders at me in my own home."

His dark brows lifted, his expression impassive. "I'll take a beer, if you have one."

I shot him the middle finger on my way into the kitchen. Adrián was a complicated man to be friends with, but so was I. That was probably the reason we got along: we both viewed friendship as a farce. We knew the truth about the world. People were inherently greedy and self-serving and capable of committing vile acts to get what they wanted.

Adrián and I were no different from everyone else. We just didn't bother to pretend otherwise.

Somehow, our mutual cynicism and disdain for the rest of humanity had fostered a strange but unbreakable bond. There was an odd sort of trust that developed in agreeing that no one was trustworthy.

I grabbed two IPAs from my fridge and joined Adrián in the living room, dropping down onto the L-shaped couch across from him. He took the beer I offered, a slight inclination of his head his only acknowledgement of gratitude.

"Are you going to tell me what you did, or do I have to guess?" he drawled.

I blew out a breath and scrubbed my hand over my beard. "I was spanking her, and I pushed her too far."

He took a drag from his beer, completely unfazed by my reference to corporal discipline. He'd been the one to introduce me to my darker perversions, inviting me to the decadent, kinky club he owned. It was a front for trafficking our product, but he still liked to indulge his sadistic needs there.

Until he stole Valentina for himself. Now, I was certain I'd never see him at that club again. She was the only one he wanted to hurt, to subjugate, to own.

I wanted to own Sofia, but my plan had been to slowly manipulate her into accepting my needs. I'd intended to train her to love submitting to my perverted lifestyle. She already thrived on praise and physical affection. It should have been a smooth process to exploit her desire to please and shape it into a desire to obey me.

"You have to be careful with her, Mateo," Adrián advised. "If you don't want to break her, you can't do anything unforgivable." He cocked his head at me. "I assume you'd prefer for her to be willing."

"Of course I want her to be willing," I snapped. "Jesus, Adrián."

He considered me for a moment, and I suspected

he was choosing his next words carefully. "Are you sure she's right for you? You've wanted her for years, but you don't really know her. If she can't handle a spanking, how can you think she'll willingly engage in what you truly want from her?"

"The spanking wasn't the issue," I admitted gruffly. "You're right. I didn't really know her before. But everything about her is even better than I could have imagined. She was made for this, Adrián, even if she doesn't understand it yet. She *likes* it."

"Then what's the problem?"

"I saw... She has a scar. I didn't handle it well."

I rubbed my fingers together, as though I could still feel the puckered furrow that had been carved into her thigh. The wash of rage that had rushed through me at the initial discovery began to surge once again.

Adrián's mouth pressed to a thin line, his eyes narrowing with disapproval. "You can't put your own shit on her. I understand why seeing her scarred might have bothered you, but a lot of people have them. Accidents happen all the time."

"It wasn't from an accident," I ground out. She wouldn't have reacted so fearfully when I asked if someone had hurt her if it weren't true. "I'll admit, I let my own shit get in the way when I first saw it. I shouldn't have made a big deal out of it. But when I asked about it, she panicked." The nauseating memory of her desperate struggle to escape my restraining hold made my fury swell. "Someone hurt her, Adrián."

His lips curved in a sharply satisfied smile. "Excellent."

"*Excellent?*" I snarled, my control tested to its breaking point. My fists clenched at my sides as I resisted the nearly overwhelming urge to punch the pleased smirk right off his pretty-boy face.

He reclined, slinging his arm over the back of the couch like it was his throne. "I was hoping you'd be like this, once you manned up and claimed her. You should see yourself right now. Positively shit-your-pants terrifying. Much better for business than the stupid expression you used to have whenever you looked at her. I need a rabid grizzly watching my back, not a cuddly teddy bear. To be honest, allowing you anywhere near Sofia has been a liability until now. She's finally yours, so you can focus on protecting her instead of mooning over her."

My mouth opened and closed a few times, at a loss for words. The insult should have heightened my ire, but hearing him acknowledge my claim over Sofia aloud helped soothe my most volatile urges. I much preferred protecting Sofia to pining for her from a self-imposed distance. I didn't have to bother with that shit anymore. I didn't have to feel guilty for pulling her into my dangerous world. Her father had done that to her when he'd chosen to threaten Valentina.

And if I was Sofia's protector, that meant someone was long overdue for a gruesome reckoning. Whoever had hurt her would be screaming in agony and begging for death very soon.

"Do you know anything about it?" I asked Adrián. "Can you think of anyone who might have hurt her in the past?"

"No. I know that's not the answer you want to hear, but I can't think of anyone who would dare to harm Caesar's darling daughter. From what I know about her, she's lived her life in a sheltered little bubble. Are you sure the scar wasn't from some sort of accident? Maybe you reacted to the mark more harshly than you think you did. You're a scary motherfucker, Mateo. She might have panicked because your reaction frightened her."

I thought back over the disturbing incident. Watching Sofia cry out my name while she came all over my hand had been the most breathtaking thing I'd ever seen. I had tensed up when I touched the scar for the first time. I'd been so intoxicated by her submission that the unexpected trigger had provoked me more easily than it would have otherwise.

You promised. Her desperate accusation knifed through my mind. *You promised you wouldn't touch me if I didn't ask you to. Please, let me go.*

I bit out a curse. Of course I'd terrified her. She'd been struggling to close her legs and begging me to let her go, but I'd held her wide open for my inspection.

"Yeah. I scared her." The awful truth was bitter on my tongue. I'd already realized that I'd fucked up by manhandling her when she tried to get away. But I'd thought my actions were justified. Because if I was able to find the person who'd hurt her and make *them* hurt, then I could make everything all better.

The fact of the matter was that no one had hurt Sofia other than me. I'd let my own damage fuck up my thought processes. The sight of a woman I cared about bearing a scar made me feel powerless, because it meant I'd failed to be there to protect her. It had happened once before, and I would die before I let it happen again. Especially not to my sweet Sofia.

But Sofia hadn't been hurt by some monstrous man. I didn't know how she'd gotten the scar, but in hindsight, it was obvious that her fear response had been prompted by my overreaction. I'd lured her into a deeply vulnerable state, and when she'd put her full trust in me to see to her wellbeing, I'd terrorized her instead.

"You're going to have to be more careful around her," Adrián advised. "She might have grown up in Caesar Hernández's house, but she's not from our world. I'm honestly surprised that you were able to spank her at all without her fighting you or weeping for mercy. She's only been with you a couple days. I figured she'd still be in a full-on meltdown."

"She's a lot more resilient than you'd think," I said, my chest swelling with pride. My little flower was soft and delicate, but she was also reasonable and adaptable. "She's more upset with Caesar than anyone else. He wounded her deeply with his lies. So deeply that she says she would actually prefer to stay here with me rather than going back home. For some reason, she doesn't seem capable of understanding what a monster I really am."

"Well, you haven't been monstrous to her, have you?"

"I scared her," I repeated, in case Adrián somehow hadn't heard me say it the first time.

He waved away my concern. "One little fuckup doesn't make you a monster. I've seen the way you look at her. You would rather cut off your own hand than harm her with it. And if she's as resilient as you say, she'll forgive you for scaring her today. You just have to prove to her that she can put her trust in you."

"You're right," I agreed. "I fucked up, but I can fix this."

"Of course I'm right. You're welcome."

I knocked back my beer, deciding not to bother

telling him he was a dick. He already knew that he was. And besides, he had given me good advice.

I knew exactly how I would earn Sofia's trust back. Then, she would willingly return to my arms and welcome my touch. I could continue with my plan to seduce her into submission.

Sofia's complete and utter devotion was still within my grasp. She was mine, and she would accept her place eagerly by the time I was finished with her.

CHAPTER 12

SOFIA

Less than twenty-four hours had passed since I'd fled from Mateo's disgusted stare, but already, I ached for him to touch me. I hadn't been soothed by his embrace in far too long. I'd only been with him for a few days, but I was addicted to his affection.

In my childhood home, affection had been earned through good behavior and meeting Daddy's expectations. I'd twisted myself into knots to please him, constantly anxious that he would withdraw his approval if I disappointed him.

Ever since I'd woken up in Mateo's house, he had offered his attention freely, even stubbornly. Now that he'd seen my scar, he'd backed off, leaving me bereft.

I'd disappointed him with the physical flaws that

I couldn't change. There was no way I could modify that particular quality and earn his affection again. I couldn't make this better with good behavior.

Although I felt moderately better now that I'd been able to style my curls and wear my own clothes, I missed the comfort of being swaddled in Mateo's massive t-shirt, enfolded in his calming scent.

He wasn't being cold or cruel this morning, but he didn't encourage me to sit on his lap while he fed me breakfast, either. It seemed that he didn't hate me or even dislike me as a person. He was genial while he cooked our meal, indicating that I should sit by the stove and watch him again. His big, warm body was so close to mine, but he was utterly beyond my reach.

After he'd seen the shameful scar that had ruined my physical appeal, I was no longer the perfect woman he'd so obviously desired. I was damaged. Unworthy. Unwanted.

I shuddered to think how he might be treating me now if he'd seen the extent of the repulsive marks carved into my thighs. He'd only glimpsed one of them, and that had been enough to earn his revulsion.

"I want to talk to you about what happened yesterday," he announced when I finished the final bite of the omelet he'd prepared for me.

My stomach dropped. I didn't want him to mention my scars or acknowledge them in any way. It was painful enough to know that he was disgusted by them. Hearing him express that sentiment aloud would crush me.

His dark eyes roved over me, assessing my body language.

I realized I'd hunched my shoulders and hugged my arms around my middle, bracing myself for the pain of his censure.

"I didn't let you go when you asked me to," he said, his tone steady and even. Despite the reassuring cadence, he made no move to reach out and comfort me physically. "I broke your trust."

"Oh." I didn't really know how to reply. He wasn't saying anything cruel about my scars, but he wasn't saying he wanted me, either.

"This is a two-way street, and I haven't been fair to you," he continued. "You promised me that I could trust you, but I failed to reciprocate. I've decided that you can go back to your classes. I'm choosing to trust that you won't try to run from me, Sofia. I hope that in return, you will choose to trust me again."

He was sending me back to my classes? I still hadn't caved to his demand that I surrender my most important contact details to him. I hadn't given him the information he needed to send the messages that would smooth over my sudden absence. He'd been so rigid and uncompromising when it came to my cooperation with my captivity.

Heat pulsed between my legs at the memory of

his discipline. He'd been serious enough about enforcing his rules that he'd spanked me in punishment for my disobedience.

But now that he'd seen only one of my scars, he was relieved for the excuse to get some time away from me. He had a life to get on with, things to do that didn't involve babysitting me.

"Okay," I agreed softly, breathing through the knifing pain at the center of my chest.

When Mateo had held me over his knee with such harsh affection, I'd been foolish enough to believe that he wouldn't withdraw that care if I disappointed him.

Why did I never learn? Time and time again, I deluded myself into thinking my world was a much brighter, more pleasant place than it actually was.

I got to my feet and stepped away from the kitchen island. Breakfast was over, and I was obviously being dismissed.

I straightened my spine and summoned up a cheery smile. "I'll go get ready, then," I announced. "I just need twenty minutes."

I kept my stride casual and my shoulders back as I walked down the hall, making a conscious effort to hide the fact that I was devastated by his rejection. If I allowed my body language to reflect my misery, I would appear even more displeasing to Mateo. No one liked a moping girl.

Once I made it to the privacy of my bedroom, I willed myself to keep up the brave front. I didn't have time for self-indulgent tears. Mateo was waiting to get me out of his house, so he could get on with his day. He'd been cordial with me over breakfast, and I didn't want to jeopardize his lingering kindness. It was all the positive attention I had left, and I would bend over backward to keep it.

I checked my reflection in the bathroom mirror, scrutinizing my appearance. Mercifully, my curls had been put back in order, the tight spirals falling around my face in an effortlessly wild, carefree style. The *free spirit* aesthetic was a carefully constructed lie, my rebellious attempt to assert my individuality and defy my mother's rigid, orderly definition of female beauty.

The amount of effort I put in to create this look was far too elaborate and meticulous to truthfully reflect the attitude of a free spirit. But the control and calm I found in methodically styling my curls had helped me gain a small sense of personal power as a teenager. I was grateful to have that shred of familiar control back, now that my entire reality had been shattered beyond repair.

My bohemian chic dress enhanced my carefree lie. I ran my fingers over the dove gray fabric, feeling the embroidered floral pattern that was sewn in subtle shades of slate. The loose-fitting garment told the world that I didn't care about showing off the shape of my feminine curves to their full effect.

But I'd spent hours shopping and sorting through dozens of outfits to select this dress. It completed the image I wanted to present to the world, the deception that I didn't care about what they thought of my appearance.

Despite my defiance of my mother's sleek, sophisticated style, I lived within the vain constraints she'd imposed upon me, my insecurities and desire for approval too deeply ingrained to eradicate.

I shook my head slightly, my artfully-designed curls swaying around my face. I might still live in an emotional cage of my mother's design, but at least I'd decorated the cramped space as my own.

Reminding myself that Mateo was waiting, I got to work polishing my look: a few coats of curling mascara, a soft sweep of blush, a neutral gloss to make my lips shine and pout.

I set down my makeup and took a final assessment.

I looked perfect, my appearance utterly effortless and carefully crafted.

I hoped Mateo liked it.

Taking a deep, fortifying breath, I turned away from the mirror and grabbed up my laptop bag, marveling that I'd been allowed to have it in my possession.

When Valentina had come to visit me yesterday, she'd brought all my clothes from my walk-in closet at my apartment, as well as my beauty products and school supplies.

I'd been wary of her at first. During our initial meeting to discuss the curriculum at UCLA, I'd gotten the impression that she was kind. But I was now aware that she was part of the criminal underworld I'd fallen into. Adrián Rodríguez was a vicious drug lord, and she was deeply in love with him.

My discomfiture was compounded by the fact that my father had kidnapped and terrorized her. She'd covered the marks with makeup, but her efforts hadn't fully obscured the bruises on her neck.

Had Daddy done that to her?

The thought of my doting father wrapping his hands around Valentina's throat made me want to vomit.

Even if he hadn't personally been the one to hurt her, he'd arranged the circumstances that had resulted in the horrific injury.

After her ordeal, the compassionate woman had come to Mateo's house to comfort *me*. She'd worried that I was distraught over being held hostage. She'd been brutalized during her abduction, whereas Mateo had been nothing but gentle with me.

Except for when he'd spanked me.

But even that hadn't been an act of violence. The

spanking had stung, but with his immense strength, he could have easily damaged my body if he'd wanted to. Instead, he'd given me the most intense orgasm of my life. My past experiences rubbing my clit with my fingers when I was alone in my bed hadn't come close to that earth-shattering pleasure.

I closed my eyes and shoved back the wash of grief at the loss of my connection with Mateo. Familiar shame twisted my stomach.

My mother had told me my body was ruined by the marks on my skin, and she'd been right.

I plastered a pleasant smile on my glossed lips and walked down the hallway to rejoin Mateo.

"Okay, I'm ready to go," I announced when I stepped into the living room.

His attention turned from the hockey game highlights he was watching, his dark eyes focusing on me. His gaze raked over my body, eliciting a small shiver. The intensity of his attention after a day of distance was so overwhelmingly gratifying that it caused palpable pleasure. I drank it in, greedy for his approval and affirmation.

"You look beautiful," he told me, the rough edge to his tone making my heart lift. Maybe he wasn't completely disgusted by me.

I was more grateful than ever that Valentina had brought me my full array of dresses and beauty supplies. "Thanks," I murmured, basking in the praise but also feeling the familiar tinge of anxiety that came along with it. Such praise could always be taken away if I failed to present myself in a pleasing manner in the future.

As much as I wanted to revel in his approval all day, I was conscious of the fact that he wanted me to leave his house. "Is one of your cars an automatic that I can drive, or should I order a rideshare?" I asked.

"No." The denial was deep and immediate, his heavy brows drawing together with an expression of censure.

I tried not to squirm at his sudden shift in demeanor. He threw me off-balance, and I didn't know how to act around him anymore. Things had been so easy between us before. Even when I'd been arguing with him—even when I'd fled from him in a bout of terror—he'd kept himself firmly in my space, captivating me with his reassuring touch. He'd felt too solid for my own good, and I'd taken his staunch presence for granted, imagining that nothing I could do would cause him to reject me.

"But I thought you wanted me to go to class," I said, my voice lilting into a questioning tone. "How else will I get there?"

"I'm going to drive you." He got to his feet, his massive body seeming to swell as he stared down at me. The disapproval in his features shifted to something equally intense, but somehow softer: sternness.

"You didn't think I was going to let you leave on your own, did you?"

I licked my suddenly dry lips. "I thought... I didn't think you'd want to come with me. I figured you could do other stuff with your day, and I promise I'll come right back here after class. You can trust me."

He took a step toward me, closing the distance between us. For a moment, I thought he would reach out and tenderly touch my face, but his arms remained at his sides.

"I know I can trust you, *dulzura*," he said. "But I won't leave you to wander around on your own. There's nothing else I'd rather do with my day than guard you."

I shrank in on myself. "Because I'm your hostage."

His head canted to the side, and I surmised that he was considering his response carefully. "Because I want to keep you safe," he finally replied. "Your father and I have arranged an uneasy truce, but he might be tempted to bring you home if I leave you exposed. I doubt he would dare to send anyone to pick you up while you're on campus. It's too public if you decided to make a scene. But I won't risk it. I'm going with you to make sure he doesn't try to take you from me."

Was I imagining the possessiveness of his statement?

All mine. I remembered the savage claim he'd made over me when he was gripping my swollen sex in his huge hand and bringing me to orgasm.

He broke the moment with a gruff order. "Come on. You'll be late for class if we don't get going."

My hand twitched toward his, longing to take it as we walked out of the house. But he didn't seem to notice the tiny movement that betrayed my pathetic neediness. I pressed my palm against my dress, fingering the embroidery to prevent myself from stupidly reaching for him.

When we stepped outside, my attention caught on the ostentatious, cherry red Porsche parked in the driveway.

"You're driving me to class in *that?*" I asked, taken aback.

He frowned, glancing at me as he opened the passenger door. "You don't like it?"

"No, I like it," I assured him, compliantly sliding into the leather seat. "It's just a really fancy car to take such a casual trip."

A dazzling grin lit his features, and his eyes sparkled as he reverently ran his hand over the aerodynamic hood of the car. I'd never seen him in this mood before: something between boyish excitement and covetous hunger.

"It's brand new, and I want to take it out for a spin. Even if we are just driving into the city. I'll take it to the track later and see what it's really capable of."

His giddy energy was baffling coming from a man who was so strong and serious. He'd been playful with me, and he'd looked at me with similar possessiveness in the past. But he hadn't pulsed with this pure, thrilled aura. Like a kid with a shiny new toy on Christmas morning.

"You can come with me," he said, more of an edict than an offer. "Have you ever been to a race track?"

I shook my head, making an effort to prevent my jaw from dropping. Mateo's joyous attitude was shocking and more endearing than my heart could bear. I wanted him so desperately, but I worried that he would never want me again. Not the way he had before he saw my scar.

"You'll love it," he informed me before he shut my door carefully.

He practically had a spring in his step as he circled the car and opened his own door. When he settled into the driver's seat, he ran his hands over the steering wheel before stroking the gear stick. My skin tingled in response. I wanted him to touch *me* with that tender reverence, like he'd done yesterday morning while he cuddled me at breakfast.

When he put the key in the ignition and the car

roared to life, he chuckled. I almost expected him to rub his hands together in glee.

Instead, he placed one hand on the wheel and put the car in gear with the other. Although I knew the sports car was capable of insanely quick acceleration, he pulled smoothly around the circular driveway at a reasonable speed.

Despite the fact that he wasn't able to test the limits of the Porsche's features, he still radiated pure pleasure.

"You really like fancy cars, huh?" I said, remembering his over-the-top collection that he kept protected in his massive garage.

He glanced over at me, sharing his tilted smile before pulling through the open gate at the end of his drive. "Guilty," he affirmed. "How did you manage to figure me out?"

He was teasing me, and I suppressed the impulse to stick my tongue out at him. It was far too easy to slip into acting playful with Mateo when he was exuding this excitable energy.

"Your collection is almost hoarder-levels of insane," I replied blandly, teasing right back. "Do you really need to own a working replica of the Batmobile?"

His rich, deep laugh boomed through the car, filling the space with warmth. I relaxed back into my leather seat, just like I wanted to snuggle into his big body.

"What man wouldn't want to own a working replica of the Batmobile? I'm living the dream. Besides." He shot me a smirk. "What else am I supposed to drive when *some* little troublemaker destroyed my favorite Ferrari?"

"Sorry," I apologized quietly, my levity melting in the wake of guilt. His flashy cars obviously brought him great joy, and I'd broken one of them. "Did I totally ruin it?"

He shrugged, the softer smile he offered reassuring. "It'll take a while to get all the parts to repair it, but you don't have to be sorry. The damage to the Ferrari was my fault for scaring you so badly. Don't worry about it. Adrián owed me a new ride, anyway. He just dropped off this sweet baby this morning." He patted the Porsche's dashboard.

My brows rose. "That's a really nice gift."

I was accustomed to my own family's limitless supply of disposable wealth, but the idea of anyone offering such an expensive vehicle as a present was mind-boggling, even for me.

"It's not a gift," he explained. "It's payment. Adrián ordered me to wreck my last one, and he made the mistake of promising to replace it with any model I wanted. I traded up."

"Why would he order you to wreck your car?" Concern furrowed my brow. In my world, a car wreck wasn't something to be taken lightly, but Mateo spoke about it so matter-of-factly. "Did you get hurt?"

He laughed. "Nothing was damaged other than my favorite Porsche. We had to ditch it when we took Valentina away from her husband. It was too conspicuous and easy to trace. Adrián made me abandon my baby to be dismantled and sold for parts. And I'd just bought her, too."

"You helped Adrián rescue Valentina?"

His expression shuttered, enigmatic. "I helped him get her away from her husband and bring her back to LA from Bogotá. She's safe from Hugo now. He'll never hurt her again. Adrián made sure of that."

I bit my lip, struggling to sort through my conflicted feelings. Adrián had always scared me, but now that I knew what he really was, he was downright terrifying.

Valentina wasn't frightening at all. She was kind and compassionate: the total opposite of Adrián, as far as I could tell.

Her love for him was obviously genuine and utterly unshakable. It was evident in her glowing expression and reverential mannerisms every time she mentioned his name. I didn't understand how she could love him, but she did.

And he must love her, too. I didn't have a full understanding of the circumstances surrounding my kidnapping by Mateo, but I did know enough to realize that Adrián had risked a lot to rescue Valentina from her abusive husband. When Daddy had stolen her to send her back into that hellish marriage, Adrián had made the ruthless decision to take me as a hostage.

Mateo had ensured that I hadn't been harmed in any way, but I understood that things were beyond tense and were balanced on a knife's edge between Adrián and my father. When I'd first woken up in his house, Mateo had warned me that things would get *very bloody* if he gave me back to Daddy.

Adrián had put himself and Mateo in a potentially deadly situation so that he could save Valentina, the woman he loved.

The complexities of this dark new world I found myself in were far more confusing than I'd initially thought. When I'd still been living in my normal little bubble, drug lords and criminals were bad men who did evil things.

I'd never thought about them being capable of love or fierce protectiveness.

"I'm glad he saved her," I said after several seconds of silence.

Mateo didn't glance over at me, and his fingers tightened around the steering wheel. "Even though it means you're my hostage?" he asked, his calm tone belying his physical tension.

"Yeah," I sighed. "This isn't how I wanted my life

to go, but if it means Valentina isn't being abused and can be with the man she loves, I can accept what's happening right now. It's not like you're being cruel to me. You're even letting me go to my classes." My jaw firmed, my teeth clenching as I focused the full force of my anger on the real culprit. "This is Daddy's fault, not yours."

Mateo relaxed, his bulky muscles going supple as he eased his hold on the steering wheel and shifted gears. "I'm glad you understand that."

CHAPTER 13

MATEO

"What classes do you have on your schedule today?" I asked to lighten the mood again. I liked when Sofia was relaxed enough to tease me. It meant she felt safe and happy in my care.

I wanted more of that.

Restraining myself from touching her this morning had taken considerable effort. By nature, I was an impulsive, greedy bastard. I'd scraped and clawed for everything I had in my life, and that habit of simply taking what I wanted through sheer force and determination had become my norm.

If I wanted to hold Sofia, my body's first instinct was to act on that desire without hesitation.

But she'd been standoffish over breakfast. She hadn't flinched away from me, but she hadn't reached for me, either. Denying myself had set my teeth on edge, but I had resolutely stuck to my plan to coax her back into my arms.

Now that I'd enacted that plan to earn her trust back, my frustration abated slightly. It had only been an hour since I'd told her she could return to her classes, and we'd made stunning progress.

I would have been content enough with her playful ribbing about my car collection, but her acknowledgement that the blame for her abduction lay at her father's feet, not mine, satisfied me to my core. I'd known that truth all along; I never would have plucked her out of her safe, easy existence, no matter how badly I'd wanted her.

Hearing her say that I was blameless for her imprisonment with me was unexpected and deeply gratifying. She trusted me over her own father.

It wouldn't be long before she welcomed my touch again. Before she begged me to put my hands on her body.

"I took a light load this semester," she replied, shifting into the more casual subject I'd prompted. She adapted to my desires so beautifully, naturally allowing me to guide her where I wanted. "I only have one class today: Alexander Technique."

"Is that the name of your class or a person?" I asked, only mildly curious. I knew Sofia studied music; a fluffy degree for a girl who didn't need a well-paying job after college. This course already sounded somewhat ridiculous.

"Both, sort of," she replied. "Frederick Matthias Alexander developed the technique. This class teaches the best posture for peak musical performance. It helps reduce anxiety and prevent injuries."

Definitely ridiculous.

"I didn't realize musical pursuits were so dangerous," I said drily.

I could practically feel her indignant glare burning a hole into my skull. I'd hoped she would read my comments as more teasing, but it seemed I hadn't been successful in masking my disdain.

"I intend to be a professional vocalist," she informed me tersely. "I train my instrument, just like you train your body to get all those big muscles. The Alexander Technique prevents vocal fatigue or even damage to my vocal cords that could end my career."

"So, you want to be a pop star or something?" I asked, trying to engage in the conversation even though it still sounded awfully silly and self-indulgent.

I only succeeded in aggravating her further.

"No, I don't want to be a pop star. But if I did, there wouldn't be anything wrong with that."

"I never said there was." I tried to placate her.

"Your tone did," she shot back. "I take my music seriously, Mateo. My program at UCLA is highly competitive, and I worked hard to get accepted. There are only twelve Music Performance majors with a focus on Voice in my year. That's the full quota the school accepts. I earned my place in this program, and I'm not taking it for granted. I don't appreciate the way you're talking about it."

"Okay," I allowed, genuinely contrite. I still believed that a career as a singer was a frivolous pursuit only available to privileged people, but I didn't like that I'd offended Sofia. "I apologize. I didn't realize you were so dedicated to your studies. If you don't want to be a pop star, what does a professional vocalist do, exactly?"

She let out a small huff, her annoyance only partially soothed by my apology. "My program mostly focuses on operatic performance. I enjoy that musical style, and training my voice is valuable. But I don't plan on pursuing opera after I graduate. My music has more of a folk vibe. I play just enough guitar and piano to get by, so I can pick out my own melodies while I'm writing songs. But instruments aren't my strong suit. I usually jam with other music students if I need more complex arrangements."

"You write your own songs?" My interest was no longer feigned.

Sofia seemed to be capable of making even the most banal things fascinating. Only moments ago, she'd been stiff and angry with me. But within a few sentences of talking about her music, she'd become animated and adorably enthusiastic.

"Yeah," she replied. "It started off as silly, angsty teenage poetry. Which totally sucked, by the way. I cringe looking at the stuff I wrote when I was fifteen. But I studied the craft, and it didn't take long for me to put those poems to a tune. I've always loved to sing, and it was a natural progression."

"Why are you in a program that focuses on opera if you write folk music?" I asked.

What had been an inane conversation about her studies was now a puzzle. I wanted to know more about the way her mind worked, why she made the choices she did, and what vision she harbored for her future.

I wanted to understand her, so that I could keep her more easily. If I knew the secrets of what motivated her and inspired her passion, then I could offer her those things. She would be not only willing but eager to remain close to me. She would have no reason to be anything less than completely devoted to me if I provided her with everything she could possibly desire.

"Daddy insisted that I go to college," she said, her bubbly enthusiasm deflating slightly. "He thinks an education is an important asset."

She waved her hand through the air, dismissing her budding consternation at the thought of her father. "But it's been good so far, and I've always liked school, anyway. I've learned so much more than I ever could have imagined. I'm definitely a way better singer than I was when I came in as a freshman."

"I'm sure you'll get a recording contract." I'd never heard her sing, but if she wanted to be a professional singer, I would figure out how to put money in the right hands to make it happen for her.

"Obviously, that would be awesome. And I hope I do. But my music isn't about making myself a big success or anything like that. Music has helped me get through some not-great stuff over the years, and I can't imagine how I would cope without it. Even if I never get a major recording contract, my work will be meaningful if it helps just one other person who's struggling to get through a hard time in their life."

I was silent for a moment, overawed by the strength of her passion and the depths of her sweet nature. Sofia didn't want to be a famous singer because she cared about being lauded or making a ton of money. She wanted to touch other people's lives, to make them better in any small way she could.

"I'm sorry," I said, my voice roughened by the profound effect she had on me.

"For what? You already apologized for diminishing my degree."

"I didn't apologize enough. I was being a dick," I admitted, shaking my head. "I've never thought about music as anything more than passing entertainment. I was being dismissive of your program because I thought you were choosing to study something that's an unimportant hobby, that it was a mark of your privilege."

I ran a hand through my hair, admitting something aloud that I'd never quite admitted to myself. "I was a little judgmental of you, because I think on some level, I envy you. But that's just my own classist bullshit, and I should have kicked it years ago. I didn't have much growing up. Studying anything at all was a luxury. If it wasn't essential for survival, it was unnecessary."

I took a breath, bracing myself for my next admission. Sofia didn't seem to realize just how different my background was from hers. She didn't understand that I was a poor kid who'd muscled his way among wealthy men and held his place there by strength alone.

"I didn't even finish high school, so the concept of paying for a college degree to study music seemed beyond indulgent to me. My choices in life have never been guided by passion, and I think I was a little jealous that you were able to do so. I trivialized it, and that was shitty of me."

She didn't respond immediately, absorbing the weight of everything I'd told her.

"I don't want you to envy me," she said quietly. "I

know that I've been spoiled and that Daddy gave me an easy life. But I don't like that you feel jealous of me. That's not a nice way to feel about someone."

Her voice was small, hurt. The thought that I might resent her or dislike her obviously caused her distress. It wasn't her fault that she'd grown up wealthy with an overbearing father who had sheltered her from anything remotely unpleasant.

"I'm not jealous of you anymore," I promised, wishing I didn't have to keep my eyes on the road. I wanted her to see the full depth of sincerity in my next words. "I'm in awe of you."

"You don't have to say that," she mumbled.

"I know I don't have to. I'm saying it because it's true." I stole a glance over at her.

Her lower lip was caught between her teeth, her gaze fixed on her lap.

"Hey," I said gently, calling her attention to me. "I mean it. I'd like to hear you sing."

"Really?" she breathed.

God, she sounded so cautiously hopeful that it made my heart ache.

As soon as I'd brought her into my home, I'd quickly discerned that Sofia thrived on affirmation. From the very beginning of our time together, calling her my *good girl* had made her so sweetly compliant. Her reaction had satisfied me because it made her easily obedient. That ensured she was a cooperative hostage, but more importantly, it fulfilled my darkest desires for her. I craved her unquestioning submission to all the dirty, perverted things I'd fantasized about doing to her lithe little body.

But I hadn't understood how fragile she would become when I manipulated her like that. Once I provided her with praise and affection, she became addicted to it. A few hits, and she put herself firmly in my power, cleaving to me and seeking more of my approval.

Until this moment, I hadn't realized just how thoroughly Sofia had placed herself under my control. I wasn't sure if she realized it, either. A cruel word from me could crush her, and if I wanted to, I could parse out my praise like a miser and make her even more malleable in her desperation to please me.

The idea made my stomach turn. If my manipulative methods had made her fragile, I would simply work that much harder to protect my precious little flower. I resolved to lavish her with praise to make up for it.

"I'm sure you have an incredible voice, since you were accepted into such a selective program," I said, not fulsome in the slightest. That was simply a fact. "I would love to hear you sing."

"You can sit in on my class if you want," she offered, shifting quickly from doubt to eagerness. "I'm sure Professor Lassiter won't mind. It's not like it's a lecture, so you won't have to sit through that. There are only seven of us taking this course, and we're all performers. You might get a little bored while we work on the theory and warm-up for the Alexander Technique, but you'll also get to hear everyone practice."

"You're the only one I care about hearing." Another completely truthful statement.

I snuck a glance in her direction to find that her cheeks were flushed, and a small, serene smile played around her pouty lips.

How could a woman look so innocently adorable and utterly fuckable at the same time?

"Everyone in the class is really talented," she asserted, shifting some of my intense admiration off her and onto others, as though she didn't believe she was fully deserving of the praise she so deeply craved.

"Only three of us are singers," she continued. "Everyone else plays an instrument. You should hear Todd play piano. He's insanely good. Like, world-class amazing."

I definitely didn't give a fuck about listening to *Todd* play the piano, especially if it incited such exuberance in Sofia.

"I'm looking forward to hearing you sing," I said instead of telling her exactly what I would do to Todd if he looked at my sweet Sofia with even a hint of interest.

Now that we were leaving the solitude of my home, I was faced with the prospect of spending time with Sofia in public for the first time since I'd claimed her. If I'd felt protective of her before, now my protectiveness was layered with possessiveness. Things could get very dangerous for her male classmates if they didn't acknowledge my claim. Especially because I was still trying to stick to my resolution not to touch her until she sought out contact. I was mindful of the fact that I'd scared her yesterday morning, and she had yet to reach for me.

That little incident would pale in comparison to her seeing my fists painted with a twenty-something pianist's blood.

I can't murder anyone on a college campus, I told myself firmly. *Not even a little.*

Violence of any kind on my part would cause problems for Sofia. I was escorting her back into her pretty little world, a world I had no place in. It seemed my impulse control would be stretched to its limit today.

***

IT TURNED OUT THAT THE *ALEXANDER TECHNIQUE* was exactly as much bullshit as I'd initially suspected. Sofia's professor droned on and on about how different joints in the body were connected, and if you paid attention to them, you could loosen them up to "widen" and "float."

All I saw were weak points on the body where I could do the most damage with my fists.

Sofia watched Professor Lassiter with rapt attention, her emerald eyes wide and serious. As though he was imparting some great, secret wisdom rather than simply using a bunch of flowery words to tell her that standing straight was good for her posture.

I leaned back in the tiny chair I'd selected by the door, removed from where the group stood in a rough semicircle at the front of the room. After Sofia had introduced me as a prospective student, the professor had invited me to join them, informing me that the Alexander Technique was "beneficial for everyone's health."

I was certain that the skinny, middle-aged man had never been nearly as fit as I was. He was wearing a fucking turtleneck, for god's sake.

I didn't need some graying, mustachioed weirdo in a turtleneck telling me how to be healthy.

Everything was going fine so far, even if it was tedious and mildly stupid. While guarding Adrián, I spent a lot of time in stillness. I might be impulsive when it came to my own selfish desires, but I was also very practiced at watching and waiting while I was on the job protecting Adrián's back.

I wasn't actively protecting Sofia from a threat at

the moment, but it wasn't a hardship to watch her. Everything about her was delicate and dainty, and I entertained myself by appreciating each of her elegant features in detail.

I observed her wiggling her slender fingers along with her classmates, "warming up" to perform.

"Don't think of it as a stretch," Professor Lassiter told his students. "Think of it as *extending your range*."

It took concerted effort not to roll my eyes.

As a group, they all started twisting their torsos from side to side, letting their arms dangle and sway loosely. Everyone looked utterly idiotic, except Sofia.

Her mahogany curls bounced around her face, her emerald eyes shining and her lush lips curved in a smile. She was clearly enjoying the class, so I was content enough with my stationary position by the door.

No matter how ridiculous their not-quite-stretches were.

"Okay," Professor Lassiter announced, stilling his twisting torso. "Now, let's slowly raise our arms and clasp our hands."

Sofia lifted her arms gracefully, like a ballet dancer. Watching her move was hypnotic enough, but when she clasped her hands together above her head and held the pose, my perverted brain went into overdrive.

I imagined her with cuffs around her wrists,

chains hanging from the ceiling to anchor her arms in place. Trapping her for my admiration and amusement. When I had my pretty hostage bound and at my mercy, would she look at me with desire? Trepidation? Trust?

Fuck, I wanted all of it. I was greedy for everything she had to offer me.

"Drop your hands, and lace your fingers together behind your head." Professor Lassiter's lilting voice sounded again, and Sofia moved to obey.

For the space of a second, my bondage fantasy was cleared away, but my reprieve was short-lived.

"Now, arch your back and let your spine stretch."

Jesus fucking Christ. Sofia's hands were immobilized behind her head, her breasts thrust out in offering and her pelvis tilted forward.

I'd imagined having her beneath me like this countless times. My good girl would keep her hands right where I told her to while I played with her pretty nipples until she arched into my tormenting touch and begged for more.

I scrubbed my hand over my beard, struggling to retain my composure.

Did innocent Sofia truly have no notion of how erotic she looked in this position?

I tore my covetous gaze from her just long enough to ensure that none of the men were looking at what was mine.

Luckily for their sakes, no one was eyeing her with hunger.

No one except me, and I was fucking ravenous for her.

Mercifully, Professor Lassiter announced an end to the warm-up exercises. Just in time, because my jeans were getting uncomfortably tight around my cock.

"Sofia," he addressed her, beckoning her into the center of the semicircle. "Let's start with you today, since your friend is here."

For the first time since class had started, she made eye contact with me. Her features illuminated with a radiant smile that was so bright it made something burn in the center of my chest.

She gave me a little wave, even though I was only a few yards away from her. I nodded back at her, the muscles in my face stretching weirdly. It took me a second to realize that I was grinning like a fool.

I tried to school my features to something more serious and intimidating. There might not be any immediate threats lurking around this room, but I'd accompanied Sofia to campus in order to protect her.

No silly smiles for me.

"What are you going to sing for us?" Professor Lassiter asked her.

I was only peripherally aware of his presence by

Sofia's side. Her stunning emerald eyes captured and held my full attention.

"*Ave Maria*," she replied to her professor. She didn't take her gaze off me.

"Okay, let's hear you go through it once, and then, we'll address how you can improve your technique on the second time around."

She nodded to acknowledge his instructions, took a deep breath, and closed her eyes. Her smile softened, her features taking on a peaceful, beatific glow.

Then, her lush lips parted, and the most beautiful sound I'd ever heard issued from her delicate body.

I forgot how to breathe, stunned by the pure, powerful notes that reverberated through the room. They sank beneath my skin and reached a dark place deep inside me. Heavy, honeyed warmth settled in my chest, filling me up and soothing tension I hadn't even realized I'd been carrying.

The sound was too ethereal to be real. I couldn't understand the language of the lyrics, but the profound sense of peace that blanketed my being couldn't have been attained through any words I knew.

The notes that had started with exquisite power flowed into a pitch so achingly delicate that I wasn't certain if it was even audible sound or simply the sensation of floating.

I filled my lungs, as though I could breathe in the

resonance of Sofia's soul along with oxygen. She felt just as essential, just as life-sustaining.

Something burned behind my eyes as a lifetime of volatile emotions were soothed by her angelic voice.

The sound softened, becoming quieter and trailing away. I leaned toward her as it receded, attempting to follow the warm peace she provided. I wanted to hold it close and wrap myself up in it, so I would never lose it.

Her perfect lips closed, but I could still feel her song in the room, gently rolling back to her like a tide flowing out to sea.

Her lashes fluttered, and her lovely eyes opened to peek up at me. The uncertainty that tightened her features for a fleeting moment melted back into the radiant smile that was bright enough to blind me.

My jaw was hanging open, but I didn't feel any shame at the unadulterated awe I displayed. I craved to close the distance between us and run my hands all over her divine form to remind myself that she was real. To remind myself that she was *mine*.

The possessiveness that had gripped my heart before I'd heard her sing now consumed me. Sofia belonged to me, my captive angel.

"That was great, Sofia," Professor Lassiter said.

She broke her attention away from me to focus on her teacher, absorbing *his* praise.

Somehow, I forced my body to lean back into the chair, restraining myself from going to her.

I couldn't punch her professor's teeth out and carry her off like my personal prize, my most jealously-guarded treasure.

This is important to her, I told myself. *Don't fuck it up.*

Sofia wouldn't thank me if I ruined her academic reputation by brutalizing a faculty member.

"Let's go through it again," Professor Lassiter prompted. "This time, I'm going to call your attention to what we've been practicing with the Alexander Technique. You'll notice a remarkable improvement."

Improvement? How the fuck did the fool think she could improve upon absolute perfection? The notion that his idiotic posture exercises would somehow affect her astounding capabilities was absurd and offensive in its arrogance.

Sofia didn't seem offended, though. She appeared focused, determined.

I gritted my teeth and stayed seated. Sofia obviously valued her academic achievements. Even if I knew her professor was full of shit, she still wanted to excel in her program.

She took a breath and began to sing, the ethereal sound filling the room once again.

Before I could relax and fall back under her spell,

Professor Lassiter placed his hand between her shoulder blades.

"Let your torso soften and widen." He spouted his nonsense over her perfect song. "Let the air come all the way down to the base of the lungs."

The fucker bracketed her waist with his hands, feeling her breaths as she created divine sound.

I tasted blood in my mouth, but I was too concerned with clinging to my tenuous control to register that I'd bitten the inside of my cheek.

"Loosen your spine," he instructed. "Don't occlude your voice box. Let your neck move freely."

His hands left her waist, only to move farther up her body. One wrapped around her nape, the other cradling her jaw to gently tilt her head back.

"That's good, Sofia," he praised warmly as she continued to sing. "Good girl."

Something snapped inside me. My world washed red, obliterating all rational thoughts.

My body swelled with possessive rage, and the space disappeared between us in five long strides.

Fortunately for Professor Lassiter, he clocked my sudden movement as soon as I started stalking toward him. He took several steps back from Sofia, holding up his hands in an instinctive show of surrender.

Her song ended abruptly, and her small hand

touched my heaving chest. The gentle warmth instantly redirected my full focus to her.

Sofia's stunning eyes were clouded with confusion, her brow furrowed.

"Is something wrong?" she asked, the barest tremor of fear making her words catch.

For half a heartbeat, I worried that she was afraid of *me*. But her fingers curved into my shirt, looking to me for reassurance.

She thought I knew about some danger she couldn't see.

I was the only dangerous thing in the vicinity, and it was safest for everyone if I took Sofia away with me right fucking now.

"We're leaving," I announced, my voice booming through the room in warning to everyone, even though I didn't take my eyes off Sofia's lovely face.

"Why?" she asked, questioning me out of worry rather than contradiction.

"It's an emergency," I told her roughly, my statement ringing with truth.

Professor Lassiter was in imminent danger if I took my eyes off Sofia for even a second. I knew it wasn't rational, but all the volatility within me that had been soothed by her song surged once again in its absence.

I hadn't properly established my claim over Sofia yet, and I couldn't leave her around other men for a minute longer without rectifying that. I knew she belonged to me, but I'd been allowing her time to come around and accept that fact on her own.

What little patience I'd possessed before was in tatters. I was taking her home with me, and we were going to settle this once and for all.

It was past time for Sofia to promise that she was mine and mine alone.

CHAPTER 14

SOFIA

Mateo's huge arm encircled my body, tucking me close to his side. The rush of relief at being sheltered in his protective hold was tainted by fear. I'd ached for his reassuring touch all day, but he offered it now because there was a threat lurking somewhere that I couldn't see.

I allowed him to hustle me out of the classroom, taking two quick strides for each of his.

"What's going on?" I asked once we exited the lecture hall and stepped outside.

"I'm taking you home," he announced, the grim note in his voice making me tremble.

He must have felt the fine tremor against his body, because his arm curved around me more tightly. The feel of his massive muscles surrounding me eased some of my fear. Mateo was solid and stronger than I could fathom. I knew he wouldn't let anyone get to me.

"You're safe with me, Sofia," he swore, his tone softening only slightly.

He was still on high alert, his body swelling with unspent aggression.

We crossed campus quickly, reaching his shiny red Porsche in less than half the time it had taken us to walk to class.

"Please," I entreated when we were both in the car. "Tell me what's happening."

His muscles bulged and flexed, and his obsidian eyes remained laser focused on the road as he started the drive back to his house.

"We'll talk about it once I get you home," he promised tightly. "We need privacy. And we're not doing this in a fucking car." He muttered the last, and I wasn't certain if it was meant for me to hear.

We drove in tense silence, and Mateo handled the Porsche with far less finesse than he had this morning. It growled and rumbled beneath us as he accelerated more quickly with each gear shift. He didn't smash the speed limit so blatantly that we attracted the attention of the cops, but it was an angry, aggressive ride.

When we pulled up to the house, he'd barely switched off the ignition before he rushed around the car to open my door. I fumbled at the seatbelt, my hands shaking. I knew Mateo would keep me safe, but whatever perceived threat that had set him off clearly hadn't abated.

He didn't allow me to waste any extra time struggling to free myself from the belt. He simply reached over my body and unbuckled it himself with no compunction about physical contact.

There was no respectful hesitation or caution in the way he handled me. He simply hooked his corded arms beneath my body and jerked me to his chest, carrying me into the house with brisk urgency.

"Are we in some sort of danger?" I dared to ask, thoroughly intimidated by his demeanor.

He shifted his hold on me, and my feet touched the ground. In the same sudden movement, he pushed the front door closed by pressing my back against the wood. His muscular form pinned me in place, and I could feel his racing heart thrumming where his torso pushed into my chest.

"No, *florecita*," he assured me, his voice rough and deep.

He trailed his fingers along the line of my jaw, his feather-light touch in shocking contrast to his overpowering weight against me.

"You're not in any danger." His dark eyes flashed, his mouth twisting in a scowl. "But everyone else is."

My stomach did a funny flip, unease stirring. "What do you mean?"

"I mean..." He said the words slowly, his free hand sliding behind my neck to grip my nape. The fingers that had touched my face so tenderly shifted lower. His big palm cradled my jaw, tipping my head back and exposing my throat.

"No one touches you but me," he finished, the furious tension easing from his muscles.

"Wait, are you upset about what happened in class?" I asked breathlessly, completely thrown by this sudden change in Mateo's behavior. "That was just part of learning the proper posture. Professor Lassiter didn't—"

His palm settled at the front of my throat, both of his massive hands encircling my neck. He didn't apply any pressure, but the assertion of dominance was clear.

"You're *my* good girl," he growled, his onyx eyes glinting. "*Mine*."

Despite his aggressive behavior, my heart leapt. "You still want me?" I asked, my voice small, hopeful.

"Of course I want you," he snarled, white teeth flashing. He pressed his hips more tightly against me, making sure I could feel his thick erection pressing into my belly.

"But I thought..." I took a breath and tried to raise my voice above a whisper. "You wouldn't touch me this morning. I thought you'd changed your mind."

He bit out a curse, grinding his hard cock against me. "That was a stupid fucking mistake, and I won't repeat it ever again. I should know better by now."

His bulk moved away from me for a split second, just long enough for him to grasp my waist and lift me over his shoulder.

"What are you doing?" I gasped, even as my body pulsed with excitement. My nipples pebbled to needy buds, and liquid heat gathered between my legs. I now recognized the scent of my own arousal, but I wasn't embarrassed at the prospect that he would be able to tell that I was turned on by his possessive actions.

"I'm going to show you just how fucking much I want you," he ground out, his hand cupping my ass and kneading my flesh, as though he had every right to handle my body however he pleased.

I shivered and sighed, relaxing into his hold as warmth flooded my being. Most of the heat was a sign of my arousal, but some of the glowing energy filling my chest was the result of sweet relief that he wasn't disgusted by me.

He carried me down the hall, passing the guest room where I'd been staying ever since he took me hostage. Instead, we entered what I assumed was his room. The stark black tones of the décor against white walls were harshly masculine, the style minimalist and devoid of any whimsical embellishments.

The world blurred around me, and my back was suddenly cushioned by his mattress. I scarcely had time to draw breath before he was on me, his huge body covering mine. My arms lifted, eager to embrace him and hold him close.

He ensnared my wrists, shackling them with one massive hand and pinning them above my head. His other hand found my throat again, pressing his thumb beneath my jaw to tip my head back.

He paused to stare down at me, his rugged features rendered harsh by hunger.

"Do you know how many times I've thought about having you like this?" The words were gravelly, his dark eyes burning. "Trapped beneath me, trembling and wet for me. Completely at my mercy."

"You think about me?" I asked with wonder. I'd pined for Mateo for five years, but I hadn't thought he was interested in me. Things had become passionate between us since he'd kidnapped me, but I'd never dared to imagine that he'd longed for me, too.

"I think about you all the fucking time," he swore just before his mouth crashed down on mine.

Mateo's kiss was ruthless. His lips conquered and claimed, shaping against my own with enough force to leave them swollen and bruised. His iron hold on my wrists and jaw kept me locked in place for his assault.

I stiffened for a moment, shocked and overwhelmed by his sudden aggression. I'd come to expect an unyielding but tender touch from Mateo.

Now, he didn't coax or encourage me to kiss him back. His teeth sank into my lower lip, drawing a gasp from my chest. His tongue surged into my open mouth, blocking my breath.

I writhed beneath him, struggling for air. But he didn't relent. He held me firm, keeping me trapped right where he wanted me and demanding my surrender on his terms.

Heat licked through my veins, pooling low in my belly. My labia pulsed, and my sex contracted, craving to be filled. My writhing shifted to wanton undulations as I rocked my hips against his thigh and rubbed my breasts into his hard chest.

I opened for him, welcoming him to take more. My head began to spin from lack of oxygen, but I craved his scorching kiss more desperately than I wanted air.

When I started to go weak beneath him, he pulled back just enough so I could draw breath. The fresh hit of oxygen sent me soaring, and I was weightless in his harsh hold. I stared up into his obsidian eyes, utterly entranced.

His thumb rubbed my swollen lips, making my sensitized nerve endings tingle and dance.

Unthinking, I rotated my hips against his thigh, seeking to stimulate my aching clit. He let more of his weight press down on me, wedging his leg between mine and forcing me to spread wide.

A needy whimper eased up my throat, and I continued to try to rub against him, my body squirming helplessly beneath his vastly superior mass.

His lips twisted in a wicked grin, his eyes glinting with cruel pleasure.

"You want more, *belleza*?" he asked, the question dripping with arrogant satisfaction.

"Please," I whispered, struggling for more friction against my sex.

He made a low humming sound that resonated deep in my body, and his head dipped toward mine. I offered my lips for another mind-numbing kiss, but his beard skimmed over my cheek as he leaned in to murmur dark words at my ear.

"I like when you beg, *dulzura*." His teeth nipped at my lobe, tugging before his tongue flicked over the abused area.

My breath stuttered, a little broken sound catching in my chest.

"Good girls ask nicely for what they want." He pressed a soft kiss beneath my ear. "And you're my good girl, aren't you, Sofia?"

"Yes," I whined.

"Tell me." The dark command rolled into my mind, compelling my truthful response.

"I'm your good girl," I promised, ragged and desperate.

"That's right." He nuzzled my neck, the tender contact belying his restraining hold on my body. "I think you've earned a reward," he murmured, his deep voice rumbling over my sensitized skin.

Keeping my wrists pinned with one hand, his other skimmed down my side, tracing the shape of my curves before caressing my thigh. His fingers found the hem of my dress, teasing beneath it.

My clit pulsed madly in anticipation, but fear tore through my lust.

"Wait," I gasped, trying to move away from his touch. He was inches away from touching my scars, from feeling the marks of my shame. I wasn't ready to lose his affection again. He'd managed to overcome the unsightliness of one scar, but he didn't know the extent of the damage.

He didn't relent. Mateo had always been gentle and careful with me, but this facet of himself he was showing me now was far rougher and more demanding.

"Mateo, stop," I begged, jerking against his hold.

He frowned down at me, his hand pausing just

above my knee. "When we're in my bed, you're not in charge, *florecita*."

The low warning made my panties grow damp with a rush of fresh arousal, but my fear didn't abate.

"I can feel your hot little pussy through my jeans," he said, his voice rough with hunger. "You like this."

He resumed his progress, pushing up my dress.

"No!" I shouted, panic slicing through my desire.

He stilled again, his massive body tensing. "I know you want me to touch you," he ground out. "Why are you fighting this?"

I cut my gaze away, my cheeks burning with shame. "I don't want you to see my thighs."

His hand instantly withdrew from my leg, coming up to cup my cheek instead. He turned my face, commanding my attention.

When I peeked up at him, I found that the sharp hunger in his black eyes had softened to something like sorrow.

He released my wrists and stroked his fingers through my hair in a soothing rhythm.

"I know I reacted badly when I saw your scar," he said, the words deep and even. "That had everything to do with me, not you. I think you're perfect."

My eyes burned. I wanted so badly for that to be true, but it simply wasn't.

"There are more," I admitted on a pained whisper.

He dropped a kiss on my lips, a sweet reassurance rather than a harsh claim.

"You're the most beautiful thing I've ever seen, Sofia."

"I'm not." The first hot tear dropped down my temple and fell into my curls. "You only think that because you haven't seen all of me."

He shifted his weight, moving off me so that he laid on the bed beside me. He didn't stop petting me, and I was so grateful for the contact that my heart squeezed in my chest.

"There is nothing you could show me that will change the way I feel about you," he swore. "Let me see."

I couldn't refuse him. Not without pushing him away. And I needed him too desperately to risk that. I could only hope that he would keep his promise.

If I bared myself to him only to be rejected, I'd break again, just like I did when I was thirteen years old. And this time, I wasn't sure if I'd be strong enough to stop myself from repeating the cycle of addiction and shame.

Closing my eyes, I fisted the soft material of my dress in both hands. I felt the swirling ridges of the pretty, decorative embroidery against my palms as I revealed the ugliest parts of my body to him.

I heard Mateo hiss in a disgusted breath, and I withered inside.

"This wasn't an accident," he said tightly.

"No," I admitted thickly, my tears coming faster. "It wasn't."

Nothing accidental could have left the neat, perfectly straight lines that marked my flesh. Some were longer than others, some deeper. Most were vertical, but a handful of horizontal and diagonal patterns broke up the monotony. The lightest scars were as thin and fine as white thread. The deepest were dark, puckered furrows. Like the one on my inner thigh.

"Who did this to you, Sofia?' he demanded, completely repulsed by the sight of me.

I cringed, wishing I could sink into the mattress and disappear.

His thumb hooked beneath my jaw, tipping my face back. "Look at me," he ordered.

My eyes opened, automatically responding to his command. Hot tears obscured my vision, and I was relieved that I didn't have a clear image of his contempt to burn into my brain forever.

"You have to tell me who did this," he insisted.

"Me," I said miserably. "I did it."

"Don't blame yourself for what was done to you," he growled. "Tell me who hurt you, and I'll take care of it."

My stomach twisted, far more painful than any of the tidy little marks I'd cut into my skin. I batted his hands from my face, pushing up onto my elbows and scooting away from him.

"I do blame myself, because I did it!" I yelled the awful truth at him, so he would understand the full horror of what I'd done. "I'm the one who ruined my body! It was a stupid, angsty teenage phase, and I ruined my body forever because I had behavioral issues." The words were bitter on my tongue, and I heard my mother's voice issuing from my own lips.

"What are you talking about?" he asked, the rough quality to his tone softened by confusion. "You hurt yourself?"

"Aren't you listening?" I demanded, furious that he was making me repeat my sin, forcing me to expound upon my shame. "*Yes*, okay? Yes, I cut myself up because I was an idiotic thirteen-year-old girl who couldn't cope with life, even though I was spoiled beyond most kid's wildest dreams."

"But why would you do that?" Mateo was utterly baffled.

Of course he was. I'd been raised in a home with everything a child could possibly want. I knew full well that my actions had been ridiculous in the extreme.

"Ask my therapist," I replied with venom. "Daddy sent me to the most expensive shrink he could find. I'm sure she could explain it far better than I could."

"I'm asking you," he said, his voice dropping to the deep register that resonated in my bones.

His arms wrapped around me. I tried to twist away, but he held me firm, tucking me against his chest. His fingers wiped at the tears on my cheeks, his unexpected, tender touch stemming the flow.

I blinked, clearing my vision so that he came into full focus. He stared down at me, his brow furrowed with concern, not disgust.

His hand rested on my thigh, touching my scars. I tensed, but he kept his palm flush with my skin, his thumb dipping lower to trace the line of the deep furrow he'd discovered when he'd spanked me.

The direct contact with the hideous marks confused me. Why wasn't he tugging my dress down to hide them from his sight?

"Explain this to me." His cadence was calm but stern.

"Like I said. It was a stupid teenage phase." The assertion was much weaker than it had been before, tinged with the pain I kept carefully buried beneath the weight of my shame.

I didn't deserve to indulge in that pain, because my behavior didn't warrant any pity or comfort. I bore the shame as my well-deserved penance.

His black gaze was steady and deep. I wanted to get swallowed up in those warm, dark pools and never surface.

"There's nothing stupid about this," he countered evenly. "You obviously did this over time. You didn't get all these marks in one day. Tell me how it started."

"It was my thirteenth birthday," I said softly, the truth compelled by his unyielding but tender demeanor. "My mom gave me my first razor and told me it was time to start shaving my legs because I was maturing as a woman. But she didn't show me how to do it properly. Mom was...pretty hands-off. So, I started from a bad angle, slipped, and sliced up my leg pretty deep. I'd never gotten cut like that before. The worst injury I'd ever sustained up until that point was a scraped knee."

I could still remember the shock of the red gash, the ruby red blood running thin in the warm water that filled the tub. I'd been so dumbfounded by the sight that it had barely even hurt at first.

"When I showed my mom the cut and asked her what to do about it, she called my nanny and left us alone to attend to the first aid. It started healing up, but it still hurt if I moved the wrong way. Or if I pressed on it. Or if I picked at the scab."

I took a breath, my cheeks burning. "I know most kids would be thrilled to live in my house growing up. I had a big bedroom of my own, chef-prepared meals, and all the toys I could possibly want. But I was fully immersed in my *poor little rich girl* persona," I said bitterly.

Mateo had told me he grew up poor. He had every reason to scorn my behavior even more than I did.

But he didn't say anything cruel or judgmental. Instead, he stroked my cheek, offering warmth and support.

"Go on," he urged. "I'm listening."

I took a shuddering breath and continued. "I didn't like that my mom dictated my style, dressing me up in frilly clothes that suited her ideal of a pretty little daughter. I didn't like that the only time she paid any attention to me was to criticize my appearance. And if she did say nice things about me, it was always loudly in front of others so that they could hear and say what a wonderful mother she was."

"And your father?" he pressed when I took too long of a pause. Mateo wasn't going to let me trail off or redirect the subject. He was steady and solid, his massive arms enfolding me and holding me with aching care while he asked me to share my most shameful secrets.

"I love Daddy, but he was busy with work." I echoed his familiar excuse. "He was sweet to me, but he wasn't around on a normal schedule, and he especially didn't have time for me if I was being difficult."

"And were you a difficult child?" There was no censure in Mateo's tone, just a desire to understand.

"I tried not to be. But I messed up sometimes,

especially if I lost control of my emotions. The cutting helped with that.

"While the accidental cut from shaving was healing, I found that if I picked at it, I could focus my frustrations and volatile feelings. The physical pain allowed me to channel my inner pain, and it provided some relief. It gave me a sense of control over my life that I'd never had before. I was able to regulate my temper, so I didn't upset the people around me with my toxic behavior."

Mateo's lips pressed together, and I suspected he was holding in something he wanted to say. But he remained silent and continued petting me, his dark eyes compelling me to confess everything.

"Once the cut fully healed, I only lasted three days before I intentionally made another. I didn't ask my mom to help me patch that one up.

"I hid what I was doing for two years. It would have gone on longer if I hadn't cut too deep. I bandaged up the one on my inner thigh, but it bled through my dress and stained Mom's fancy upholstered dining chair.

"Daddy sent me to therapy, and I started writing poetry to deal with my emotions instead. If I'd just done that from the very beginning, I wouldn't have ruined my body."

He stroked his fingers over my thighs, rubbing my

damaged flesh as though it didn't bother him in the slightest.

"You keep repeating that phrase. You didn't ruin your body, *belleza*. These marks don't make you any less beautiful."

"But they do," I countered, my heart aching. "I... I'm ashamed of them. I'm ashamed of what I did."

His rugged features firmed to solid granite, but his touch on my thighs remained gentle. "You have nothing to be ashamed of. You were a child in pain, and you did what you could to ease the hurt. Someone should have protected you."

I let out a hollow laugh. "Protected me from what? Myself?"

He cupped my cheek, trapping my face so I had no choice but to see the sincerity in his deep, dark eyes. "From loneliness. From indifference. You should have been loved, Sofia."

"Daddy loves me." The assertion hitched in my throat.

"I believe he does," Mateo agreed. "But he wasn't there for you. Not like he should have been."

He rubbed his thumb over my lips and traced the lines of my cheekbones, as though he was memorizing every detail of my form.

"I'm here for you now," he swore. "You're mine."

CHAPTER 15

MATEO

I'd always assumed Sofia had lived an easy, blissfully happy life. I'd thought she'd been handed everything she wanted on a silver platter by a doting father who showered her with love.

He might have provided for her, but Sofia hadn't been loved. Not like she should have been.

She'd been lonely and so desperate for her father's affection that she'd chosen to cut her soft skin. She'd hurt herself in order to regulate her emotions, so that Caesar wouldn't think she was being *difficult*.

No wonder she'd become attached to me so quickly. I lavished her with the praise and attention she craved so deeply that she'd been willing to bleed for it.

My hatred for Caesar swelled. He might not

realize how his behavior had tormented Sofia, but that didn't excuse what he'd done to her. He wasn't forgiven, and I wouldn't forget.

Sofia was convinced that she'd *ruined her body*. I suspected those were her mother's cruel words, inflicted on an anguished young girl who was already consumed by the longing for approval.

No wonder Sofia was so sweet and innocent. She'd conditioned herself to be pleasant and bubbly, seeking to befriend anyone and everyone. And it was now obvious that she'd remained innocent because she was too deeply ashamed to show a man her body in an intimate way.

The qualities that I revered were rooted in her pain.

I couldn't erase what had been done to my precious little flower, but I was determined to soothe that pain.

She remained cradled in my arms, her emerald eyes so wide and hopeful that it made my chest ache. She wanted to believe what I was saying—that I truly did think she was perfect, and that I would take care of her.

I'd fucked up by giving her space this morning. She'd interpreted my distance as rejection. I'd been trying to manipulate her into willingly returning to my arms, but I understood now that Sofia's surrender didn't require games like that. She needed to be held, reassured that I wouldn't discard her for any reason.

When Adrián had given me permission to take her, I'd claimed her to indulge my own selfish desires. I'd plotted how I would cage her, lure her in so that she thought she was choosing her captivity.

Devious schemes had never been necessary. All Sofia needed was my promise that I wanted her, and she would cling to me and never let go.

My darkest desires for her were easily within my grasp, and she was better suited to my twisted tastes than I could have dared to hope.

She thrived on structure: punishment and reward. Clearly demonstrating my expectations brought her a sense of stability. She would never have to feel insecure or guess how to behave in order to please me.

I owed her a very special reward for sharing her secrets with me.

I shifted my hold on her willowy body, taking her lush lips in a kiss as I guided her back down beneath me.

Fuck, she felt so good in this position; captured for my pleasure and helpless to resist me.

I'd handled her aggressively when I'd pinned her in place for our first kiss. She'd struggled at first, overwhelmed and intimidated. Her surrender had been exquisite.

The damp spot on my jeans proved the intensity

of her arousal. Her body was mine to play with as I wished, and I wanted to taste her.

She shuddered and sighed, melting into my hold. Her head tipped back, inviting me to explore her more deeply. I claimed her mouth with firm strokes of my tongue, my cock aching to penetrate her tight little pussy at the same rhythm.

My jeans were painfully tight around my dick, but I knew better than to strip when I had Sofia like this, pliant and wet for me.

No penetration of any kind. Adrián's warning was an unwelcome voice in my head, denying me what I desired so keenly that I hovered on the edge of pain.

I grasped Sofia's slender wrists and directed her hands behind her head, pulling back from her hot mouth at the same time.

She stared up at me, her pouty lips swollen and her eyes dark with lust.

"Keep your hands there," I commanded, my voice roughened by my own suppressed need.

"Why? I want to touch you," she said, soft and slow. She appeared drunk off my kiss, and the sight of her intoxicated bliss made my own satisfaction swell.

"Because I said so," I replied sternly. "This is what obedience means, Sofia" I stroked her cheek, and she leaned into my touch. "You'll obey me because you want to please me. Isn't that right, *dulzura*?"

She nodded, closing her eyes and nuzzling her cheek into my hand like a needy little kitten.

The pleasure that pulsed through me was more than simple lust. This was what I'd craved from the moment she'd relaxed into my hold when I'd kidnapped her and tied her to a chair to be terrorized. She should have been horrified, but she'd drifted off in my arms.

"Good girl." I pressed my lips to her throat, feeling her low moan vibrate against my mouth.

Mindful that my control over my own body was tenuous, I forced myself to leave her dress covering her breasts. I wanted to grip the soft fabric in my fists and rip it away, but I couldn't allow my impulsiveness to distract me from my purpose.

I moved down her slender form, pushing her legs wide and settling between them.

"What are you doing?" she asked breathlessly, staring down at me with curiosity and dark intrigue.

I pushed up her dress and nipped at her inner thigh, drawing a sharp yelp from her. My hands wrapped around her hips, pressing her into the mattress. I kept her trapped with my teeth, watching her jerk and struggle to escape.

Despite her resistance, my good girl kept her hands behind her head, as though it didn't even occur to her to try to move them.

I kept my eyes locked on hers as I waited for her surrender.

"Mateo," she whimpered, her body going still.

I released her from my punitive bite, licking the tender, red mark I'd left on her tanned flesh.

"No more questions," I rebuked. "Just submit."

I ran my tongue along the line of her scar, the one I'd first glimpsed when I'd spanked her. She stiffened, but I held her firm and continued at the pace I desired, kissing the marks as I made my way up her thighs. With each brush of my lips over her damaged nerve endings, she relaxed. The tension in her muscles melted away, and she went supple beneath my tender attentions.

I eased her dress over her hips, and the sinful sight of her barely-there white panties drew a growl from my chest. I trailed my fingers over the pretty lace, and she arched and gasped when I brushed her clit.

Acting like the animal I was, I caught the delicate fabric in my teeth and curled my fingers into it, shredding the barrier that hid what was mine.

I fisted the ruined underwear and shoved them into my jeans pocket, a trophy to keep for later.

My hands curved beneath her ass, tugging her body toward me and spreading her for my admiration. I traced the line of her slit with my tongue, groaning at the first taste of her arousal.

She cried out at the new sensation, bucking against my mouth.

My fingers sank into her cheeks, holding her hard enough to mark her. She whined, and I could feel her muscles dancing and fighting to move.

I lowered my lips, so they hovered just above her clit.

"Are you trying to get away from me?" I asked, my question deepened by cruel amusement. "Or are you trying to get your hot little pussy closer to my mouth?"

"I..." She strained and tensed, but my good girl kept her hands exactly where I'd told her to. "*Please*," she begged.

"*Please*, what?" I mocked, reveling in her predicament. I nuzzled her inner thigh, letting her feel the heat of my breath teasing over her swollen, soaked lips. "What do you want, *florecita*?"

"More," she whined.

I flicked my tongue over her clit, making her gasp and writhe. I repeated the teasing contact, tracing her folds with my fingers at the same time.

Fuck, she was so soft and wet for me. I wanted to plunge my fingers inside her and find the sensitive spot at the front of her inner walls that would make her weep for orgasmic release.

I can't break her hymen.

I tongued her clit with more force, some of my

frustration with my limitations bleeding out into ruthless aggression on the most tender part of her body.

The primal need to stake my claim threatened to overwhelm reason. I couldn't fuck her, and I couldn't handle her delicate pussy as roughly as I wanted.

I dipped my forefinger just inside her slick opening, gathering up her arousal without driving deep.

There was a vulnerable part of her untried body that I could penetrate without leaving any visible sign of my transgression. I'd promised Adrián I would keep my cock in my pants, but I would allow myself this one possessive act.

Every part of Sofia belonged to me. I'd claimed her mouth with my tongue and explored her pussy as much as I was allowed. I was greedy for more, and I had a very limited capacity for restraint.

I maintained my firm grip on her ass with one hand, trapping her in place, so I could play with her how I wanted. Keeping my mouth on her clit, I lifted my gaze to her face. I was hungry to watch her reaction when I slipped my desire-slicked finger past her swollen folds.

The instant I touched her asshole, she jolted beneath me.

"Mateo!" She shrieked my name in protest, but it ended on a strangled cry when I nipped at her clit.

I eased off slightly, but I held her like that, immobilizing her with the threat of my teeth around her sensitive bud.

She stared down at me, her sparkling eyes wide with alarm and her lush lips parted around panting breaths. Her hands were still locked behind her head.

She was being so good for me, so perfect.

I brushed my finger over her asshole, forcing her to accept my touch on the most vulnerable part of her virgin body.

She whimpered, her eyes clouding with confusion as she watched me with a mixture of trepidation and fascination.

I applied pressure, and she tried to clench to keep me out. I growled a warning against her clit, and I felt a fresh wash of her hot arousal on my palm.

I didn't have to issue a verbal rebuke to make her relax; her most sensitive, secret places were thoroughly under my control. All I had to do was watch her and wait, rubbing her tight little hole so that she understood I wouldn't back off until she gave me what I wanted.

After a few seconds of ruthless stimulation, she eased enough to allow me to penetrate her. I barely pushed in before withdrawing, playing with her tight ring of muscles and teaching her how good it could feel to surrender this part of herself to me.

I removed the threat of my teeth and placed a

kiss on her clit. She gasped and lifted her hips, drawing my finger deeper inside her.

"See how sensitive you are, *dulzura?*" I cooed, tonguing her tight bud to reward her good behavior.

I slowly pumped in and of her ass, pressing a little farther with each gentle thrust. Keening, broken cries issued from her perfect lips, and she began to rock toward my hand, inviting me to claim her.

"This is all for me," I told her, intoxicated by her complete submission. "All mine."

My possessive words pushed her over the edge, and her liquid heat coated my hand as her tight muscles squeezed my finger. She screamed out my name and ground her hips against my face, pulling me deeper inside her ass and seeking more stimulation on her clit.

I allowed her to writhe through her release, giving her enough freedom to move against me in desperation, her little body greedy for all the pleasure I could wring from her.

Her scream softened to a whine, and she collapsed beneath me, spent and sated.

I released her clit and slowly withdrew my hand. Before I moved away, I dropped more kisses on her scars, worshipping her perfect body.

She let out a contented sigh, and I glanced up to find her eyes closed, a serene smile curving her lips.

"I'll be right back," I murmured against her

marked flesh, pressing one last kiss on her thigh before slipping into the bathroom to quickly clean up.

When I returned to the bed, she lay exactly where I had left her: legs bared, pink pussy on display, and her hands cushioning her head.

I stretched out beside her, grasping her wrists and freeing her from the position I'd shackled her in with no more than a command. She rolled over and snuggled into me, breathing deeply, as though she couldn't get enough of my scent.

I let her cuddle up as close as she wanted, even though her nearness caused me physical pain at this point. My dick was still rock hard, my balls aching for release.

She tucked her face against my chest, her hands roving over my body. She'd never touched me like this before, her dainty fingers tracing the shape of my muscles in a lazy, lust-drunk exploration. Her small hand curved over my arm, as though testing how much of my girth she could fit between her extended thumb and little finger.

"You're so big." She made a happy humming sound.

"That's because it's my job to keep you safe. I'm supposed to look scary," I murmured, dropping a kiss on her forehead.

"You're not scary," she said with a child's innocence. "You're just big."

A low chuckle rumbled from my chest. "I'm glad you feel that way."

"Mateo..." She hesitated, suddenly shy.

There wasn't anything shy about the way she tilted her hips into mine, pressing tight against my throbbing erection.

Without thinking, my palm firmed on her lower back, trapping her there.

"I know you're big," she continued softly. "That makes me nervous. But I...I want you. Will it hurt a lot?"

I bit back a groan. She wanted me to take her virginity.

The wait for Ronaldo to die was going to kill me.

"I'll make sure you're ready for me," I promised roughly, my lust for her setting my teeth on edge.

"Okay," she breathed.

Her touch skimmed over my abs, her fingers fumbling at the button on my jeans.

I grabbed her hand, jerking her away more roughly than I intended.

She peeked up at me, her eyes tight with uncertainty. "Do you want to be the one to do that? I can take off my dress, if that's better for you?"

Jesus. She wanted to do this right now.

"I can't—" I cut myself off before I said *I can't fuck*

you. That language was too crass for her first time, and I would have to let her down gently. I didn't want her to think I was rejecting her by delaying.

"We can't have sex," I said instead. "Not today."

"What?" A wrinkle appeared between her brows. "Don't you...Don't you want me?"

"I want you more than anything, sweet Sofia," I promised, pressing my hard-on against her for emphasis. "But I can't take your virginity yet."

The wrinkle drew deeper. "How do you know I'm a virgin? And what do you mean by *yet*?"

"Your engagement to Ronaldo is the answer to both of those questions." I couldn't help the anger that bled into my tone. The fact that Ronaldo thought he still had a claim on her made me see red.

"Engagement?" She pulled back, putting a few inches of space between our bodies. "What are you talking about?"

All the air was knocked from my chest. "You don't know?"

"Know what?" she demanded, her voice growing louder with her own anger and a note of fear. "Who is Ronaldo?"

"That fucking bastard," I seethed. My hatred of Caesar was poison in my veins, a burning sickness driving me to the brink of sanity.

He'd sold Sofia to Ronaldo without asking for her consent. Without even telling her it was a done deal.

She scooted away from me, her lovely eyes wide with panic. "Explain what's happening. Right now, Mateo!" she shouted when I didn't answer immediately.

"You're engaged." I couldn't help snarling the words.

"Are you crazy?" she demanded shrilly. "Trust me, I would know if I was engaged. I've never even had a serious boyfriend."

"That's because your piece of shit father didn't tell you, apparently," I barked. "He arranged for you to marry Pedro Ronaldo."

Her head shook back and forth, her curls swaying wildly. "I don't know anybody named Pedro Ronaldo."

I spat a curse, rage at Caesar riding me hard. "Ronaldo controls one of the Mexican cartels that traffics our product into the States. Caesar arranged the marriage six months ago. I assumed you'd agreed to it."

"Why would I agree to marry someone I've never met? Daddy was going to hook me up with a *drug lord?*" She shook her head more forcefully. "This is insane. It's not true."

"That's what you said when I told you that your father had kidnapped Valentina," I reminded her harshly, my tenuous hold on my anger slipping in response to her disgust at the idea of being with a drug lord.

Sofia seemed to keep forgetting that I was a criminal, just like her father. Just like Ronaldo.

She paled, her jaw going slack. My cruel retort had shocked her like a slap to the face.

"I won't do it," she said on a horrified whisper. "I'm not going to marry a stranger."

"No," I agreed, some of my ire fading. "You're not going to marry Ronaldo. He'll be dead soon, and then, there won't be anything to keep you from me."

Her eyes met mine, the horror focused in my direction. "*Dead?*" she repeated. "Why will he be dead? I'll just tell him I won't marry him."

"That's not how this works, *belleza*." I tried for a gentler tone. "If your father cared about your opinion on the matter, he would have asked you."

She pushed off the bed, standing on shaky legs. "You knew about this." It wasn't a question. It was an accusation. "You knew I was engaged, and you... touched me anyway. Because..." She swallowed, as though fighting down nausea. "Because you knew Ronaldo would be dead soon. What if I had wanted to marry him?"

"But you don't want to marry him," I snapped, knowing that she wouldn't like my truthful response: that I didn't give a fuck if she wanted to marry Ronaldo. As soon as I'd taken her as my hostage, her fate had been sealed.

"You said we couldn't have sex because I'm engaged," she continued, as though I hadn't responded. "But if you know I'm not going to marry him, why does that matter? Why did you say we couldn't have sex *yet*?"

She was picking at this, her mind wading through her horror and anger to seek out an answer I didn't want to give her.

"You're a virgin," I said, as though that would explain everything, as though I wouldn't have to say more.

"So?" she demanded. "Why does that..."

Her mouth snapped closed, and her eyes began to shine. She was starting to put things together, and the truth was going to be agonizing for her.

"Daddy always said how important it was to wait for marriage." I wasn't certain if she was aware that she spoke the disturbing words aloud. "And Mom said no one would want me if they saw my scars. So I never..."

Her eyes narrowed at me, a fresh wave of anger surging in my direction. "Daddy wanted me to be a virgin when I married this Ronaldo guy. But I want you to tell me why that matters if you aren't intending for me to go through with the marriage."

"Sofia, I was just trying to protect you." I attempted to placate her. "Those men who came to the house—the ones you saw me fight—didn't come to take you away. Your father sent them to deliver a message. Caesar intends to keep his alliance with Ronaldo. He wanted to make sure I don't take your virginity, so the marriage could still go forward. I was never going to give you to Ronaldo," I swore before she could even question it. "But Adrián had to promise your father that I wouldn't... He promised that your virginity would remain intact. That's why Ronaldo has to die. Once he's dead, there is no arrangement, and there won't be anything keeping us apart."

Her lower lip trembled. "You made a deal with Daddy and Adrián about my virginity? You all traded my body like a bargaining chip between you?"

I took a step toward her, but she threw up her hands to ward me off.

"I didn't have a choice," I reasoned, not wanting to acknowledge the lie on my tongue. "If we hadn't made this agreement, there would have been war. You would have been in danger. I was protecting you."

"Protecting me?" she shrieked, her eyes wild. "Is that what you call what you just did to me? You couldn't take my virginity without my father's permission, but you could put your mouth on me and..."

She couldn't seem to finish articulating what I'd done to her without being sick. Her features were pale and pinched, her delicate body shaking.

"This doesn't change anything between us." If I said it out loud, maybe it would be true.

"There is *nothing* between us," she hissed. "Just your lies and my stupidity for blindly trusting you."

"No." My refusal was harsh and immediate. I wouldn't let her pull away from me. I wouldn't lose her trust.

I closed the distance between us in one long stride, wrapping my arms around her and pulling her close to my chest.

"Don't touch me!" She tried to shove me away, but she didn't have a chance at physical resistance.

"I won't let you go," I ground out, keeping her pinned against me. "I won't make that mistake again. You need me to touch you."

"Stop it!" she insisted, breathless from her struggles.

"I've got you, Sofia," I swore, not giving her an inch. "You're mine."

She went completely still, and I could practically feel her body solidify to ice. "If you force yourself on me, I will hate you forever."

My muscles flexed around her, my body rebelling at the prospect of releasing her.

"Let me go." She bit out each venomous word.

Somehow, I summoned up enough willpower to peel my arms away from her trembling form. As soon as she was freed from my cage, she stumbled back, putting space between us.

She took a deep breath and straightened her spine, finding the strength to present defiance even though tears streamed down her cheeks.

"I will stay here at your house," she declared coldly. "I'll be a compliant little hostage, because being trapped with you is a slightly less horrific nightmare than facing Daddy right now." She lifted her chin, her bright green eyes searing into me. "But I will never make the mistake of trusting you again. I will never let myself forget who you really are."

"You know who I am." I rasped the lie.

"I do now," she agreed. "You're a criminal. You're my jailor. And nothing else."

CHAPTER 16

SOFIA

I touched my thumb to the base of my ring finger, a habit that had become obsessive over the last twenty-four hours. But the absence of a diamond ring didn't take back the awful revelations about my *engagement*.

My brain's default defensive mechanism was to deny what Mateo had told me.

I'm not engaged to a drug lord I've never met. Daddy wouldn't do that to me.

But denial wouldn't make this go away.

It was agonizing enough to accept that Daddy had arranged this marriage, but thinking about Mateo's part in the bargain made me want to vomit.

I'd trusted him enough to let him...*touch me* in ways I'd never considered before. I'd shared my scars with him. My secrets. My body.

But he'd bartered for the rights to my body days ago, working out a truce with my father and a second, clandestine deal with Adrián that would allow him to claim my virginity when it was no longer problematic for their criminal enterprises.

No one had asked my opinion. No one had asked for my consent.

Mateo's heavy fist hit the bedroom door, the booming knock a feeble veneer of respect for my personal space. He hadn't forced his way into my bedroom since I'd shut myself in yesterday, but I could sense his mounting frustration each time he brought one of my meals.

"What?" I demanded, setting down my songwriting journal.

"Valentina and Adrián are coming over for dinner." His deep voice penetrated the closed door. "We're eating in twenty minutes."

"I'm not hungry." That wasn't true, but I didn't want to deal with company right now. Especially not Adrián Rodríguez, even if I did like Valentina.

"I didn't ask if you were hungry," he retorted, terse. "I expect you to eat dinner with us."

"Whatever, warden," I snapped back.

There was a long, ominous pause. "Your attitude now changes nothing, Sofia," he warned darkly. "Disobedience means consequences. Be at the table in twenty minutes."

He didn't have to say *or else* for the threat to come through loud and clear. I wasn't certain how he would discipline me, but something unpleasant would happen if I defied him.

"Fine!"

A low growl slipped through the door, and I knew the barrier wouldn't serve to keep the beast at bay if I riled him further.

I held my breath, nervous tension gripping my body, until the angry thud of his heavy footfalls signaled his retreat down the hall.

My fingers trembled slightly when I picked up my pen, so I firmed my grip. My hand cramped in protest. I'd been writing song lyrics for hours, scribbling out my fury non-stop. Most of what I'd written wasn't remotely cohesive, but this was the only way I knew to purge the toxic emotions roiling within me. If I didn't put pen to paper, I might be tempted to use the razor in the bathroom and siphon off my pain a different way.

My fingers tensed around the pen, and a dark navy blotch bled onto the page.

I'm not doing that. I'm not going to cut.

I didn't stop writing until I heard the doorbell ring. Adrián and Valentina had arrived, and that meant I needed to get to the dining table.

I hadn't made note of the time, and all I could do was hope that I was within the twenty-minute deadline that Mateo had imposed.

I set aside my journal and got to my feet, stretching out the kinks in my muscles from remaining curled up on the bed for too long.

When I poked my head into the hallway, the incredible scent of Mateo's cooking wafted toward me.

A heartless criminal shouldn't be capable of making heavenly-smelling tamales.

Mateo isn't heartless, the stupid part of my brain told me.

I mentally smacked down that ridiculous naivete. It kept getting me into trouble, and I wouldn't make that same mistake again. As nice as it would be to pretend that Mateo was a sweet, gentle man, that simply was not an accurate assessment. Pretending and wishing wouldn't make that fantasy a reality.

"It smells wonderful, Mateo." I heard Valentina's soft voice as I made my way toward the delicious scent. "I didn't realize you knew how to cook."

"Mateo isn't a man of many talents, but he's incredibly accomplished in his limited areas of expertise," Adrián said drily.

"Do you want dinner or not, asshole?" Mateo shot back.

"Do you want my help or not?" Adrián drawled. "I'm doing you a favor. Dinner is the least you can offer me in order to express your gratitude."

I lingered down the hallway, listening in on their conversation to ascertain the purpose of this visit.

"Adrián, I came here for Sofia," Valentina insisted, her tone sharper than I ever would have dared with the terrifying drug lord.

"You're very sweet, *conejita*," he purred. "But Mateo is taking up the time I'm supposed to be spending alone with you. That's invaluable, so it's going to take a lot more than home-cooked tamales and a shitty attitude to repay me for this."

"How is she?" Valentina asked, ignoring Adrián and directing her questions at Mateo. "Do you think she'll want to see me?"

I wasn't certain what the dispute between the two men was about, but it was clear that Valentina had come to Mateo's house for the sole purpose of comforting me.

I was stunned by her concern about my wellbeing as a hostage when my father had condemned her to brutal abuse. Valentina's kindness compelled me to join the group, even though Mateo's nearness grated on me.

"I told her to come out for dinner," Mateo said. "She should be—"

"*She's* right here," I announced coldly, striding into the open-plan living room/kitchen space.

I felt Mateo's black gaze like sandpaper on raw

skin, and I resolutely suppressed the reflex to cringe away from him.

Adrián's striking, luminous green eyes were almost as unbearably intense as Mateo's.

I focused intently on Valentina. The petite brunette had warm, chocolate eyes and a sympathetic smile. She slipped out of Adrián's hold to offer me a hug, her arms outstretched but waiting for me to come to her.

The tiny woman was several inches shorter than me, but her embrace was fierce; a comfort to me and a warning to the men. Solidarity had been declared.

"I'm so glad to see you, Sofia," she said, giving me an extra little squeeze before stepping back. "I've been thinking about you constantly. Mateo promised Adrián that you were comfortable here, but I want there to be a direct line of communication between you and me. Can we get to know each other better over dinner and exchange numbers after?"

"Yeah," I agreed, my heart twisting at the vehement declaration of concern and support. "I'd like that."

"That's settled, then," Adrián announced, impatient. He grabbed Valentina's wrist and tugged her back to him, jealously guarding her attention. "Let's eat."

He started walking in the direction of the dining room, as though he was in his own home. Valentina shot me an apologetic smile, but she edged closer to Adrián, clearly loving his harsh affection.

When I didn't move right away, Mateo reached for me, like he expected to hold my hand, too.

I recoiled, panic spiking. I wasn't afraid that Mateo would hurt me; I was afraid of how I might react if I allowed him to touch me. It would be so much easier to forget all the awful things he had done to me—kidnapping me, bargaining for my virginity—if he held me with tenderness.

His hand curled to a fist, his huge body coiled tight.

"You're already late," he informed me in a clipped tone when I didn't follow Adrián and Valentina to the dinner table. "Don't test me."

My stomach flipped, the little thrill elicited by his low threat caught somewhere between arousal and fear. I remembered how good it felt when he'd disciplined me before, when he'd spanked me and put his big hands all over my body. But to melt beneath his touch now might break me. If he forced his attention on me, I was certain my body would react, whether my mind welcomed it or not.

I followed after Valentina, skirting around Mateo's bulk. He caught up with me in a few long strides, arriving at the dining table in time to pull out my chair for me. As I shifted to lower myself into it, he brushed his palm against the small of my back, pushing my boundaries with the guise of support.

I jerked away from him, too frazzled to retain my balance properly. His hands bracketed my waist before I could stumble. I stiffened and tried to twist out of his hold, my heart hammering against my ribcage. His thick fingers curved into my hips, branding my flesh through my clothes.

"Let me go," I demanded. His proprietary hold felt far too good, and his refusal to release me heightened my distress.

"No," he growled. "I'm not going to let you fall."

"Let *go*." I shoved at his granite chest.

His black brows drew together, his mouth harsh with grim determination. "I know you want me to hold you."

"Stop it!" I insisted, panicking.

Adrián sighed loudly, but Valentina jumped straight into the conflict.

"Back off, Mateo!" she commanded.

Adrián didn't seem to realize just how incensed she was on my behalf, because he didn't move quick enough to restrain her from coming to my aid. She inserted herself directly into Mateo's hulking shadow, glaring up at him. Her chocolate eyes were dark with rage, her full lips drawn thin with fury.

"Valentina," Adrián said, her name sharp with censure. "This is Mateo's business, not yours."

She rounded on Adrián. "I will not allow this to continue," she seethed, her small body practically vibrating with righteous rage. "I know what it's like being the object of a man's obsession when the attention is unwelcome. I'm not going to sit here and make nice over Mateo's tamales if he's forcing himself on Sofia."

Mateo hissed and dropped his hands from my body as though I'd burned him.

"It's not like that," he ground out.

Her ferocious glare softened when she focused on me, but the aggression didn't ease from her petite frame. "Do you want Mateo to touch you?"

"No," I whispered, so grateful for the woman's intervention that tears sprang to my eyes.

"Then he won't." She issued the edict with another hard glare at Mateo. She held the scathing look for several long seconds before turning back to me with a gentler expression. "Can we eat dinner, just the two of us? The men will give us privacy, and we can talk. Is that okay with you?"

"Yeah," I agreed, swiping a stray tear from my cheek. "Thanks."

"Adrián." She addressed the fearsome man with a much more deferential tone. "Could you and Mateo eat in the kitchen, please?"

"This isn't what we talked about," Mateo countered roughly.

Valentina fixed him with a frigid stare. "You asked for my help. I am helping Sofia."

"I'm not a threat to her," he argued.

"That's enough, Mateo," Adrián snapped. "You're really fucking up my entire day. If you want to live to see the end of it, do as Valentina says. And serve me the fucking dinner you promised me. I'm starving."

Mateo dug in his heels, his black eyes flashing.

"Kitchen. Now," Adrián bit out, staring down the much larger man.

Mateo spat a curse and stormed out of the dining room, his bulging muscles flexing with frustration.

"Thank you, Adrián," Valentina said, all softness and gratitude now that the threat had retreated.

He dropped a quick kiss on her forehead, pulling her into a firm embrace. His unnerving, pale green eyes fixed on me.

"I'll make sure Mateo doesn't step out of line," he swore.

His intense gaze shifted back to Valentina, including her in the promise. "I won't allow him to abuse Sofia. I know what this means to you. I'll take care of it."

My gut twisted into knots. Mateo hadn't abused me, and I didn't think he ever would. Not really.

But if he subjected me to his mercilessly tender attentions, I would fall for him. I would get hurt again and again, deluding myself into forgetting he was a bad man only to be reminded by cruel circumstances.

My heart wouldn't survive it.

Valentina's staunch solidarity and Adrián's promise were all I had to prevent me from succumbing to Mateo's allure and suffering under his achingly gentle hands.

CHAPTER 17

SOFIA

Three Weeks Later

I missed Mateo so much.

Every day, I saw the criminal who wore his face, but I longed for the man I'd thought he was: the domineering, gentle giant who told me I was perfect.

Don't be stupid, I ordered myself every time I was tempted to fall back into his strong arms.

I was done being a stupid little girl. I was done being willfully ignorant.

Mateo had told me I was a fool for trusting everyone, and he'd been right. Just because he'd been sweet to me didn't make him trustworthy. It didn't make him a good man.

A good man wouldn't have bargained for the rights to my body in a power struggle between drug lords. He wouldn't plot to kill a rival just so he could claim my virginity for himself.

No part of that equation was good.

I walled off my heart—a practice that I'd never attempted before.

It was hard to remember to keep those walls up all the time. Like when Mateo cooked for me. Or when he drove me to class in one of his insanely expensive cars. Or when he brushed my body with his hand, sending unbidden heat pulsing through my system.

He only touched me occasionally, and I mostly believed it was accidental. But a few times, I'd caught him watching me when he made contact, as though assessing if I might welcome more.

I never did, even though forcing my body to move away from his caused a deep ache in the center of my chest.

The only thing that had kept me sane over the last three weeks was Valentina's daily visits. We spent hours together every evening after I finished my classes. I introduced her to my favorite bands, and she introduced me to telenovelas—her guilty pleasure. I'd thought they were silly at first, but I was now completely absorbed in the drama.

We talked about everything from our favorite clothing designers to our hopes and dreams. I'd never had a close female friendship like it. I didn't have to pretend with her or put on my best face. She'd seen me at my lowest point, and she still offered her friendship.

"Valentina's coming over tonight," I reminded Mateo as we pulled away from campus in his cherry red Porsche.

The polite thing to do would have been to ask for permission to invite a guest into his home. But there was nothing polite about him holding me hostage, so I wasn't going to tiptoe around him and try to please him. I was done with such accommodating behavior.

"No, she's not," he informed me. "Adrián texted me while you were in class. Valentina is too stressed out about the wedding, and he won't let her come over tonight. The rehearsal dinner is tomorrow, and she needs to rest and relax."

"Oh," I replied, my heart sinking. I'd come to rely on her daily company.

I hadn't known her long, but Valentina obviously valued our friendship, too. She'd even asked me to be maid of honor at her wedding. Adrián had thrown boatloads of money around to arrange an LA wedding in a month. Apparently, he was impatient to make her his wife, and he was only allowing her this much time to plan because he wanted her to have a beautiful day to celebrate their union.

Her relationship with the cruel drug lord was very confusing to me, but we mostly avoided awkwardness over the subject. He made her happy, and that was what mattered. I was looking forward to standing beside her on her wedding day.

Even if it meant Mateo would be standing opposite me, taking his place as Adrián's best man.

"I want to show you something," Mateo said, his hands tense around the steering wheel. "I think I owe it to Adrián to do this before the wedding." He cut his eyes over to me. "We're going to have to be near each other for the ceremony."

"It'll be fine." I waved away his concern, even though my anxiety had been building for days. I would have to take Mateo's arm when we processed out of the church after the ceremony.

I could handle touching him for a few minutes just to make sure Valentina's pictures looked nice.

"Maybe," he allowed. "But before the big day, I'm going to try to make it so that you hate me a little less."

"I don't hate you," I said truthfully before I could think about holding the words back.

"No," he said on a low rumble. "I don't think you do. You hate the idea of me you've built in your head over the last three weeks. You don't hate the man I was when we were together."

My heart twisted at the mention of that man. I wanted so badly for him to be real.

"I'm going to show you something that I never wanted you to see," he continued, his huge body coiled tight from some invisible strain. "It might help you understand me better. I won't pretend that I'm not a criminal. And I won't lie to you and take back anything I told you about the circumstances surrounding your engagement. I did make a deal for your virginity. I would do it again if it meant keeping you from Ronaldo." His knuckles turned white. "But I've decided to provide you with more context, so we're taking a little field trip."

"Where are we going?"

His rugged features twisted in a grimace. "Hell."

We drove for half an hour, the tension growing thicker until the atmosphere inside the Porsche was nearly suffocating. The shining skyscrapers of the LA skyline fell into the distance as we drove away from the glittering, opulent parts of the city and into ramshackle, impoverished neighborhoods.

Vibrant murals in bold colors broke up the wash of gray cement blocks and fading paint that flaked off dilapidated buildings. Graffiti was scrawled everywhere, the hastily-drawn marks so different from the artistry of the murals.

There were vast gaps between the buildings, sometimes taking up as much as half a city block. The spaces stood vacant; flat expanses of bare concrete behind chain-link fencing.

"That's the new money coming in," Mateo explained in a monotone, noting the direction of my gaze. "The only thing the gangs in this neighborhood hate more than each other is gentrification. Developers are buying up land they don't even have a use for yet. They bulldoze the housing and pour concrete to mark their claimed territory. They're pushing out the undesirables, displacing the communities steeped in crime that will damage their future business ventures." He sneered the last, his disdain for the wealthy discernable in his disgusted tone.

Did he feel that same scorn toward me for my wealthy background? Mateo had told me he'd grown up poor, but now that he worked for Adrián, he had the same comforts and expendable income as my family did. He wasn't poor anymore, but his feelings surrounding money were more complex than I could have fathomed.

I remained quiet, uncertain what to say. It was becoming clear to me that Mateo hated this place. It was also obvious that this was where he'd been raised.

He resented the rich men who were coming in and transforming the neighborhood, but he also held deep-seated contempt for the area.

As we drove past crumbling houses and old, beaten-up cars, Mateo's scowl drew impossibly deeper.

The Porsche slowed in front of a sprawling, single-story building. It was utilitarian and blandly beige, and the only mark of character was the cartoon lion emblazoned on a banner that hung by the wide, glass front doors.

"This is where I went to school. For a while." Mateo's dark eyes were fixed on the building, as though he was focusing on some disturbing scene I couldn't see.

"You see those prison bars around the grounds?" he asked bitterly, drawing my attention to the tall iron fencing that served as a barrier around the property. "They're not to keep dangerous people in. They're to keep the criminals *out*." His mouth pressed to an angry slash. "They don't work."

He tore his gaze from the school, and the Porsche started moving again.

"So, what do you think?" he asked coldly, not deigning to glance over at me. "What are your first impressions of *home sweet home*?"

"This isn't your home," I murmured.

The angry, resentful man in the car beside me wasn't the Mateo I knew. Not even the criminal version that I'd been living with for the last three weeks. This man was full of bitterness, and despite the way his massive muscles flexed and bulged, there was something weak about him. I sensed that his rage had no outlet, no clear target, and it ate at his insides.

"It's the place that made me what I am," he countered grimly. "I'm the kind of man who hurts people for money and makes deals to claim innocent little virgins. And I don't feel guilty about any of it."

At the outset of this journey, he'd told me he was trying to help me understand him better. I'd assumed that his intent was to make me more sympathetic to how and why he lived his lawless life.

But now that we were here, surrounded by the ghosts that clearly haunted him, he seemed to have lost track of his objective.

The anger that masked his pain was far more effective at drawing forth my compassion for him than any manipulative spin he could have put on this place.

"I'm not sure what you want me to say," I replied quietly. He wasn't intimidating me, and I didn't feel any disdain for his impoverished upbringing. Mateo was bleeding inside, and he was giving me a glimpse at the trauma that had wounded him so deeply.

He remained silent for a moment, stewing in his dark emotions. "I don't know what I want you to say, either."

We pulled up outside a dirty, cream stucco apartment complex with roof tiles the color of dried blood. He put the Porsche in park, glaring at the rotting building.

"This is where I lived for the first seventeen years of my life." He made the admission as though it was acid on his tongue.

I kept my expression carefully neutral, not wanting to display any sort of emotion that might derail him from sharing.

Before he'd announced this *field trip*, I'd had no desire to open my heart to Mateo or get to know him better. Keeping him at a distance was the only way to protect myself from getting hurt again.

But now that he was revealing his secret past that caused him such anger and shame, I wanted to learn more. I couldn't feel compassion for the criminal who had been holding me hostage, but I could sympathize with this man who was making himself vulnerable by allowing me to witness his hidden anguish.

I was starting to put pieces together, bridging the gap between the man who had abducted me and the boy who had grown up in this hellhole.

Mateo had been seventeen the first time I'd met him. The young man I'd instantly swooned for at one of my father's lavish parties must have only just moved out of this decaying apartment building. He'd appeared aloof that night—a muscular, sexy enigma.

How foreign he must have felt in our multimillion-dollar mansion, surrounded by people wearing designer clothes and sipping champagne.

I was beginning to suspect that despite his new wealth, Mateo still didn't feel like he belonged there.

"You see that graffiti there?" he asked, pointing at one of the numerous black scrawls painted onto the stucco. "One of my gang members tagged the place. Marking our territory."

I noticed how he said *our*, how his eyes were shifting out of focus as his brain pulled him back into a dark place he'd kept locked away for years.

Without considering my actions, I reached over and placed my hand atop his clenched fist.

He blinked and looked down at where I touched him, as though baffled by the contact.

"You don't belong here," I told him. "You're not part of this place anymore."

His black eyes lifted to mine, his brows drawn in a challenge. "Only because I fought my way out. I escaped violence with more violence. But at least with Adrián, I'm free to make my own choices. And I have the resources to keep the people I care about safe."

"How did you end up with Adrián?" I pressed, seeking more information to connect the dots.

His scowl returned. "Why do you care?" he lashed out, pushing me away from his pain.

I kept my hand on his, refusing to break contact.

"You brought me here to give me context," I reminded him calmly. "Explain this to me."

He looked down at our hands again, staring at my much smaller fingers clasping his meaty fist. After a tense moment, he unfurled his fingers and turned his palm so that it pressed against mine. He took a breath and briefly closed his eyes, as though my touch brought him palpable peace.

"My gang dared me to steal from Adrián," he began, rubbing his thumb over my wrist as he spoke, feeling my pulse. That seemed to soothe him even more, and the tension eased from his huge body. "I was getting jacked by then, and I was throwing my weight around, using my size to instill fear and provide security for my mom. If everyone was terrified of me, they wouldn't go near her.

"Adrián is the scariest motherfucker in the city, but I'm one of the biggest. I was taunted into trying to humiliate Adrián, and I couldn't back down once the challenge was issued. Not without losing face and weakening my reputation. My mom needed me to protect her, and I couldn't risk her by letting anyone think I couldn't stand up for myself."

"She lived here with you?" I asked when he paused to glower at the dilapidated building again, as though he wished he could destroy it with his fists.

"Yeah." He spat the confirmation. "But not after that night. I went to steal from Adrián at his club, even though I knew that walking into his territory and insulting him would end with me dead if he caught me. Once my mom's safety was on the line, I had to risk it.

"Of course, he did catch me. Adrián commands a small army of ruthless killers, and he's not stupid enough to sit around undefended. I managed to take down five of his best men before I got knifed."

My fingers tightened around his palm, an automatic reflex to the idea of Mateo being gravely injured.

He continued stroking my wrist, and I wasn't sure which of us was soothing the other anymore.

"Adrián could have killed me right then and there," he continued, "but he hired me instead. He handed me a fat roll of cash, and I managed to stay on my feet long enough to come back here and pick up my mom. We left that night and never looked back."

"Where is she now?" I asked, knowing Mateo wouldn't have left her unprotected. Not after everything he'd just told me. His affection for her had been obvious ever since I'd woken up in his house and he cooked breakfast for me that first morning. He'd told me how she taught him to cook, how he'd helped her with chores while growing up in this rotting apartment.

He might hate where he came from, but he loved her.

"I bought her a house in Santa Monica." His chest swelled with pride when he told me how he provided for her. "Now, she lives in the comfort she deserves."

"Do you want to show me?" I realized that it would be important to him if I could see the safe home he'd procured for her, especially after showing me this decaying place where his demons lived.

He hesitated, fresh tension gripping his brawny frame.

"I'd like to see the house you bought for her," I pressed gently. "You've shown me the place where you grew up, but this isn't context that helps me understand who you are. It tells me where you came from, but not who you are."

He gave my hand a little squeeze before reluctantly releasing me, so he could put the car in gear. "Okay," he agreed. "I'll take you to meet my mom."

Something about the prospect of our meeting troubled him, but he didn't offer further insight.

We were both so preoccupied with the intensity of Mateo's confessions that neither of us noticed when a burgundy SUV followed the Porsche out of the neighborhood, ghosts from his past trailing after us.

CHAPTER 18

MATEO

As we drove away from old nightmares in Boyle Heights, I struggled to break free of the toxic emotions that clouded my thought processes. I'd planned to share just enough of my past so that Sofia could understand that my world was about survival, not cruelty. It still wasn't a pretty place, but my motivations might make me less of a monster in her eyes.

But as soon as we'd driven into the neighborhood, the ugly emotions that had ruled me when I lived in that hell had surfaced from where I'd buried them deep. My formative years had been fueled by hunger, hatred, and resentment of anyone who had more than I did. Even when I'd built my body to be bigger and stronger than anyone I knew, I'd still been pathetically weak.

The gang had locked me within its confines from an early age, preying on my fears for my mom to trap me in a cage of guilt and duty masquerading as safety and brotherhood.

Adrián had freed me from all that. As long as I watched his back, he paid me mind-boggling amounts of money. When I wasn't on the clock, my life was my own, with no obligations to anyone else. I could do whatever I wanted with my time, buy whatever pleased me with my newfound wealth.

And I could finally keep my mom safe. I would never have to be scared that I might come home to find her broken and bleeding on the floor.

I would never fail her again.

Sofia was quiet while we drove to Santa Monica, but I didn't sense any judgment or disgust in her silence. When I'd started losing my shit while parked out front of my childhood home, she'd remained calm and reached for me. Offering me comfort.

My delicate little flower possessed more strength than I'd thought. Given the volatile way I'd behaved, she should have been frightened or repulsed. Or both.

Instead, she'd held my hand and asked for more information. She'd asked to meet my mom.

My stomach knotted with familiar guilt as I pulled up in front of Mom's house: a pretty four-bedroom home in a safe neighborhood. I'd tried to get her to live farther outside the city, somewhere I could hide her down a long drive secured by a big gate. But she wanted to be close to the beach, and she'd lived through enough misery that I would give her anything that might make her happy.

So, we'd compromised on this Spanish-style bungalow in Santa Monica. Only the roof of the house was visible over the ten-foot, solid wooden fence. An equally high hedge guarded the other three sides of the property. No one would be able to get close to my mom without breaching those barriers or tripping the highly advanced security system I'd installed.

I parked my Porsche on the street, pulling up to the curb a few car lengths down from her front door. Another disadvantage to this city property: no garage to shelter my expensive vehicles.

When I got out and went to open Sofia's door, she took my offered hand without hesitation.

I'd completely fucked up my plans for how I was going to manipulate her by showing her my old neighborhood, but my shitshow breakdown seemed to have worked even more effectively to win her back.

She followed where I led, and we crossed the short distance from my Porsche to Mom's house. I paused before I keyed in the code that would unlock the solid metal gate set into the fence line.

"I should warn you before we go in," I said,

speaking the words aloud to convince myself to continue. "My mom has scars on her face. They can be alarming to someone who's never seen her before. I thought you should know. She gets self-conscious when people stare."

Mom barely even went out in public. She lived with enough physical pain every day without dealing with the anguish of being gawked at.

I lifted my hand to the keypad set beneath the gate handle, but Sofia's slender fingers closed around mine.

"Mateo." I felt her say my name like a soft caress on my cheek. I hadn't heard her speak to me in this sweet tone since the night she'd found out that I'd made a deal for her virginity.

I turned to face her, grasping both of her dainty hands in mine. I was hungry for more of this softness from her, and now that she offered it, my first instinct was to draw her close and keep her there.

Her lovely green eyes sparkled in the golden sunlight. For the first time in three weeks, she actually looked at me, peering straight into whatever I had left of my soul.

"You said my scars upset you at first because of something to do with you, not me," she said quietly. "You thought that someone had hurt me, and that's why they upset you. Did someone hurt your mom?"

My jaw clenched, a physical reaction to hold in

painful admissions.

But Sofia was touching me. She was looking at me.

I couldn't lose her again.

"Yeah," I rasped. "Someone hurt her."

"Will you tell me about it?" She wasn't asking out of morbid curiosity. Now that I'd been stupid enough to lose control in front of her in my old neighborhood, she wanted to know more of my dark secrets.

But my fuckup had somehow brought her back to me. I could give her more if my confession would keep her close.

"Her boyfriend beat the shit out of her when I was fifteen." The words were drawn from me, compelled by Sofia's nearness. "He'd been supporting us for ten years, keeping my mom as a side piece and providing just enough money for rent and food. He was a gangbanger, and his relationship with her meant protection for both of us. She made him swear that he would leave me out of it.

"That promise lasted until my tenth birthday. He got me to start dealing for him, threatening to leave us high and dry if I didn't comply or if I told Mom. So, I did what he wanted. Over the next few years, I grew bigger, stronger. He started asking me to do heavier shit, and I did. But one day, Mom found out."

Her abject horror at the sight of blood on my hands was burned into my mind. For five years, I'd managed to hide the truth from her. She'd thought I was living as easy of a life as she could possibly provide for me, and seeing the bloody evidence of what I'd become had broken her heart.

I suppressed a shudder and continued on. "She confronted her piece of shit boyfriend, so he beat her and left her to die for daring to question him. I came home after dealing one afternoon to find her…"

I stopped myself before I confessed the nauseating details to Sofia. It would be upsetting enough for her to see my mother's disfigured appearance. She didn't need a graphic description of the gory sight I'd come home to. The man had taken his time hurting Mom, using his knife and his fists.

"I called an ambulance, and they got to her in time," I said. "While Mom was recovering in the hospital, I hunted down the motherfucker who hurt her and made sure he would never do it again."

More gory details Sofia didn't need to know. The day I'd tortured him to exact my retribution had been the day I'd realized that there was no bloody task I was too squeamish to carry out.

"After, I kept Mom as comfortable as I could in that shithole apartment, but I couldn't leave the gang. They were the only protection we had left, and I needed the money from dealing to support us. Meeting Adrián was the best thing that ever happened to us."

By the time I finished, Sofia's vibrant eyes were shining. "Mateo," she said tremulously, a tear sliding down her cheek.

I brushed it away with my thumb, and she leaned into my hand.

"Your life is…more complicated than I realized." She bit her lip, thinking through what she wanted to say. "Thank you for sharing with me."

I stroked her cheek, tracing the path of her tears until my fingers touched beneath her chin. She tipped back at the lightest pressure, inviting me to take the kiss I'd been craving for weeks.

The distinctive hiss of an aerosol spray paint can —a familiar sound from the ugly past I'd just revisited —was a gunshot to my senses, jolting me to instinctive action.

I pushed Sofia out of harm's way, tucking her between my back and the fence behind us as I searched for the threat.

Several yards down the street, my pretty Porsche was being vandalized. One of my former *friends* was tagging my brand-new baby, scrawling our gang sign onto the perfect, cherry red paint job.

I roared out a curse and launched myself at the motherfucker. Ruiz had either forgotten just how fast I could move, or he'd gotten slower with age, because Shit-for-brains didn't drop the paint can quick enough to put distance between us.

I tackled him to the pavement before he got three steps, and ruby blood sprayed onto the sidewalk when his front teeth busted against it. I turned him roughly onto his back. I wanted him to see my face when I killed him. No one fucked with what was mine.

My hands wrapped around his throat, letting him feel the vise closing. "You thought you could follow me *here* and fuck up my shit?" I seethed, enraged that a demon from my former life had tailed me to the safe place I'd bought for Mom.

His eyes rolled in terror, his mouth opening and closing in desperation to draw the breath that I denied him.

Sofia's soft cry hit me like a grappling hook, yanking my body away from Ruiz to slaughter whoever had frightened her.

My stomach dropped to the pavement, and I froze in place. Medina, another one of my former demons, held a knife to her throat. Her lustrous curls were trapped in his fist, yanking her head back and baring her vulnerable artery to his blade.

Rage and panic wracked my system, making my body vibrate with impotent fury. I couldn't risk an attack, because he could slice her open before I even got close.

"Give Ruiz your keys," Medina ordered, the command harsh with malice. "You were stupid enough to think you could drive through your old hood and show off your fancy shit. You think you're better than us, Ignazio?"

I held up my hands, the show of attrition utterly foreign to me. "Let her go," I snarled, knowing there was no power in my demand. From this distance, I couldn't do anything to stop him from slitting her throat.

"Give us your ride, and we'll leave," Medina sneered.

"If you hurt her, you're a dead man." He was already dead, but I would have to wait until Sofia was out of harm's way. Medina wouldn't live to see the end of the day.

"Consider it a trade, then. Your whore for the Porsche."

An enraged, purely animal sound tore from my chest. He would die extra slow for that insult to my sweet Sofia.

"Keys. Now." I heard Ruiz's rasping voice behind me. He'd gotten back on his feet while I witnessed my nightmare playing out before me.

I managed a stiff nod and retrieved my keys from my pocket, moving slowly so I didn't spook Medina. My heart slammed repeatedly against my ribs, pumping enough adrenaline through my immobilized body to enable me to face an army.

I kept my focus trained on Medina and the knife

at her throat. If I allowed myself to look into her lovely eyes, her terror would break me, and I might do something impulsive that would get her killed.

I let my keys drop from my fingers, sensing that Ruiz caught them before they hit the pavement. I couldn't take my attention off Medina, even though it made my skin crawl to have Ruiz at my back while I remained motionless, neutralized far more effectively than he could have managed with a gun to my head.

"Let's go," Ruiz wheezed to Medina, his throat bruised from my crushing grip.

I was glad I hadn't killed him quickly. Once I had Sofia safely inside the house, I could return to the hellhole where I was born and eviscerate Ruiz properly.

"Move." Medina pulled on Sofia's curls, forcing her to walk with him to my Porsche. He used her as a shield, knowing that I'd tear him apart the moment he released her.

Her soft whimper as he yanked at her hair pierced my chest and twisted as cruelly as the blade that threatened her life.

Ruiz unlocked the Porsche and slid into the driver's seat, his freshly-ruined teeth flashing in a red, broken grin.

Medina moved awkwardly when he reached the car, maintaining his hold on Sofia while fumbling at the passenger door handle. As soon as he managed to open it, he shoved her away from him and slammed the door. The Porsche's roar echoed my own savage rage as Ruiz pushed the car to accelerate, as though putting distance between us would somehow save them from me.

Sofia stumbled, and I barely managed to catch her before her knees hit the sidewalk. I lifted her into my arms, crushing her close to my chest to shield her from further harm. Her delicate body shook, and she tucked herself against me, seeking protection.

My muscles bunched and flexed, already anticipating the slaughter of the men who had dared to frighten her.

Focusing the feeble capacity for conscious thought that remained, I rushed her to safety, never releasing her for so much as a second as I unlocked the front gate and hustled her into the house.

"Mateo?" Mom called out, the fearful hitch in her voice stoking the imperative to mete out violence.

She must have heard me shouting outside her house. Ruiz and Medina had terrorized two of the three people in the world who mattered to me. The only two who were completely defenseless without my protection.

Impotent rage pounded through my system. I hadn't felt this debilitating powerlessness since the night I'd met Adrián. The only thing tethering me to sanity was the knowledge that Ruiz and Medina were going to beg for death very soon.

I rushed toward the living room, where Mom liked to spend her afternoons reading. When I entered the room, I found her struggling to stand, trying to come to me and offer solace. The pain that twisted her ruined face incensed me, driving me to new heights of fury I'd never known before.

"Don't get up." My command was so gravelly that I wasn't sure how she understood me.

Mom eased back down onto her couch, grimacing at the permanent agony inflicted by the man who'd almost destroyed her.

I shot a glance at her live-in caregiver, who was dithering at Mom's elbow, assisting her in getting into a more comfortable position.

"Get out," I snapped at the woman, making her kind gray eyes widen in alarm.

Beatrice was a quiet, nurturing woman with a round face and gentle manner. She knew nothing of my criminal enterprises, and I intended to keep it that way. I'd hired her to make Mom's life as easy as possible, and revealing dark truths to Beatrice would complicate things.

"What's wrong, *mijo?*" Mom asked as soon as we were alone. Her chocolate eyes were dark with worry, the scars carved into her face drawn deep.

I took a breath, struggling to function on a civilized level. I at least needed to reassure her before I went tearing off after the men who had threatened Sofia.

"Ruiz and Medina followed me here," I ground out, clutching Sofia closer to my chest, as though the men might materialize and try to take my precious possession away from me again.

"Are you hurt?" she asked, but her concerned gaze shifted to Sofia.

My little flower was still trembling in my arms, but she reassured my mom. "I'm okay."

Her emerald eyes fixed on mine. Tears still glistened on her pale cheeks, but she wasn't crying anymore. Her delicate features were soft and calm, all traces of tension and anxiety gone.

She lifted her hand to my face, tenderly caressing my cheek. My sweet girl was comforting *me*.

"I'm okay," she promised, her voice low and soothing.

The crushing panic that had weighed on my chest lifted, and I drew in a calming breath. My rage didn't abate, but she grounded me enough to harness it, focusing my wrath with purpose. My fury was a tool, fuel that would sustain me while I destroyed the men who'd threatened her. The sense of powerlessness that had debilitated me faded, and I was fortified with renewed strength and white-hot purpose.

"I have to take care of this," I told her. I would

spare her the details of my brutal plans for Ruiz and Medina, but she had to know that I would ensure they could never touch her again.

"You're going after them." She knew my response, and it wasn't a question. "You shouldn't go there alone," she said quietly. "That place isn't safe for you."

"I can handle myself," I vowed. "I'll come back to you without a scratch on me."

Her thumb traced the line of my cheekbone, and her eyes darkened with something like sorrow. "That's not what I meant."

Her concern hit me like a blunt force to the chest, knocking the air from my lungs. Sofia was worried for my emotional wellbeing, not my physical safety. She'd seen firsthand how that place had fucked me up, and she didn't want me to hurt anymore.

Something hot and bright surged through my being, eclipsing my rage. I pressed a kiss to her forehead, an instinctive display of my affection for her.

She didn't flinch away.

"You don't have to worry about that," I murmured, inhaling her rosy scent for the first time in weeks. "I have you to come back to. I don't belong there anymore."

I echoed her assertion that she'd uttered while we visited the shithole where I'd been raised.

"I have to go." Calm settled over me, centering me. With my primal, volatile emotions soothed, I felt stronger than ever before. "They know where Mom lives now. I have to send a clear message that no one comes here without facing consequences. They can't threaten either of you without suffering for it. I'll keep you safe."

"I understand," she said softly. "Be careful."

"Sofia can stay here with me," Mom said. I didn't have to introduce Sofia for her to recognize the woman in my arms. I'd been consumed by desire for my little flower for years, and although I didn't often emote, Mom was well aware of my obsession.

"We'll be fine, *mijo*. Sofia and I can get to know one another while you take care of this." Mom was reassuring me gently, too.

When I was a boy, she'd tried to spare me from a life of violence, but she'd long since accepted what I'd become. She loved me unconditionally, and there was no gruesome task I wouldn't carry out in order to protect her.

"You can put me down now, Mateo," Sofia urged. "I'm safe here."

I was reluctant to break contact after being denied her nearness for long, cold weeks.

But the imperative to punish the men who had frightened her was more powerful than my desire to continue holding her. Touching her was a selfish impulse, but protecting her was an absolute necessity.

I carefully shifted her in my arms, keeping my

hands bracketed around her waist once I set her on her feet. When she stood steadily, I allowed myself a single, swift taste of her lush lips. She tipped her head back, returning my kiss without hesitation. I could lose myself in her, but my prime objective was more consuming than my hunger to take more.

I forced myself to release her, so I could go eviscerate the men who dared to threaten what was mine.

I SLIPPED BACK INTO MOM'S HOUSE, MOVING quietly so I didn't call attention to my arrival. I'd taken several hours with Ruiz and Medina, and bits of them clung to my clothes.

The sun had set, and I'd managed to conceal my bloody clothes from the neighbors by sticking to the shadows. It had taken me less than thirty seconds to cross the distance between my parked, reclaimed Porsche and my mom's front gate.

I would have to replace her Lexus that I'd ditched back in Boyle Heights, but recovering my Porsche had been symbolically important. I could afford to leave behind the luxury sedan that was rarely driven, anyway.

Besides, her Lexus' upholstery would have been ruined by the blood that had soaked into my jeans and t-shirt. The Porsche's black leather interior would wipe down clean.

I'd successfully evaded the prying eyes of the neighbors, and I would spare Mom and Sofia from the gory sight of me, too. I kept spare clothes in one of the guest bedrooms, so I intended to sneak past the women, take a shower, and return to them with clean hands.

Before I made it past the threshold to the living room, I caught the sound of my name. I paused, lingering just down the hallway, where I could eavesdrop and remain totally out of sight.

"Thank you for sharing all this with me," Sofia said. "Mateo told me about some of it, but I don't think he would ever open up this much. He probably wouldn't want to tell me everything you went through in order to provide for him."

My stomach turned. Had Mom told Sofia all the dark details about her past? About how she paid our passage into America with her body and continued selling herself to keep food on our table?

"My son has always been quiet," Mom told her, talking about me as though I was still a child. "He doesn't say much, but he's a sweet boy. He has a good heart."

"Yeah," Sofia agreed on a sigh. "I haven't been fair to him. I understand him better after today. I was just scared of getting hurt again. All of this is so new to me, and the transition has been hard. I still don't like that I'm part of this world, but that's not Mateo's fault. I'm conflicted about him working for Adrián, but I can see now that he's a good man."

I looked down at my body, considering my appearance through Sofia's eyes.

She wouldn't say I was a good man if she could see the guts on my clothes and the torn flesh embedded beneath my fingernails.

Maybe she could accept that I'd gone after Ruiz and Medina to protect her. But I was certain that she couldn't begin to fathom what I'd done to their bodies, how I'd made them suffer and scream before I'd finally allowed them to die.

A good man wouldn't have killed them at all.

A man with a shred of goodness in him would have granted them a quick death.

I was not a good man.

And I'd been touching my sweet, pure Sofia with greedy, bloody hands.

Ever since I'd taken her as my hostage, I'd placed the blame at Caesar's feet. I reasoned that I never would have ripped her out of her safe, happy existence and dragged her into my dark, dangerous world.

I might be blameless for pulling her into this world, but I wouldn't be innocent if I kept her trapped in it.

I'd been so pleased for the excuse to act on my

selfish desires, to claim and cage the woman I'd always wanted without having to accept any of the guilt.

She wouldn't be married off to Ronaldo, not even over my dead body. She wouldn't be given to any criminal.

Including me.

Until Caesar had forced Adrián's hand and I'd kidnapped Sofia, she'd lived completely separate from our criminal organization. She had her simple college life, plenty of creatively-minded friends, and a dream for a future where she pursued her passion for music.

That life still existed, waiting for her to step back into it. Once Ronaldo was dead, I could put her back there. I'd have to make it clear to Caesar that she was to remain outside our world, or he would suffer at my hands.

But I could return her to safety and a life untainted by moral compromises. Even now, I could hear her making excuses for me, rationalizing how it would be best for her to give me a chance.

I was going to have to break this infatuation that I'd fostered if I was going to ensure her future happiness.

Sofia was better off without me in her life, and it was time for both of us to accept that unpleasant truth.

CHAPTER 19

SOFIA

I still wasn't thrilled that Mateo had made a bargain to claim my virginity, and I would rather not think about all the killing and maiming that was part of his job, but everything I'd witnessed today had softened my heart toward him.

Mateo might do bad things, but he wasn't a bad man. He didn't hurt people for fun. This was how he'd survived the hell he'd been raised in. It was how he'd saved his mom.

I didn't like the dark underworld I'd found myself in when Daddy had chosen to kidnap Valentina, but I'd always been part of it, even if I hadn't been aware.

Transitioning into this reality would be a difficult process going forward, but I was willing to face it. With Mateo's help and support, I would survive it. I knew he was strong enough to carry me through it and shelter me from the worst parts of it.

He was quiet on the journey home, but I didn't press him to talk. I sensed that his dark mood lingered; the aftermath of revisiting his traumatic childhood. I wanted to at least hold his hand to offer silent support, but that was hindered by his attention to driving.

When we pulled up in front of his house, he got out of the Porsche and walked straight to the front door. He didn't open my car door and help me out.

Even when I'd been emotionally withdrawn from him over the last three weeks, he'd still opened the door for me every time without fail. No matter how often I refused his offered hand.

My heart ached for him, knowing he must be completely trapped in the nightmares inside his head. That was the only explanation for his sudden neglect.

In the past, I would have overanalyzed this behavior and interpreted it as rejection. I would have shrunk away and settled for scraps of affection when he deigned to give them to me.

Not this time. Mateo was in pain, and my insecurities paled in comparison to his anguish.

He had encouraged me to lean on him for support numerous times. He'd held me and coaxed me to confide in him about my cutting, reassuring me that my scars hadn't ruined me forever. Even though I'd shut him out after that night, my internalized shame and disgust had abated.

Today, he'd revealed his own scars. It was my turn to prove that he could lean on me, too.

I got out of the car and hurried after him, walking through the doorway he'd left open for me. By the time I closed it, he'd already made his way into to the kitchen and grabbed a beer from the fridge.

"Hey," I said softly, trying to call his attention to me.

He popped the cap and tipped the bottle back, draining half of it in one go.

I closed the distance between us and put myself firmly in his space. He didn't so much as glance down at me.

I grasped his wrist when he raised the bottle to take another gulp. He could have resisted me with zero effort, but he froze as soon as I made contact.

"Mateo." I said his name slowly, calmly demanding his attention. "Look at me."

His black eyes snapped to mine, and I caught a flash of longing in their depths before his expression smoothed to something cold and hard.

I lifted my hand to his face, trying to ground him with my touch. When he'd held me after I'd been threatened, I'd been able to soothe him with tender contact.

He scowled and snatched my hand, forcing me away from him.

He'd lashed out at me while we'd been parked outside his rotting childhood home. I hadn't flinched then, and I wouldn't give up so easily now.

I reached for him with my free hand, but I barely brushed his cheek before he slammed his beer down on the counter and captured that wrist, too.

"Back off," he growled.

I lifted my chin, meeting his dark glower head-on. "No."

"*No?*" he repeated, a dangerous hiss.

"That's right." I defied him. This could earn me some consequences, but if that was the kind of interaction he needed right now, I was willing to engage. "*No.*"

He blinked, and his eyes went cold. Rather than reacting with aggression, he simply dropped my hands, turned from me, and walked away.

The familiar sting of rejection cut at my heart, but I resolutely followed him. I grabbed his corded forearm, but he kept walking, shaking me off like a gnat.

I darted around him, blocking his path and refusing to allow him to retreat from me.

"I know today wasn't great," I said firmly. "I'm not exactly thrilled about being held at knifepoint, and I don't like that visiting your old neighborhood was so difficult for you. But don't shut me out right now."

His muscles tensed, his massive frame swelling to tower over me. "Move."

"I know you're upset, but—"

"I'm only upset because you won't take a hint," he barked over me. "I don't want you in my space, Sofia."

I pressed my lips together to prevent them from trembling. Tears burned behind my eyes, but I pushed through.

"Why are you being like this?" I demanded. "I thought you took me to your old neighborhood to win me back. Well, you did. I want to be with you, Mateo."

"No, you don't," he snapped, his white teeth flashing like a predator baring its fangs. "The man you want to be with is a lie I created to lure you in. Returning to where I came from today reminded me who I truly am."

I straightened my spine, standing my ground. "You might have been raised there, but you don't belong in that place. Your life is better now. You're better, even if you still do bad things for Adrián."

His lips curved in a mocking smirk. "*Bad things*. You have no idea what I do for Adrián. You have no idea what I did to Ruiz and Medina."

I shook my head. "You're right. I don't know. And I don't *want* to know. I can't change how you live your life, and I can't change the fact that I was born into this nightmare, even though Daddy hid it from me. I understand that now. I understand it, and I still want to be with you."

The cold smirk twisted into something harsher, meaner. "What your father says about me is true, Sofia. I'm an animal. I'm ruled by my base urges, and I take what I want. I wanted *you*. So, I manipulated you into choosing to accept that you're mine. But you never had a choice. I claimed you for myself, and I never had any intention of letting you go."

His words were icy, but his eyes glinted with a feverish light. He still wanted me, but he was pushing me away. I wasn't certain which specific event today had triggered this change in him, but I resolved to persist.

"I don't understand how taking care of me and respecting my boundaries is manipulative," I reasoned. "You showed me who you really are today, and the man I see isn't an animal."

"That's because you only see what I've wanted you to see," he countered, the rasp in his voice caught between menace and desperation. "You don't know what I'm capable of. Your pretty little brain couldn't even imagine the twisted things I want from you, what I planned to do to your deliciously delicate body as soon as I obtained Adrián's permission to fuck you.

You have no idea what it would really be like to be mine."

Mine. He caressed the final word, as though he savored the taste of it on his tongue. He'd declared his claim over me like this several times since he'd taken me hostage. It obviously meant more to him than simply being in a romantic relationship with me. The term was utterly possessive, irrevocable.

The intensity unnerved me, but I wouldn't permit him to pull away because I was too cowardly to fight for him. Mateo was bleeding inside, and now that he'd shown me the wound, I couldn't walk away.

"Fine." I flung the word at him like a challenge, goading him. "I don't know what it would be like to be *yours*. So, show me."

He made a harsh, animal sound, gnashing his teeth. I'd provoked the beast, but I had to trust that he wouldn't hurt me.

"You don't know what you're asking for," he growled. "I've given you a pretty little fantasy version of how it would be between us. You don't want to see the truth."

"Yes, I do," I insisted. "Show me. Make me yours."

His features sharpened to something almost feral. "You'll regret this," he warned, the bulge in his jeans signaling my victory. "Go get changed. Put on the most revealing dress you own. Nothing sweet or innocent will do for where I'm taking you."

I shrank back slightly, off-balance. This wasn't the direction I'd expected the conversation to take. "Where are we going?"

He flashed his teeth in a wicked, hungry grin. "If you're mine, you don't question my decisions. You obey."

I swallowed hard and managed a shaky nod.

"We're leaving in half an hour. For the rest of the night, you do exactly as I say. You don't even speak without my permission."

My lips parted, but I locked down my protest. If Mateo was trying to scare me off, he was doing a really good job of it. He'd been bossy before, but our interactions had always been playful.

He wasn't playing right now.

I pressed my lips together, demonstrating my willingness to comply with his demands.

His black eyes glinted, his mouth taking on a cruel twist. "Good girl."

Despite his unnerving energy, the words were an instant, visceral trigger. The wash of pleasure that rolled through my system was strong enough to draw a small moan from my chest, and my panties grew damp with arousal. I swayed toward him, my body drawn to his as though he was magnetic.

His brow creased in confusion, and he stepped back, as though he was trying to escape an answering pull toward me.

He shook his head, attempting to clear it.

"Thirty minutes," he muttered, turning and stalking away from me.

I remained rooted to the spot for several seconds, my mouth watering as I admired his muscular frame. Mateo had always been sinfully sexy, but suddenly, I was ravenous for him. My body pulsed with desire, my nipples pebbling to hard buds. All that prevented me from chasing after him and climbing his big body was his demand for my obedience.

Whatever I'd just agreed to engage in was more than a little frightening, and the intensity of my response was even more disconcerting.

For Mateo, I would face these fears.

And judging by my current state of arousal, I would enjoy it.

Mateo had never looked more dangerous or more irresistible. His tight black t-shirt, dark wash jeans, and heavy motorcycle boots were no different than usual, but he pulsed with dark, powerful energy that made me want to fall at his feet and worship him like my own personal god.

I didn't even consider teasing him for selecting the Batmobile as our ride for the evening. He didn't utter a single word to me for the duration of the forty-minute drive to our destination, but his reticence didn't worry me. If anything, his aloof demeanor intensified my arousal.

Every time the impulse to chatter to fill the silence popped into my mind, his order for my absolute obedience weighed on me more heavily, sinking in to my psyche and setting off an arousal response in every sensitive spot on my body.

Good girl.

Obeying him felt *so good*. I didn't have to twist myself in knots to try to win his approval, because he'd told me exactly how he expected me to behave. The knowledge that my compliance pleased him elicited physical gratification.

By the time the Batmobile came to a full stop, my fresh pair of black lace panties were ruined, and my nipples ached where they rubbed against my silky red dress.

Mateo got out of the car and tossed his keys to the valet. I watched his every move with minute attention to detail, drooling over the way his muscles shifted and flexed as he walked around the car and opened my door.

He offered his hand, and I snatched it, pulling myself toward him and tucking my body close to his. I stared up at him, drinking in his dark, rugged features as I fell deeper under his thrall.

He frowned down at me, gripping my chin

between his thumb and forefinger to capture my face for his inspection.

"You're not supposed to like this so much," he said gruffly.

My voice was already fully harnessed by his order for silence, but I rubbed my aching nipples against his hard chest, clinging to him to demonstrate how much I wanted him.

He bit out a curse and stepped away from me, breaking the intimate contact and holding only my hand. I craved more, but I'd agreed to this arrangement for the evening. Mateo was completely in control, and so far, I'd loved every second of it.

A bouncer opened a heavy, metal door with a familiar nod to Mateo.

He led me inside, and we stepped into a short, mirrored corridor. Our reflection surrounded us on all sides: Mateo dark and massive, and my much smaller frame draped in red silk that revealed more than it concealed.

I'd never dared to step outside of my bedroom in this dress before. I'd purchased the designer garment for a ludicrous amount of money, considering I'd never had the guts to actually wear it in public.

"I shouldn't have let you leave the house in this dress," he muttered, low enough that I suspected he was speaking to himself.

The mirror directly in front of us swung outward, opening to admit us into the club.

The deep, pulsing bass hit me first, thrumming into my body and making my heartbeat match its hypnotic rhythm. A whiff of cigar smoke and a heavier, muskier scent permeated the air: an intoxicating, decadent perfume.

I pressed myself closer to Mateo, but he stepped forward, leading me out of the reflective corridor and into the most shocking scene I'd ever witnessed.

At first, I thought he'd brought me to a high-end strip club. Two completely nude women wound their bodies around silver poles, undulating in an erotic dance that matched the pulsing music. A third woman wore some sort of strappy leather harness that accentuated her nakedness, highlighting the most sensuous parts of her body as she sauntered around on black stilettos, balancing a tray of martinis.

I hesitated, my steps faltering. Mateo didn't spare me a glance or pause to check in on me. He simply continued walking, tugging me along in his wake.

We moved deeper into the club, scantily-clad bodies parting to make way for his bulk. I became aware of low, unmistakably sexual groans mingling with the rhythmic bass.

My stomach sank. Had Mateo brought me to a sex club?

He'd warned me that he was going to show me

the kind of man he really was. Did he intend to push me away by showing me that he came here to fuck other women whenever he pleased?

If that was his plan, I wasn't certain if my heart would survive it.

He tugged my hand sharply, making me stumble forward. He caught me before I fell, his hands sinking into my hips as he shifted my body into the position he desired. One brawny arm hooked around my belly, pulling my back flush with his rock-hard chest. His erection pressed into my ass, long and thick.

Keeping me pinned against him, he lifted his other hand to my throat, wrapping his fingers around my neck and forcing me to focus on the scene before us.

Another naked woman was on display, the crowd we'd waded through surrounding the spectacle in a loose circle. This woman wasn't dancing. She was bound, her wrists cuffed and chained above her head, forcing her up onto her toes. Her breasts rose and fell with her heavy, panting breaths, her nipples peaked with desire despite her predicament. Her flushed cheeks glistened with tears, and when the man looming behind her dipped his hand between her legs, I realized that the sensual groans had been issuing from her lips.

I tried to edge away, overwhelmed by the sight. I

knew that some people engaged in kinky sex, but being faced with a public display of bondage went far beyond anything I'd ever experienced.

Mateo held me fast, his body an iron cage around mine. I felt his hot breath tease over my skin as he dipped down to whisper dark words in my ear.

"You see? This is what I want to do to you. I want you just like that: bound and trembling and weeping for release. If you were mine, this is how it would be between us. Your pretty little body would be my plaything. I would make you scream for me and beg for more of whatever I wanted to give you: pleasure or pain.

"That's what it means to be mine. Absolute submission. I would own you."

I shivered in his hold, and I felt his cock jerk in response to my tremor. Heat pooled between my legs, my desire rising to match his.

"This is who I am, Sofia," he declared, low and fierce. "This is what you're agreeing to when you say you want to be with me. Is this what you want?"

I squirmed in his restraining hold, my blood too hot in my veins. His hand firmed around my throat, and I stilled on a whimper. Wet arousal slipped down my inner thighs, my clit aching.

"I don't know," I squeaked, utterly confused by the intensity of what was happening.

He abruptly released me, only to grip my shoulders and spin me around to face him. He grasped my nape, pulling me close and trapping me beneath his black, maddened stare.

"It's *yes* or *no*," he seethed. "Either you want to be mine, or you don't."

"Mateo, I—"

"Is this Caesar's sweet angel?" a new voice purred, masculine and far too close. "I'm shocked you chose to bring her here, Mateo. He won't be happy if he finds out."

Mateo grabbed me, and I found myself trapped in his possessive arms once again. He held me in front of his body, one hand splayed on my stomach while the other wrapped around my thigh. His touch was proprietary, but he didn't tuck me behind him to shelter me from a threat. He held me on full display, showing the newcomer that I belonged to him.

I hadn't agreed to be his. Not yet. Desire pulsed through my system in response to all these new stimuli, but my brain hadn't caught up enough to process what was happening.

The man who had recognized me as Caesar's daughter regarded us with keen interest. His eyes were black like Mateo's, but they held a mean, conniving glint that reminded me of a shark.

Other than the shade of their eyes, the two men couldn't be more different. Mateo was wild and untamed, whereas everything about the stranger was perfectly tailored, from his sharp suit to his designer stubble.

"What are you doing here, Duarte?" Mateo demanded.

"I'm in town for the wedding, of course." The man shook his head ruefully, his perfect grin white and sharp. "How many times do I have to tell you to call me Stefano? We're good friends, aren't we?"

"Play your bullshit games with Adrián," Mateo said tersely. "I'm just the muscle."

Stefano sighed, as though very put-upon. "I can't, because Adrián refused to meet me here. He's no fun now that he's all loved up. But running into you is an unexpected pleasure. As is your lovely companion."

Mateo's fingers flexed into my tender flesh.

Stefano ignored his low growl and dared to address me directly. "You must be Sofia. I've heard so much about you." His shark's eyes roved over my face and down my body. "I can see what all the fuss is about."

"If you want to lose an eye, keep looking at her like that," Mateo threatened.

Stefano beamed at him. "No offense intended. I'm on your side, remember? No one is happier about your little romance than I am."

I wasn't certain if there was anything at all romantic about the way Mateo was snarling over me like I was his favorite toy that might be taken away.

I would own you.

My skin pebbled with a chill of fear, but my body still burned beneath his hands.

"If you didn't come over here to tell me that Ronaldo is dead, then I'm not interested in anything you have to say," Mateo ground out.

Stefano winked at me. "Your Neanderthal is very impatient, it seems."

I had no idea who Stefano was, but it was abundantly clear that he was somehow part of the fucked-up negotiations surrounding the sale of my virginity.

My indignation must have been evident in my expression, because he offered an apology.

"I'm sorry. I can see that I've upset you by talking about such a delicate topic. Please know that while I'm very invested in your relationship, I think waiting for marriage is a laudable virtue. An innocent little lamb like you doesn't belong in a place like this." He cut his cold eyes to Mateo, all pretense of a smile disappearing. "Don't fuck this up for me, Ignazio."

Stefano walked away, leaving me staring at the bound woman who was still on display for the amusement of the crowd. The man who had been tormenting her was now winding a coil of rope around her, knotting it in complex patterns around her breasts. I didn't understand why he would bind her when she was already immobilized by the cuffs around her wrists.

As the man drew the rope taut, the woman's lashes fluttered, and she let out a husky moan.

I felt the phantom embrace of rope around my own body, and hazy memories drifted back to me. Mateo had tied me up when he'd drugged and kidnapped me. I'd been bound and disoriented while Adrián threatened my father over the phone.

"Is that what you did to me?" I asked, forgetting his command for my silence. "When you kidnapped me. I remember you tying me up. Was it like this?"

The woman's breasts were caught between the intricately knotted rope, trapped in a lewd display. The thought of Mateo putting me in a similar position to intimidate my father made my stomach roll with nausea.

Mateo's entire body tensed at my back.

"I shouldn't have brought you here."

He shifted his hold on me, wrapping his arm around my shoulders and pulling me close to his side as he started striding toward the exit.

"No," I agreed softly. "You shouldn't have."

CHAPTER 20

SOFIA

Smile, I reminded myself, arranging my features into a joyous expression.

I stood in the chapel vestibule, waiting my turn to process down the aisle. I didn't want to ruin Valentina's pictures by revealing my angst on her big day.

Just get through the wedding, and deal with everything else after. I repeated the plan that had become my mantra over the last thirty-six hours.

Mateo and I had barely spoken since he'd hustled me out of the perverted club. We'd returned home, gone to our separate rooms, and I'd stewed in uncertainty. My feelings for him hadn't changed since he'd taken me to meet his mom. But there was a huge leap between wanting to start a relationship with him and…whatever that was in the club.

I would own you.

I suppressed a shiver at the overwhelming statement that had been burned into my mind. Ever since Mateo had taken me as his hostage, my life had spun completely out of my control. I'd ceased to be a human being with a will of her own; I'd been reduced to a pawn in power plays between ruthless, amoral men.

A few times since we'd left the club, I'd felt a surge of anger toward Mateo. After he'd taken me to that deviant place, it had become impossible to gloss over the fact that he'd claimed the right to my body, my virginity, without my consent. I cared for him deeply, but that was still a bitter pill to swallow.

Yesterday had been fully booked with my class schedule, followed by a women's sleepover at Valentina's house the night before the wedding. The activities had given me a welcome reprieve from discussing the club incident with Mateo. That conversation was going to be emotionally raw and potentially painful.

I could deal with it after the wedding.

The organ music that signaled the beginning of the ceremony filled the chapel, the notes powerful enough that the space practically vibrated with the jubilant tune.

Valentina's sister-in-law, Samantha, tucked her copper hair behind her ear in an anxious gesture. Despite her nervous energy, she kept her spine straight and shoulders back as she stepped out of the vestibule, starting the procession.

A few beats later, it was my turn as maid of honor. The entire wedding party included Samantha, me, and Mateo. Valentina's brother—Samantha's husband—Andrés had arrived in town just in time to walk the bride down the aisle.

With so few of us involved in the proceedings, it would be even more challenging to divert my attention from Mateo.

I took a breath and braced myself to face him, clutching my blue hydrangea bouquet more tightly than necessary.

As soon as I stepped onto the red carpet leading up to the altar, my attention caught and fixed on Mateo. Taking his place as best man, he stood next to Adrián, and I couldn't keep him out of my field of vision.

He was as darkly gorgeous as ever, but he appeared endearingly uncomfortable in his tux. He'd made an attempt to style his black hair with some sort of product, and it wasn't quite as wild as usual. He tugged at his jacket sleeves and shifted his massive shoulders, frustrated within the confines of so much extra fabric. I was certain he'd much rather be dressed in his usual cotton t-shirt and well-worn jeans.

His onyx eyes widened when they landed on me,

his fussing over his tux completely forgotten. His jaw dropped for a second then clenched tight when his features drew harsh with familiar hunger.

My heart leapt into my throat, and my carefully crafted smile faltered. I continued my smooth progression up the aisle, but I was no longer moving toward the altar with the proper purpose in mind. I should have been focused on my duties as maid of honor, but my body was being pulled toward his. I felt as though I had a rope knotted somewhere low in my belly, and Mateo tugged on the opposite end, compelling me to come to him. His magnetic energy made my sex pulse with awareness, and my nipples pebbled against the structured bodice of my organza gown.

When I reached the front of the chapel, Adrián suddenly shifted to the side, edging his body to an angle that intercepted my view of Mateo.

The groom's pale green eyes glinted in warning, his small frown belying the joyous occasion. He didn't need to utter a word to make his message crystal clear: *Don't fuck up Valentina's perfect day.*

I swallowed hard and summoned up my smile, gliding into place beside Samantha. My new vantage point provided me with a view of the seated guests, and my stomach dropped. I kept my smile in place through sheer force of will, but it felt fragile enough to shatter at the slightest additional pressure.

Daddy was sitting three pews back, his emerald eyes shining with unshed tears. Mom was artfully arranged at his side, her body language the perfect posture of an adoring, supportive wife. They both appeared grief-stricken to see me, as though my absence from their lives caused them great anguish. I suspected that Daddy's feelings were genuine, whereas Mom's expression was a carefully constructed mask designed to win the sympathy of everyone around her.

I'd been so focused on preparing myself to face Mateo that I hadn't stopped to consider my parents' presence at this event. Things were beyond tense between Adrián and Daddy, but they were close business associates. I supposed it would have been perceived as a grave insult if Adrián hadn't invited my father to his wedding.

Even though the men hated each other, the delicately balanced power dynamics within their organization dictated this façade of respect, if not friendship.

I was certain Daddy wouldn't tolerate this false cordiality if he knew that Mateo and Adrián were plotting to have Ronaldo killed in order to free me from the marriage he'd arranged without my consent.

My emotions were on overload, and it took every ounce of strength and practice to maintain my outwardly happy demeanor. For the rest of the ceremony, I remained resolutely focused on Valentina, studying every breathtaking detail of her couture gown. By the time she kissed Adrián, sealing their union, I'd become desperate enough for the distraction that I'd started counting the thousands of seed pearls sewn into the ivory lace.

The organ music swelled again, and Valentina and Adrián started to make their way out of the chapel. That meant it was time for me to take Mateo's arm and follow them to the limos that would carry everyone in the wedding party to the reception venue.

He paused in the aisle, waiting for me to come to him. His black eyes were tight with uncertainty, and I found myself immediately taking his arm to soothe him.

As soon as I wrapped my hand around his massive forearm, the tension that had stretched me to my breaking point melted away. Mateo was warm and solid and stronger than I could fathom. The comfort I found in his presence provided such relief that tears sprang to my eyes.

I could feel my lower lip quivering, and I blinked hard to stop myself from weeping.

Just get through the reception, I commanded myself. I could break down with Mateo in private, once the wedding was over and we could talk everything out back home.

"Please don't cry, *dulzura*," he rasped.

I choked on a sob, his concern shattering my resolution to remain poised.

We reached the vestibule, and I hastily stepped away from him. "I need to go to the ladies' room," I murmured, my vision wavering with the torrent of tears I was struggling to hold back. "I'll meet you at the limo in a few minutes."

"Okay." His agreement was strained, but I couldn't waste time puzzling through his mood. I had to duck away from the cameras and compose myself.

I rushed down the steps that led to the basement level beneath the chapel, where the restrooms were located. Luckily, no one was around to witness my distress as I stumbled into the ladies' room; all the other guests would be making their way out of the chapel and over to the reception venue. I should have a few minutes of solitude to pull myself together.

I grabbed several tissues from a box on the sink counter, blotting at the wetness on my face and praying that my professionally-applied makeup would survive this meltdown.

"Sofia, you're going to ruin your mascara." My mother's judgmental voice echoed the tone of my own thoughts.

Dread pooled in my stomach. I didn't want to talk to Mom right now.

"It'll be fine," I said thickly, patting my cheeks dry with the tissue. "It's waterproof."

"That just means it'll be harder to touch up if you smear it under your eyes," she criticized.

"I'm not smearing it!" I snapped, suddenly feeling like I was thirteen again.

I took a breath and reminded myself that I was an adult, and I didn't have to let her pointed critiques get to me.

"What do you want, Mom?" I asked bluntly. She definitely hadn't come down here to comfort her distraught daughter.

She pursed her full, red-painted lips, her baby blue eyes narrowing at me. The rest of her face didn't move much; she'd been nipped and tucked and injected until she'd become the frozen embodiment of *aging gracefully*.

She stepped beside me to face the mirror, needlessly smoothing her perfectly-styled, platinum blonde hair. "Can't a mother come check on her daughter?" she asked, not even glancing away from her own reflection to consider me.

"We both know that's not why you're here." I was rarely rude to my mother, but I didn't go out of my way to be nice to her, either. Not like I did with Daddy.

There was no point trying to earn Mom's love and

approval, because she simply wasn't capable of offering it.

"Your father is worried about you." She didn't bother to include herself in the statement of concern. "He wants to talk to you, but his number has been blocked from your phone." She smoothed on a fresh coat of red lipstick and made an exaggerated pout at her reflection.

"That's because I don't want to talk to him."

Her blonde brows managed to lift slightly, and she finally focused on me. "Why not? He's been devastated ever since you were taken hostage."

I rolled my eyes. "Of course you only care about how this affects him. You have to play the part of simpering wife and keep him happy so that you can keep your claws in him. Have you even once wondered if *I* might be devastated at being taken hostage?"

She lifted her chin, too haughty to stoop to my level. "I don't appreciate your tone, Sofia."

I threw up my hands. "I don't know why I'm even bothering with this conversation. Tell Daddy whatever you want. I'm not interested in talking to him anytime soon."

"Don't disrespect your father," she scolded as I stormed out of the bathroom.

I stepped into the hallway and jerked to an immediate stop.

"*Princesa.*" Daddy held out his arms, expecting me to step into them for a hug.

His tall, slim body blocked my way to the stairs, trapping me in a conflict I wasn't ready to face. I tried to ease back, distancing myself from the painful prospect of confronting him about his lies.

Mom's slender arm draped over my shoulders, urging me toward Daddy. "Your father has been worried sick about you," she told me in a falsely kind tone. "He wants to see that you're okay."

A hollow laugh echoed through the basement, the spiteful sound issuing from my own lips.

"*Okay?*" I demanded, glaring into my father's bright green, watery gaze. "You lied to me my entire life! It was awful enough learning that you're a criminal, but what you did to Valentina..." My stomach turned. "How could you do that to her?" I railed, the full force of my anguish ripping through me. "How can you be the kind of man who does something like that?"

"Sofia." His voice cracked on my name, his distress genuine. "I'm still your father. You're still my little girl. I didn't want you to be troubled by my business dealings, and I'm sorry that you were pulled into this. But nothing has changed between us. I love you, *princesa.* Always."

His promise of love tore at my heart. I craved it so badly.

"And what if I don't agree to marry Pedro Ronaldo?" I challenged. "Will you still love me if I refuse the future you've arranged for me without even asking my opinion?"

His jaw went slack, as though my objection had never occurred to him. "I was only thinking of what's best for you," he insisted. "Ronaldo is a wealthy man. He has a vast estate. You will be comfortable and provided for."

"He's a *drug lord*. And he lives in another country. How could you think I would be okay with marrying a criminal stranger who lives in a country I've never even visited?"

Daddy's jaw firmed, and he fixed me with his disapproving frown, the one he reserved for the times when I was being especially difficult. "Now, Sofia. Ronaldo will keep you in a life of luxury, and you won't have to worry about anything. You don't have to know about his business dealings, just like you haven't known about mine."

"I don't want to be a kept woman," I insisted. "I would never be happy in an arrangement like that."

"Don't be ungrateful," Daddy rebuked. "I arranged this marriage so that you can have everything you could possibly want. You enjoy your musical hobby, right? Ronaldo will be able to support you so that you can spend your time however you wish."

"Hobby?" The word was soft, small. Most of the air had been knocked out of my chest.

All these years, Daddy had just been indulging me. He didn't take my music seriously. I'd been stupid and desperate enough to think that he actually believed in my talent.

"You don't have to worry about anything, *princesa*," he cooed, completely ignoring the fact that he had inflicted the pain he was attempting to soothe. "I'll sort everything out with Adrián soon, and then the wedding can move forward as planned. You won't have to be trapped with that animal for much longer."

"Don't call him that!" I snapped.

How dare Daddy speak about Mateo as though he was sub-human? The old man standing before me was far more of a monster than I'd ever realized. He possessed less humanity than the man who'd been holding me hostage.

Daddy's slate gray brows rose. "You can't possibly *like* Ignazio." He uttered the words as though they were distasteful. He shook his head, hardening his resolve. "This just proves how important it is for me to take care of you. If you think Ignazio is anything more than an animal, then you're a poor judge of character. The life Ronaldo will provide for you is what you need."

"Why aren't you listening to me?" I shrieked,

feeling like a little girl screaming futilely at my locked bedroom door. "I don't want to marry Ronaldo!"

"Sofia, you're being very disrespectful," Mom scolded. "Apologize to your father."

Suddenly, Mateo came barreling down the stairs, his black eyes wild. He was laser focused on me, and he didn't even seem to notice that my father was an impediment to his path. When Daddy tried to stand his ground, Mateo simply shoved him aside.

Daddy shouted in pain when he slammed into the wall, but Mateo didn't notice that, either. He came straight for me, and Mom darted into the safety of the bathroom.

"I heard you scream," he said, his voice rumbling with unspent aggression.

I flung myself at him, closing the short distance between us. His corded arms enfolded me, and I leaned into his warmth and strength.

"Take me home," I whispered, tucking my face against his chest, breathing in his intoxicating scent.

"All right, *dulzura*." He dropped a kiss on my forehead. "We'll go home. I've got you."

CHAPTER 21

MATEO

Adrián would be annoyed that I'd skipped out on his wedding reception, but Sofia needed me. She cried softly the whole way home, and I was anxious to park my BMW so I could soothe her. She responded to my touch far more powerfully than any words of comfort I could offer.

As soon as I picked her up out of the passenger seat, she tucked her face against me and clung on tight. Her tears wet my shirt as I carried her into the house and settled us both down on the couch. I tried to position her beside me, but she cuddled closer, indicating that she needed me to hold her.

I hated her tears, but her willingness to turn to me for support made warmth pulse in my chest.

Ever since I'd ushered her out of Adrián's kinky club, I'd been tormented by the very real prospect that she would leave me, now that I'd pushed her away for her own good. Letting her go was the right thing to do, because it was what was best for her happiness, not mine.

But her emotional distance over the last two days had shredded me.

"You were right," she sniffled against me, speaking for the first time since we'd left the chapel. "Daddy doesn't care whether or not I want to marry Ronaldo."

"I'm sorry, *florecita*."

My touch on her soft skin remained gentle despite the anger that surged. I loathed her piece of shit father, but she still had enough love left for him that he was able to wound her deeply with his betrayal.

I regretted that I hadn't taken the time to hurt him more. He'd stood in my way when she was in distress, so I'd resolved that little issue by shoving him aside. If I'd stopped long enough to register that he had been the one to make Sofia scream in anguish, I would've done a lot worse.

"You're not an animal," she said quietly, her dainty fingers catching my shirt to hold me impossibly closer. "You told me my father was right to call you that. He's not." She looked up at me, her emerald eyes wide and shining. "You're a good man, Mateo."

Her words were a knife to my heart. More than

anything, I wished they were true. I wanted to be the man she thought I was, but I never would be.

"I know you want to believe that, *dulzura*." I rubbed my thumb over her pretty, plump lips, memorizing their softness. "But it's not true. You say you want to be with me, but you're making excuses for who I really am so that you can justify your decision. That's why I took you to Adrián's club. I need you to understand that I'm not a good man. And being with me isn't good for you. Once Ronaldo is dead, I'm going to make sure you can go back to your old life."

A wrinkle appeared between her brows. "My old life is over. It was never real, anyway."

"I can make it real for you," I swore. "I'll make sure you father doesn't fuck with you. You'll be separate from all this violence and cruelty."

"Why are you doing this?" She pressed her palm to my cheek, commanding my full attention and honesty. "I know you want me. I know you care. Why are you pushing me away when I want you too?"

My fingers encircled her wrist, but I couldn't find the strength to pull her hand from my face. "Because I don't deserve you."

Her lovely eyes drew tight, as though she felt my pain in her own chest. "You do deserve me, Mateo. You deserve me, because you earned me. When you first took me as your hostage, you claimed the right to my body and imprisoned me in your house. You could have done anything you wanted to me, but you chose to take care of me. You...made me better."

She guided my hand to press against her thigh, right over the expanse of flesh where she'd cut herself to earn her father's love.

"You've taken care of me, and you've never asked for anything in return. Even now, you're trying to push me away because you think it's what's best for me. But it's not. *You're* what's best for me. I know who you are, and I know what you do for Adrián. I still want to be with you. I want to be yours, Mateo."

Mine.

My hunger for her twisted my insides, my denied craving causing me physical pain.

"I showed you what it means to be mine," I ground out, wrestling against my consuming desire to take what she offered without question. "It frightened you."

"Not all of it," she admitted. "It was just a lot to take in. You didn't present it to me in the subtlest way, either." She caressed my cheek. "But I trust you. You would never hurt me."

"Never," I vowed.

Holding me steady with her gentle touch on my face, she leaned in and pressed her lips to mine. My mouth remained firm beneath hers for the space of a few seconds, but I didn't have a chance of resistance. Not when Sofia offered herself to me.

Not when she refused to take *no* for an answer.

I'd rejected my sweet Sofia to try to spare her, knowing my withdrawal would hurt her. But she'd managed to overcome her crippling fear of rejection to stand her ground and fight for me. For us.

There was no going back for her now.

My fingers slid into her hair, tugging her voluminous curls, so I could kiss her more deeply. She shivered and melted in my arms, giving me everything I demanded and offering more.

Like the greedy bastard I was, I took it all. I toyed with her body, teasing and petting in the places she liked best. I savored her little tremors, her gasps for breath, her needy whimpers.

My cock strained against the slacks I wore. They were less confining than my jeans, but that didn't make my denied craving to bury myself in her wet heat less agonizing.

She shifted in my hold, her hand snaking between us to caress my dick. The slacks provided a barrier between us, but even that light touch was shocking enough to make my entire body jerk beneath her.

I grabbed her wrist, pulling her away more harshly than I intended.

"You can't do that, *florecita*," I warned. "I can barely control myself as it is. Don't make this harder on us both."

She stared up at me, her emerald eyes wide and

earnest. "It doesn't have to be hard. I want you, Mateo. I want to give myself to you. Not because you've staked a claim over my body, and not because Adrián gives his permission. This is between you and me and no one else."

I pressed my forehead to hers, grounding myself so I wouldn't be tempted to madness. "I want you, too, Sofia. From the moment I first saw you, I've wanted you. But I can't put you at risk. If I defy Adrián and force him to break his word, the truce we've established falls apart. Things will get bloody. You could get hurt in the fallout."

She wrapped her hand around the back of my neck, anchoring herself to me. "I know Adrián is important to you. He still frightens me, but I won't betray him. No one will know if we're together, Mateo. I'm not going to tell anyone. And once Ronaldo isn't a threat anymore, we won't have to hide it."

"If you were to get hurt because I couldn't keep my dick in my pants, I would never forgive myself," I rasped, wanting so desperately to give her what she asked.

Her eyes began to shine, imploring. "Please. I know I'm asking a lot, but I want this to be my choice. Knowing that my virginity was traded like a commodity has been devastating. I need to do this on my terms. I need you on my terms, Mateo."

She'd found the exact words to break me.

I'd been truthful when I'd told her I didn't regret bartering for her virginity. I still didn't, not if it meant keeping her from Ronaldo. But I did regret that my actions had hurt her.

This would always remain a sore spot between us, a resentment built into the foundation of our relationship.

I wasn't willing to build our future on her pain. No part of belonging to me should be painful for her.

"All right, *dulzura*," I agreed. "This is between us and no one else."

I skimmed my palm up her thigh, pushing the floaty layers of her dress out of the way so I could stroke her pussy. She gasped and arched at first contact, her lacy panties already soaked for me.

"I'll show you how good it feels to be mine," I swore, teasing her clit.

"Yes," she cried, her legs falling open in offering. "Make me yours, Mateo."

She wasn't taunting me this time; she was begging.

The last shred of my restraint snapped. I shifted my hold, cradling her against my chest as I carried her into my bedroom. Sofia's first time wouldn't be a rough fuck over the couch.

When we reached my desired destination, I set her down on her feet, steadying her with my hands around her waist. She went up onto her toes, pulling me in for a hungry kiss.

Her aggression shocked me, but my body responded in kind. I growled against her mouth, nipping at her pouty lower lip. She let out a shuddering sigh and opened for me, welcoming my harsh claim.

I started tearing at her dress. The strapless gown was secured with a long row of buttons down her back. I kissed her in a frenzy, my thick fingers fumbling at the tiny impediments to stripping Sofia.

By the time she had my shirt unbuttoned, I lost patience. Grabbing the structured bodice of the dress in my fists, I yanked it apart with my full strength.

Dozens of little, organza-covered buttons popped free and bounced all over my bedroom floor.

Sofia giggled against my lips, the sound of her delight rolling into my body. It filled me with joy so hot and bright that it consumed me, her purity scouring the darkest parts inside me.

I shoved the ruined remnants of the dress away and moved farther down her body, hooking my thumbs beneath the band of her panties. Once I slid them down her legs, I pressed a reverent kiss against her scarred thigh.

Her fingers threaded through my hair, and her lower lip quivered with the force of her emotions. Her eyes were shining, but she wasn't sad. Sofia had spent her entire life being told she wasn't good enough, that her appearance wasn't pleasing enough. Her shitty mother had planted the insidious idea in her head that she had *ruined her body*.

"You are breathtaking, Sofia," I promised. "You're perfect."

After lavishing the marks with my tender attentions, I picked her up again, so I could lay her down on my bed—*our* bed.

I took a minute to drink her in, burning the sight into my brain. Sofia's lovely body was pure, mouthwatering perfection straight out of my obsessive fantasies. But it was her soft, shy smile that transformed her into my personal goddess.

"I want to see you, too," she whispered, her sparkling eyes raking over my bared chest like a tactile sensation.

She'd never seen me naked, not even shirtless. Now, her hungry gaze roved over my tattoos, meandering along the swirling, stark black patterns I'd chosen to ink into my skin: symbols of strength and power.

Her gaze dipped lower, and her white teeth sank into her lip when her attention dropped to the bulge in my slacks.

I bit out a curse and hastily shucked off the rest of my clothes, eager for her to see all of me.

Her wide-eyed stare and parted lips were a snapshot out of one of my wet dreams. She swallowed hard, not diverting her attention from my erection for a second.

"You're really big," she said, her soft tone caught between wonder and fear.

Everything about her reaction was more perfect than I could have ever imagined.

Shock tore through me when she propped up on her elbows and reached for me, her slender fingers stroking my length in a curious exploration.

I hissed at the delicious contact, and I grasped her shoulders to press her back down into the mattress.

"You'll make me lose control, Sofia," I explained tightly to allay the little furrow in her brow.

I'd waited for her, wanted her, for too long. I wouldn't ruin this by rutting into her like a teenage boy.

I settled my body over hers, pinning her beneath me. My cock jerked against her soft belly, tormented by the feel of her. She lifted her hips, grinding her clit on my thigh in an attempt to stimulate herself. Her wet arousal painted my skin, her body slick and ready for me.

She would need more preparation this first time. I doubted I could take her virginity completely painlessly, but I would make damn sure she loved being mine.

I captured her lips in a punishing kiss, claiming her mouth while I played with her hot little pussy. Her folds were swollen, her clit a needy bud. I explored her at my leisure, memorizing her shape, every stroke that made her gasp and writhe.

When I finally eased one finger into her virgin channel, I released her mouth and indulged myself in her perfect breasts for the first time. I learned their weight and shape in my palm, teasing her nipples with my thumb.

Unable to resist, I leaned in and flicked my tongue over the tight peaks. I groaned when her inner muscles squeezed my finger in response. Testing her, I grazed her nipple with my teeth.

She cried out my name and arched her back, inviting more. With a low, animal growl, I bit her tender flesh, rubbing her g-spot and pressing my thumb down on her clit at the same time.

She came in a rush, writhing beneath me as ecstasy washed through her body. Her pussy squeezed my finger, and I stroked her until her orgasm faded and her inner muscles relaxed.

Satisfied that she was prepared, I grabbed a condom from my nightstand. Sofia wasn't on birth control, and I wasn't going to take any stupid risks with her.

I sheathed myself quickly and settled my weight over her once again.

"This might hurt a little," I warned, my voice rough with my own denied need. "I'll go slow with you."

She caressed my cheek, and I leaned into her touch. "I trust you."

I kissed her palm and lined my dick up with her slick opening. Her velvet heat felt heavenly enough to make my eyes roll back in my head, but I resolutely focused on her as I pressed into her tight channel.

Her delicate features pinched with discomfort when my cockhead breached her. I gritted my teeth and paused to pet her and praise her, running my hands all over the places where she liked to be stroked best.

When I tweaked her pretty nipples, she gasped and relaxed enough to let me sink an inch deeper.

Easing into my sweet Sofia was exquisite torture. Every time she whimpered in pain, I slowed my progress and played with her until she flowered open for me.

When I pushed in the final inch, locking our bodies together, she shuddered beneath me, her lithe frame trembling from overwhelming sensation.

I stroked a stray curl from her sweat-slicked brow. "Good girl."

She moaned, and her tight muscles squeezed my dick before relaxing, her body adjusting to my size.

I pulled out slightly and rocked back in, letting her feel my full length stretching her.

"This is all mine," I growled, drunk on her surrender.

I withdrew and tested her with a more forceful thrust. She handled it beautifully, her lashes fluttering in bliss.

I began taking her in long, slow strokes, reveling in her soft cries as she tentatively moved against me.

"That's it," I encouraged as she learned to match my rhythm. "You like my cock filling up your tight little pussy, *dulzura*?"

"Yes!" she cried, rocking her hips toward me with new confidence and hunger.

I wrapped my hand around her throat, an instinctive, primal act as she pushed me toward the brink. I applied only a fraction of pressure, just enough so that she was fully aware of my palm pressed snugly against her neck.

Her inner walls contracted around my dick, and she made the most exquisite, sexiest whimper.

I fucked her harder, taking her more roughly for my final, brutal thrusts.

"Tell me you're mine," I snarled.

"I'm yours." Her fingernails scoured my back, urging me on. "Please…"

I crushed my lips to hers, coming on a rough

shout. As my pleasure crested, I pinched and tugged at her nipples, drawing out her answering ecstasy.

I drove deep, holding myself inside her as we both gasped for air. I wanted to stay buried in her soft heat forever, feeling her pulse racing beneath my hand on her throat.

Sofia had given herself to me, and there was no going back now. Her fate was sealed.

CHAPTER 22

MATEO

One Week Later

"I got you a present, *florecita*," I murmured, closing the front door behind us.

"You didn't have to get me anything."

My hands bracketed her hips, preventing her from turning to face me. I nuzzled her neck and nipped at her soft skin in the way that made her shiver and sigh.

"It's just as much for me as it is for you." I cupped her breast, hungry to explore her body now that we'd returned to the privacy of our home. "I'm still a greedy bastard. But you'll like this, too."

She pressed back against me, rubbing her pert ass

against my cock with brazen desire. "Does this present involve an orgasm?"

I chuckled, dropping a tender kiss on her shoulder. "Maybe. If you're good for me, I'll let you come."

"I have been good." She huffed, her petulance exaggerated and designed to goad me. Sofia really would have excelled in a Drama degree.

I grazed her ear with my teeth, my fingers flexing around her breast and hip. "I think you're greedy too, *belleza*." I hummed against her throat, and her skin pebbled beneath my lips. "I wonder how many orgasms I can force from your pretty little body before you beg me to stop."

"Is there such a thing as too many orgasms?" she teased breathily.

"You tell me. You can count them for me until it's too much." I gripped her pussy, grinding my palm against her clit and dipping my fingers between her legs. "And then, I'll take more. We don't stop until I'm satisfied."

Her low moan was purely wanton, and she shifted into my hand, offering herself to me. It was probably for the best that she couldn't see my savage, merciless grin. My innocent little flower had no idea how she could suffer in ecstasy.

I withdrew my touch, and she whined at the loss.

"Not yet, greedy girl." I nipped at her throat. "Present first. Orgasms later."

I reached into my pocket and withdrew the length of black cloth I'd stashed there before we left the house this morning. I'd planned this little surprise a few days ago, and everything had been delivered and set up for her while I'd guarded her on campus.

I dropped the cloth over her eyes. She tried to twist away on instinct, but I knotted it firmly behind her head. My grip returned to her hip and breast, pinning her in place as she squirmed.

"Settle," I commanded, tweaking her nipple through her thin cotton dress. "Trust me."

She trembled and went still, submitting to my control.

Over the last week, I'd played increasingly kinky games with her, testing her responses and training her to please me. She'd been amply rewarded for her good behavior, and she'd loved every second of being tamed to suit my desires.

I took a few minutes longer to caress her, demonstrating my approval. Her head dropped back against my chest, and she sighed in contentment.

Sofia loved being my good girl.

"Are you ready for your present, *dulzura*?" My voice came out slow and deep, her intoxicating effect on my body profound and addicting.

"Yes, please," she whispered, soft and pliant beneath my hands.

I finally stepped away from her, releasing her body so that I could capture her hand in mine.

"Come," I urged, leading her where I wanted.

Her first steps were hesitant, nervous. With the blindfold robbing her sight, she was off-balance.

I rubbed my thumb over her palm. "I've got you," I promised, continuing our progress through the house.

She steadied, putting her trust in me. I wouldn't let her stumble and fall.

Warmth pulsed in the center of my chest, spreading outward through my body with each steady beat of my heart.

I walked slowly, savoring her complete reliance on me, her absolute surrender.

When we reached the new space I'd set up for her —transforming one of my useless guest bedrooms—I squeezed her hand and ordered her to stop.

I positioned myself beside her, hungry to study her expression when she saw what I'd procured for her.

I tugged at the knot on the blindfold, pulling it away from her face.

She squinted and blinked, her eyes taking a second to adjust to the light. As soon as the room came into focus, she gasped, her features going slack with wonder.

I'd purchased a baby grand piano and three

guitars for her, so she could write her songs and practice at home. I wasn't certain which guitar she would like best, so I'd gone with the most highly recommended options I'd found in my online research. I'd had plenty of time to arrange everything from the convenience of my smart phone while she attended her classes.

"You did this for me?" she asked, her voice small, as though she hardly dared to hope that the gifts were for her and that they didn't come with conditions.

"And me," I said truthfully. "I want to hear you sing every day."

She flushed with pleasure, her radiant smile hitting me square in the chest. "Thank you. You didn't have to do this."

"Yes, I did," I countered. "How else are you going to prepare for your gig if you can't practice?"

Her brow furrowed. "My gig?"

I nodded. "I booked a show for you at a cocktail lounge. It's not huge, but I think you'll like the venue."

"What?" she asked faintly, as though she couldn't wrap her mind around what I was saying.

"I recorded you singing during your class last week. I contacted a few venues around town. This place offered the most money, so I booked it for you."

I didn't need to bribe anyone to secure a gig or a

recording contract for Sofia. Her incredible talent would ensure a successful career. I was simply nudging her along.

Her emerald eyes began to shine. "You believe in me?"

I pulled her into a firm embrace, reinforcing my promise with a reverent touch. "More than anything." I brushed a tear from her cheek. "There's something else I got for you. It's on top of the piano."

"Mateo." Her voice hitched around my name. "This is too much."

"No, it's not." I continued petting her, grounding her. "I know part of you is still scared that I'll take these things away from you. That I might withdraw from you if you disappoint me." I captured her face in both hands, forcing her to stare into my eyes and read the depth of my sincerity. "Nothing I give you comes with conditions. I will never leave you, Sofia. Nothing you could do would ever cause me to reject you. I'm not going anywhere."

I sealed my promise with a kiss, claiming her lips with harsh passion. I kept her trapped in my embrace until every trace of tension melted from her willowy frame.

When I gave her enough space to draw breath, she trembled against me, her emerald eyes sparkling with the pure devotion I'd so savagely craved ever since I'd taken her as my hostage. The sight soothed something inside me, quieting my volatility even more profoundly than her powerful singing voice.

"Time for your last present," I murmured, taking another kiss from her lush lips. "Then, you get your orgasms."

She shivered, her senses already overwhelmed by my intense attentions. I was equally affected by her, perhaps more so.

I intended to prove my devotion to her beyond a shadow of a doubt.

I guided her to the piano, placing her hand atop the drawing I'd had commissioned for her.

She took a sharp inhale, and her fingers traced over the fine, elegant lines drawn in stark black ink. I could practically feel that phantom touch on my chest, and I craved it more strongly than I'd ever desired anything.

"This is for me?" she asked softly, stroking the delicate curve of one of the flower's petals.

"It's my next tattoo," I told her, my voice coming out rough and deep. "I wanted you to approve the final artwork before I book it."

Her bright green gaze lifted to my face, her lips parted in shock. I rubbed my thumb over those lush lips, reveling in her softness. I lifted her hand from where it stroked the drawing and pressed her palm against the center of my chest, directly over my heart.

"I'm getting the tattoo right here," I declared with the weight of on oath. "What do you think, *florecita?*"

"I love you," she said in a rush. Her jaw went slack, as though she'd just taken herself by surprise. Then, her features illuminated with an ecstatic grin. "I love you, Mateo!"

She flung herself against me with a jubilant laugh, squeezing her body tight to mine.

"I love you, sweet Sofia," I vowed, breathing in her addicting scent.

The imperative to conquer robbed my next, brutal kiss of any finesse. I always treated her delicate little body with care, but I needed to push her to her limits; I needed to claim her completely.

After today, there would be no question that I was the master of her body and soul.

Never releasing her lips, I grasped her hips and lifted her up onto the piano.

She squirmed against me and tried to protest. "Wait! We'll break it."

"If we do, I'll buy you a new one." I bit her shoulder with enough force to leave a mark.

Her sharp cry sounded over the harsh rip of her cotton dress giving way beneath my fists.

I'd buy her another one of those, too.

Anything Sofia could possibly want, I would provide.

I shoved aside the ruined garment, stripping her for my hungry gaze. With a few more savage tears, her lace bralette and panties fell away, laying her body bare for my pleasure.

My fingers sank into her heavy curls, capturing the lustrous locks in a cruel grip. At the same time, I penetrated her tight pussy with two fingers, abruptly taking her in hand. She gasped, clutching at my shoulders for support.

Her gorgeous eyes were wide, her expression of innocent shock perversely perfect enough to provide a lifetime of dirty fantasies.

I pressed my thumb down on her clit and rubbed my fingers against her g-spot, holding both of her pleasure triggers. Her inner muscles fluttered around my fingers, and her wet arousal dripped onto my palm.

A savage grin twisted my features.

"Do you feel that, *belleza*?" I asked, exerting a fraction of pressure. She bucked into my hand. "Usually, I like to take my time with you. But I don't have to. I can make you come whenever I want. You're *mine*."

I stimulated her mercilessly, rubbing her g-spot and clit to wring an orgasm from her body. She cried out, her eyes tight with confusion at her rapid response.

"Hmmm..." I mused, easing off after she peaked.

"I wonder if I could train you to come on command for me. If I press down right here..." She writhed in my grip, but I held her trapped for my cruel game. "*Come.*"

Her inner walls squeezed my fingers, and she jerked beneath my hands.

"I told you I would make you count them," I reminded her, my voice coming out slow and deep. I was becoming intoxicated by her surrender, by my absolute control over my sweet Sofia. "How many orgasms was that?"

"Two," she squeaked, her muscles spasming weakly.

"That's not nearly enough, is it?" I teased, loving toying with her. "Should I make you work for the next one?"

"Mateo." My name was caught somewhere between an adorable protest and a plea.

"As much as I like it when you whimper my name, that's not an answer, *dulzura*. It's a *yes* or *no* question."

She licked her lips, her brow furrowed with confusion. Her skin was flushed with pleasure, but her mind was still struggling to comprehend the full power I held over her body.

"I don't know," she whispered.

I brushed a tender kiss over her cheek. "Then I'll decide for you, sweet girl."

I forced her to orgasm, ruthlessly stimulating

the pleasure points she'd surrendered to me. I brought her body to climax three times in rapid succession, leaving her shaking and gasping in my arms.

"You're supposed to count them," I reminded her, stoking my fingers through her slick, swollen folds as she shuddered in my arms. "Otherwise, how will we know if there's such a thing as too many orgasms? How many are we up to now?"

"I..." she panted. "I don't know."

"Poor *florecita*," I cooed, nuzzling her neck. "You didn't realize what you were getting into, did you?"

"No," she whined, trembling against me.

I nipped at her shoulder. "Do you want to beg for mercy?"

"Yes," she implored on a broken whisper. "Please."

My teeth grazed over her artery on a wicked grin. "That's too bad. I'm not feeling merciful."

I withdrew my hand from her abused pussy, only so I could grab her hips and flip her onto her front, pressing her down so that she was bent over the piano.

I kept her pinned with my hand on the small of her back, and I petted her puffy folds, playing in the wetness her orgasms had left behind.

The *crack* of my hand slapping her pert ass resounded through the room, mingling with her shriek.

"Stay." I delivered two more stinging slaps to reinforce my command.

While I stripped off my own clothes, my good girl waited exactly where I'd left her, quivering and wet for me.

I quickly retrieved a condom from my jeans pocket and sheathed my cock.

I roughly grabbed her hips and pulled her toward me, driving deep in a single thrust. Her inner walls squeezed me hard enough to make me see stars, and a feral sound rumbled from my chest. My fingers dug into her hips, holding her harshly, letting her feel how helpless she was.

"You're going to come for me again, *belleza*," I told her, a dark promise.

A soft sob jolted through her body, but her greedy pussy contracted around my dick. My sweet girl liked this cruel game every bit as much as I did.

I gathered up more of her slick arousal, coating my fingers in the wetness between her legs. I brushed my thumb over her clit, drawing another sob from her chest as I stimulated the hyper-sensitized little bud. At the same time, I pressed my desire-slicked finger against her asshole.

She tried to clench to keep me out, but her body was already too exhausted to fight. It only took a few seconds of stroking her tight ring of muscles for her to ease open and allow me to penetrate her.

She squirmed as I filled her up, impaling both of her tight little holes for my pleasure.

"Such a good girl," I praised when she accepted me fully, her willowy frame trembling and pliant.

Her broken whine and the helpless way her inner walls fluttered around me drew a satisfied rumble from my chest.

I started to fuck her at the pace I desired, taking my time to enjoy her body. I ruthlessly stimulated her clit and played with her ass, keeping her on edge as my own pleasure crested.

"Are you ready to come for me?" I asked roughly, driving hard and deep.

"Yes," she cried. "Please, Mateo…"

"Come," I commanded, rubbing her over-stimulated clit.

Her pussy squeezed my dick, and I threw back my head to release a roar of savage satisfaction, reveling in the perfection of the woman I loved.

CHAPTER 23

SOFIA

Two Weeks Later

"I can't believe you posted on my Instagram about this," I half-groaned, torn between overwhelming gratitude and pre-performance jitters.

Mateo grinned, unrepentant. "You shouldn't have given me your phone passcode if you didn't want me to log onto your app and make a post about your first gig. Your legion of adoring fans is waiting to hear you sing."

I leaned into him, loving how solid he was. I would never have to worry about anything, as long as

I had Mateo to support me. "There's only one adoring fan I care about."

He captured my chin between his thumb and forefinger, tipping my face to his. "Good. Then I don't have to worry about eliminating any competition."

He dropped a swift, firm kiss on my lips, drawing back before either of us could get lost in it.

"You should probably go," I prompted, even though I would have preferred for him to stay with me until the moment I had to walk onstage.

But this "backstage" area was cramped enough as it was. The space was little more than a broom closet with a vanity mirror and a guitar stand, and bulky Mateo did not fit. I needed to do some of my warm-up exercises to mitigate my mounting anxiety.

"I'll be front and center," he promised. "Tonight and every night from now on."

I grinned like a fool. "I love you. Thank you for arranging all this for me."

"Everything was booked based on your talent," he reminded me, as he'd done multiple times over the last two weeks.

"I still wouldn't be here without you believing in me. I love you so much, Mateo." I couldn't say it often enough.

"I love you, Sofia."

God, I couldn't get enough of hearing him say it,

either. Those rumbly words in his deep voice made me all warm and shivery. I went up onto my toes and offered one final kiss before shooing him out of the cramped space.

Mateo had been gone less than a full minute before someone knocked on the door, interrupting my stretches.

Puzzled, I opened it to find a stranger on the other side. The woman offered a bright, perfect smile.

"Hi," she introduced herself. "You must be Sofia. I'm Carmen, the assistant manager."

I took the hand she offered and shook it, even though I was a bit confused by her presence. "I thought Steph was the assistant manager?"

The statuesque, raven-haired beauty with the sleek, polished style was completely different from the bubbly blonde I'd been introduced to earlier this evening.

"Shift change," Carmen explained with a little wave of her red-manicured fingers. "I brought you a complimentary tea," she announced, raising the steaming white mug she held in her free hand.

"Oh?" I asked, my interests piqued. I wrapped my hands around the warm mug and sniffed at the hot beverage. "What kind? I love tea."

"I know," she replied with a smile. "I noticed your tea-lover hashtags on your Instagram, and I thought you might like it. It's ginger tea with a little honey."

"Perfect combo," I approved. "Thanks so much. That was really thoughtful of you."

"Let me know if you need more honey in it," she prompted.

I took a tentative sip, testing the temperature and flavor on my tongue. "This is awesome as-is," I confirmed. "Thanks again! I really wasn't expecting free tea. I'm just so grateful to get this gig."

"I heard you sing in some of your videos posted on your social media. You have a remarkable voice."

"Thank you." I took a long sip to hide my flush. I'd spent my entire life training my instrument to be good enough to warrant praise, but accepting it still made me uneasy. Mateo was helping me learn to let go of my anxiety that the praise came with a price or expectation, but I still had a lot of bad habits to break.

"This is your first gig, right?" she asked, making polite conversation.

I wished she would give me a little space to breathe before I had to perform, but I didn't want to be rude to the assistant manager of the venue that had hired me.

"Yeah." I took another big sip. "I'm so thrilled for the opportunity. I really appreciate it."

"I'm sure you'll be very happy in your musical

pursuits, wherever you end up. You obviously have a great passion for it."

That seemed like kind of a weird thing to say, but I couldn't focus on picking at it. My anxiety must be hitting overload, because I was feeling far too hot and a little dizzy.

I practiced the deep breathing exercises I'd learned in therapy, but they didn't help clear my head.

"Careful," Carmen warned, plucking the mug from my hand before I could drop it.

I pressed my palm to my forehead, willing the room to stop wavering around me. I'd never had anxiety like this before.

"I don't feel good," I admitted, struggling to practice my breathing exercises. I kept losing track of what I was trying to accomplish.

"You just need some fresh air." Her slender arm hooked around my waist, and she guided me out of the backstage area.

The world began to spin, so I closed my eyes. Cool air kissed my cheeks, rousing me for a few seconds.

I was in an alley behind the venue, leaning heavily on Carmen as she guided me toward a black Audi.

"Wait," I slurred, my feet dragging.

She kept walking, grunting slightly at the effort of hustling me along. A man got out of the car, and he hurried toward us.

I tried to recoil when he picked me up, relieving Carmen of the burden. I only managed to fall into his burly arms.

My eyelids were too heavy to keep open. The world went dark again, and I heard car doors shutting and locking.

"Where's Mateo?" I managed to murmur, wanting him desperately.

"You don't have to be afraid of that animal anymore," Carmen promised, as though she was offering great comfort rather than dragging me into my nightmare.

❦

I CLAWED MY WAY BACK TO CONSCIOUSNESS, fighting the drowsiness that had been forced upon me. In my fleeting moments of lucidity, I knew I was being separated from Mateo. I was desperate to get back to him, frightened of how much time might be passing and how far I might be carried away from him.

Finally, I managed to force my eyes open, groaning against the wash of light that seared my vision. I didn't dare blink, in case I couldn't find the strength to wake again.

I squinted, willing the world to materialize around me.

"You're okay, Sofia," a female voice reassured me. "I'm sorry for drugging your tea. I didn't mean to cause you so much distress. Your father said you wouldn't know who to trust, and I couldn't risk a delay in case Ignazio saw me and realized who I was."

I turned my head, searching for the woman. It felt too heavy, as though my skull was filled with sand. My body sank into a soft mattress, lethargy pinning me down.

"You should sleep it off," Carmen advised kindly. "You're safe now. I'm right here with you, and no one will touch you. Ignazio can't get to you here."

"No," I protested, my tongue too thick in my mouth. I swallowed and tried again. "I want Mateo."

Carmen's angular, stunning features coalesced above me. Her full, red-painted lips were pursed in a frown.

"Caesar warned me you might be confused. You've been Ignazio's hostage for some time, and your father said you seemed to have developed a misguided attachment. I'd hoped he was misreading the situation. I don't want this to be difficult for you. I'm trying to help you."

Confusion sapped my already fogged brain, and I struggled to piece together what was happening. Carmen didn't seem to be threatening me. If this was some sort of misunderstanding, I could clear it up. And I would have to do so quickly, before Mateo went on a rampage to get to me. If Carmen truly didn't wish to harm me, I couldn't allow her to stand between me and Mateo. That wouldn't end well for her.

I could fix this. I just had to get my thoughts in order.

"How do you know my father?" I tried to puzzle out the connection. "Did he ask you to get me away from Mateo?"

"Yes," she confirmed, her dove gray eyes softening. "I've known for weeks that Ignazio was holding you hostage. I wanted to come for you sooner, but things were too tense. Caesar promised me that you would remain untouched as long as we stood down, and I didn't want you to suffer if things went sideways."

"Who are you?" I didn't understand why this stranger would care about my wellbeing or how she knew about the terms of my captivity.

"I'm Carmen Ronaldo. I'm going to be your sister-in-law." She reached out and covered my hand with hers, giving me a reassuring squeeze. "I'll keep you safe, Sofia. We're family now."

"No, wait." I pushed up onto my elbows, wincing when the world tilted. "You think you're helping me, but you're not. I don't know what my father has told you, but I want to be with Mateo. I don't want to marry Pedro Ronaldo. Daddy arranged the marriage without my consent. I didn't even know about it until Mateo told me."

"What?" Carmen demanded, her gentle demeanor honing to something sharp and forbidding.

Regaining some of my balance, I managed to sit upright and assess my surroundings. I was in an opulent, unfamiliar bedroom. Varied shades of blue contrasted elegantly with ivory, creating a sumptuous atmosphere. Two huge bay windows broke up the damask-patterned wallpaper, but the light that filled the room was cast by the crystal chandelier; it was dark outside, a crescent moon shining bright against the black night sky.

"Where am I?" Panic constricted my throat. I had an awful suspicion where I was, and what that would mean if Mateo tried to come get me. Things would get violent if I didn't talk my way out of this.

"This is our estate," Carmen replied briskly, her attention still fixed on my declaration that I didn't want to marry her brother. "We're close to the port of Lazaro Cardenas, which our family controls. Otherwise, we're isolated out here. The compound is completely secure."

My stomach grew heavy with dread as my worst suspicions were confirmed.

"You have to let me leave," I implored. "Mateo won't let you keep me here. He'll come for me, and a lot of people will die."

If Mateo was willing to conspire to kill Pedro to prevent me from marrying him, I shuddered to think what he might do to anyone who stood between us now.

"You're scared of him," Carmen surmised, her tense posture easing. "Don't worry. This place is a fortress. No one can hurt you here."

"I'm scared *for you*," I corrected her. "I'm not sure what my father has told you, but he refuses to accept that I don't want to marry Pedro. I never agreed to the marriage, and I never will. I love Mateo."

Carmen crossed her arms over her chest, her features pinched with uncertainty. After a few seconds of consideration, she shook her head, dismissing my assertions.

"You're young, and you've been in a distressing situation with Ignazio. Your perceptions are clouded by what he wants you to see, and whatever he told you was no more than a means to control you. I guarantee it.

"Love is a lie that men use to trap you and destroy you. I understand that you've been sheltered from the truth about our business dealings, so the concept of an arranged marriage might seem odd to you. But I promise that our family will provide for you and protect you. That's what matters. Love isn't real. Safety and stability are."

"You have to listen to me," I begged. "This will

not end well for you if you don't send me back to Mateo right now. Please, I—"

The bedroom door opened, and Daddy cut through my desperate plea. "*Princesa.*" He beamed, as though thrilled to see me after a long vacation. He walked toward me with open arms, seeking my embrace.

I scrambled back, getting to my feet and using the four-poster bed as a defensive barrier between us.

His jaw went slack, his bright green eyes clouding with hurt.

"What have you done, Daddy?" I demanded, a rush of rage clearing the last of the cobwebs from my mind.

"I coordinated your rescue, of course," he said, baffled by my reaction. "After Ignazio got violent with me at the wedding and dragged you away, I knew I had to save you from him. I've been working to arrange your extraction ever since. Adrián will be furious, but I couldn't leave my little girl with that animal. My good friend Pedro has agreed to help me push Adrián out of power. You'll be safe here from now on."

"Mateo didn't *drag me away*," I shot back, unable to wrap my mind around Daddy's delusion. "I asked him to take me home. He only pushed you out of the way because you'd cornered me and wouldn't listen to me when I told you I don't want to marry Pedro." I turned my attention on Carmen, reinforcing my assertion. "I don't want to marry your brother."

Daddy fixed me with his deepest, most disapproving frown. "You're acting very foolish, Sofia. It's past time I separated you from Ignazio. He's dangerous."

"Aren't you going to introduce me to my bride?" a new voice drawled.

A strange man stepped across the threshold, his cold gray eyes fixed on me. He was short in stature—maybe an inch taller than me—but he was broad, his bulk evident beneath his tailored slacks and blue dress shirt. His lips pressed together, all but disappearing beneath his thick, black mustache.

"Sofia, this is Pedro," Daddy said firmly. "The wedding is tomorrow. It's all been set up for your arrival."

"My *arrival?*" I choked. "More like abduction. I don't consent to any of this." I met Pedro Ronaldo squarely in the eye. If Daddy wouldn't listen, maybe this stranger would. "I don't want to marry you. I love Mateo."

"No, you don't!" Daddy barked, his face going red with rage.

My fists curled at my sides, my own fury riding me hard. "Denying it doesn't make it any less true," I hissed. "I love Mateo, and I won't marry anyone else. You can't make me."

Pedro scowled at Daddy. "You didn't tell me she was infatuated with Ignazio. You said he was holding her hostage."

"He was," Daddy insisted. "Sofia is just confused. She's an impressionable young girl, and she thinks the best of everyone."

"Not anymore," I seethed. "I definitely don't think highly of you, Daddy."

"You also told me she was respectful and meek," Pedro accused, his mounting anger fixed on my father, discussing my character traits as though I wasn't even in the room with them.

"*She* can speak for herself," I insisted. "Let me leave and get back to Mateo before he does something drastic. He's not going to allow you to keep me here."

Pedro sneered. "If Ignazio is foolish enough to try to attack me in my own home, he'll find that it's well-defended. He'll be dead before he can get anywhere near me. If he possesses more than two brain cells, he'll focus on protecting Adrián instead of coming here to die."

His icy eyes narrowed, pinning me in place. "This alliance between your father and me is a done deal. We're going to war. Caesar will take America from Adrián, while I eliminate Stefano Duarte here in Mexico. You will be an obedient wife and play your part without complaint. I didn't get to where I am today by tolerating insubordination."

My stomach turned, and I took a step back. Pedro didn't care if I consented to this marriage any more than Daddy did. My gut knew what he meant by *playing my part*, even if my brain didn't want to fully acknowledge the threat of rape.

"Pedro, we should talk about this," Carmen insisted, the flash of fear in her eyes belying her assertive posture. "Caesar lied to us about Sofia's willingness to marry you. What else isn't he telling us? We can't go to war without considering the risks."

"I've told you everything," Daddy countered, but he appeared shaken, too. He placed his hand on Pedro's shoulder, a friendly, reassuring gesture. "I didn't understand how badly Ignazio had warped my little girl. We should postpone the wedding until she's had a chance to calm down. She's not thinking straight."

"There's no point postponing it, because I will never agree to it." My declaration wavered with fear, but I had to stand my ground on this. Daddy seemed to realize that Pedro did not have my best interests at heart. My father might have betrayed me, but in his mind, he was doing all this for my own good. If I could get him on my side, he would protect me.

I lifted my chin and met Pedro's fierce scowl head-on. "I will never marry you. I love Mateo."

His icy blue glare turned on Daddy. "Maybe Carmen is right. What else have you been lying about, Caesar? Is my bride even a virgin?"

"Ignazio promised—"

"I'm not," I cut Daddy off. "Mateo makes love to me because I ask him to. Not because he bargained for the right to my body in some sick power negotiations. I will never give myself to any man who claims me in an illicit deal without my consent."

Pedro's frigid stare made my blood freeze in my veins. "I don't care about your consent. This marriage is happening. The wedding goes forward tomorrow as planned. Anything else would cause public embarrassment at this point. I'm not going to be a laughingstock because a silly woman has notions about romance. That's not how the world works. Your Daddy might have indulged you in the past, but I won't be humiliated just to spare your feelings."

"Now wait, Pedro," Daddy cajoled. He wiped sweat from his brow. "I won't let you talk to my little girl that way. You promised me she would be provided for and treated well."

"And you promised me a virgin," he shot back. "The terms have changed. You'd better pray this doesn't get out. If a rumor goes around that Ignazio deflowered my bride, I will find a way to vent my displeasure."

"I don't agree to these new terms." Daddy swelled

with fury, his protective instincts finally rising to defend me. "Our deal is off. I won't allow my daughter to marry a man like you."

Pedro moved faster than I could comprehend, and I caught a flash of silver just before Daddy bellowed in pain. Pedro got in his face, their chests nearly touching as my would-be fiancé snarled at my father.

Pedro stepped back abruptly, and Daddy dropped to the hardwood floor with an agonized yell. The blade at Pedro's side dripped crimson, and a matching shade bloomed on Daddy's white shirt.

I rushed to him, my scream echoing through the room. I dropped to my knees beside him, but my hands fluttered uselessly around his bleeding body.

"He'll live," Pedro announced, wiping the bloody blade on his slacks and returning it to the holster at his back. "If you agree to marry me without putting up a fuss. That way, I won't have to hurt you to make you cooperate, and Caesar can heal up to carry through his end of the bargain. I won't be made to look like a fool because of a woman's willfulness. You exist to serve my needs. Tell me you will cooperate, and I'll call for medical attention for your father. We can still salvage this deal."

Daddy struggled to push himself up, only to drop back to the floor with an agonized cry. He reached for me blindly, gripping my hand in his.

"I'm sorry, *princesa*," he rasped, his eyes shining with anguish.

"Daddy," I whispered brokenly, my heart shredding in my chest. Everything was happening too fast, and my brain was paralyzed by the horror of the events unfolding around me.

"This isn't what we talked about, Pedro," Carmen interjected, her voice edged with anxiety. "And it's not a sensible strategy. If Ignazio feels the same about her as she does about him, he will fight for her. You've seen what he's capable of. Do you want to invite that threat into our lives?"

I tore my eyes from the blood pooling beneath my father's body, so I could focus on my only ally in the room. Carmen was trying to reason with Pedro. Maybe she could help Daddy and me.

"If Ignazio tries to come for her, I'll put him down," Pedro declared. "And if he's not alive to guard Adrián Rodríguez, it'll be that much easier to take control of America."

He fixed her with a contemptuous glare. "I know your angle, and it won't work, Carmen. You have a soft spot for this girl, but I won't be manipulated. You stand beside me, or I'll find another way to make you useful."

Carmen's bronze cheeks paled, but she advanced on her brother, positioning her body as a shield between us. "I'm not going to allow you to force yourself on Sofia."

Pedro lashed out, swift and vicious. The sickening impact of his hand against her cheek cracked through the room, hitting her with enough force that she dropped, her body sprawled out next to my father's.

He towered over her, spittle flying from his lips as he vibrated with rage. "Miguel Armendariz would be a much more loyal dog if I gave you to him as a treat. He's been begging me to give you back to him for years. Is that what you want?"

Carmen gagged, and I wasn't certain if it was from the sickening injury he'd inflicted or from the stark terror invoked by his threat.

His attention riveted on me, his gray eyes glinting with malice. "Do you want to save your Daddy's life? Promise me you won't give me any trouble, and I'll get him the medical attention he needs to survive."

I nodded vigorously, the world blurring with my tears. No matter how Daddy had betrayed me, I couldn't let him die.

"I promise."

"Pedro..." Carmen groaned, struggling to get to her feet.

He shoved her away, sending her crashing back down.

"Call the doctor to see to Caesar," he commanded her coldly. "I need him well enough to walk her down the aisle tomorrow. Don't let him lose too much blood."

His fist caught in my curls, and he dragged me to my feet. I shrieked as I was pulled free from Daddy's weak grip on my hand.

Pedro jerked my head back, forcing me to stare up into his merciless, storm cloud eyes. "We're going to get to know each other better, my pretty bride," he threatened softly. "There's no point waiting for our wedding night, since Ignazio sent me damaged goods. You're going to prove to me that you can be my obedient wife."

Bile rose in the back of my throat, and I trembled in his cruel grip. "Please, I—"

He silenced me with a slap across my cheek, the shock of sound registering before the stinging pain.

"No more talking," he hissed. "I have other uses for your mouth."

He yanked on my curls, coercing me to follow where he led. My world blurred with horrified tears, and I heard Daddy wheezing my name as my future husband dragged me off to teach me my new wifely duties.

CHAPTER 24

MATEO

"Less growling, more breathing," Adrián ordered coldly. "You need to get your shit together, Mateo. We're almost there."

I hadn't breathed properly for hours. Ever since I'd realized Sofia had been taken from the venue where she was supposed to perform for the first time, I'd been suffocating. My impotent rage was all but debilitating, consuming me without an outlet. I was only functioning now because I'd been able to unleash my fury with a clear purpose back at Caesar's house.

That was where I'd gone to look for her first. I'd left a gory mess behind, slaughtering everyone who'd dared to guard the place. I finally extracted a confession from one of the dying men: Caesar had taken Sofia to Pedro Ronaldo's estate in Mexico.

Caesar's fancy mansion would be little more than a smoldering ruin by now. I'd torched the place where he'd tormented Sofia as a child. She would never go back there, and neither would he. Luckily for her mother, she was away on vacation. Otherwise, I might not have spared the bitch.

"Sofia won't be harmed," Adrián tried to reason with me for the dozenth time, his ice-cold clarity the only thing tying me to sanity. "If Caesar is with her, he'll make sure she's safe. Ronaldo has nothing to gain by hurting her. We will hit the perimeter hard and fast. No firepower on the house until we're inside and have eyes on the ground. Duarte's men will attack the southern defenses. Ronaldo doesn't have the manpower to stop all of us."

This full-scale assault was exactly what Adrián had tried to avoid by making our truce with Caesar regarding Sofia's virginity. The attack would be costly and bloody, but the relationship with Caesar was completely unsalvageable now that he'd brazenly stolen Sofia from me.

"She's not a virgin," I admitted to Adrián on a rasp, my fear for her eating me up inside. "What if Ronaldo finds out before I get to her?"

Adrián bit out a curse. "You'd better hope he doesn't."

We both knew the ugly truth: Sofia had far less value to him as a sullied bride. He might be keeping her comfortable right now if he still planned to marry her, but if he thought she didn't have to remain pure for their wedding night...

"Breathe," Adrián snapped. "Snarling like a feral animal isn't going to get Sofia out of this safely. You have to use your head, Mateo. Focus. We rendezvous with Duarte in thirty seconds, and then everyone gets into position. I need you lucid right now. I didn't come down to Mexico with you because I intend to die tonight."

Our slow progress made me want to tear this truck apart from the inside. Adrián's private jet had gotten us to a nearby airstrip, but we had to take a quieter approach down the winding dirt roads to reach Ronaldo's remote estate. I would have much preferred to drop straight onto his property with a chopper, but Adrián had called out my plan as idiotic the moment I voiced it.

He was right, of course. Sofia could get hit accidentally if I incited a firefight right on top of her.

Adrián was a better strategist than me on my best day, and with Sofia in danger, I was barely clinging to my humanity.

The truck came to a stop, and Adrián hopped out. I did the same, joining him in the thick darkness of the forest that surrounded our convoy.

Stefano Duarte's perfect grin flashed in the

truck's headlights. His black eyes flickered over my face and down my body.

"You look positively terrifying, Mateo," he approved, as though he was paying me a high compliment. "The blood of your enemies is a good look on you."

I flexed my fists, feeling the dried blood cracking around my knuckles. The strange tightness on my skin told me that my forearms and face were covered in gore, too.

Things had gotten messy back at Caesar's house.

"Cut the shit, Duarte," Adrián commanded. "This isn't a fucking dinner party."

Duarte's smile curved with malice. "I promise you I'm approaching this situation with deadly seriousness. But you can't blame me for feeling a little celebratory."

Adrián fixed him with a frigid stare. "After tonight, the debt between us is paid. Our relationship goes back to how it was before."

"Adrián, we've always been good friends, and we always will be," Duarte promised. "I look forward to this new era in our working relationship."

Duarte was about to seize control of all of Mexico, eliminating his rival Ronaldo so that his cartel was the sole organization trafficking our cocaine into the States. He was pulsing with excitable energy, like he'd just won the goddamn lottery.

Before I could throttle him for daring to find joy in Sofia's abduction, my phone buzzed in my pocket, startling me.

No one should be contacting me right now. Unless...

My phone was in my hand before I could fully process the decision to answer.

"Sofia," I rasped, hardly daring to accept that her contact details had indeed flashed on my screen.

"This is Carmen Ronaldo," a female voice responded. "Am I speaking with Mateo Ignazio?"

"I want to talk to Sofia," I demanded.

Adrián glared at me, mouthing: *hang up the phone.*

I ignored him, and he knew better than to try to physically wrest the phone away from me.

"Listen, I made a mistake, but I want to help," Carmen said quickly. "Caesar lied to me. I thought I was saving Sofia from you. But now I... You have to come get her. I'll help you do it."

"Put it on speaker," Adrián hissed.

I managed the presence of mind to comply. This conversation was taking a turn my addled brain couldn't follow, and I needed his clear head to sort out our next move.

"Why would you help me?" I asked, holding the phone in front of my chest, so Adrián and Duarte would be able to hear her response.

"Because I didn't know Sofia hadn't agreed to

marry my brother." Carmen's voice sounded through the silent woods.

I caught another flash of Duarte's white teeth as he recognized the caller's identity. Suddenly, I was grateful for his presence, too. If he could help me think through this, I could ensure Sofia's safety in the coming violence.

"I'm willing to help you get her out, but it can't be traced back to me," Carmen continued. "And I want your boss' word that I am acknowledged as the head of the Ronaldo Cartel in exchange for this favor. If you come to my estate, I'll let you inside. You, and no more than four others. Just enough to make it look like a surprise extraction and get Sofia out safely."

"Why would I trust you?" I ground out. "You could be inviting me into a trap. Why shouldn't I just destroy your entire organization to get Sofia back?"

"Because Pedro will use her against you if he realizes he's under siege," she countered. "He's...not being gentle with her."

A beastly roar ripped through the night, an animal sound of rage and pain. Adrián dared to grab my shoulders and shake me hard enough that I focused on his steady, pale green stare.

"You have my word," Adrián told her, agreeing to Carmen's terms and letting her know he was listening in. "You control the Ronaldo Cartel now, Carmen. Tell us how we can access your estate."

It took twelve agonizing minutes to get everything into position. If Carmen had been alarmed to learn that we were waiting just outside her gates to launch an assault by the time she called me, she hid her surprise from her tone.

Duarte seemed more excited than ever, his wide grin practically maniacal and plastered as a permanent fixture on his face. He'd come to some sort of arrangement with Adrián while we'd moved in on the estate, but I'd been too consumed by fear for Sofia to focus on what they were saying.

He's not being gentle with her.

Carmen's sickening admission played through my mind on a maddening loop, making my stomach churn. I tasted fresh blood in my mouth where I'd caught my cheek while gnashing my teeth.

Adrián risked touching me again, gripping my upper arm hard enough to harness my attention.

"When we get inside, Carmen will tell us how to get to Sofia. You go straight for her. I'll have your back, and so will the rest of the team." He jerked his chin in the direction of the two most dangerous killers in his employ, who rounded out our extraction team. "Duarte will deal with Carmen. After Sofia is safe with you, we burn this place to the ground. No one gets out alive," he swore, his panther's eyes glinting through the darkness. "Not after challenging me."

Caesar's brazen challenge for control of Adrián's territory wouldn't go unpunished. An example would be made tonight.

Right on time, a light flashed from atop the defensive wall that surrounded Ronaldo's estate. Our group moved through the night, swift and silent. As promised, Carmen had disabled the motion-sensor floodlights to enable our approach.

It seemed she'd been completely honest in her intentions. She was willing to betray her brother in exchange for control of the cartel.

She would live to regret that decision.

Just as we reached a reinforced steel door set into the defensive wall, it swung inward to admit us.

Carmen Ronaldo was a slender, lone silhouette in the threshold. I heard her sharp gasp the instant she saw my blood-streaked body barreling toward her. She made the mistake of changing her mind, trying to close the door to keep me out.

I slammed my weight against the metal, knocking her back with the force of my entry.

She stumbled and fell onto the grass lawn, and our team breached the defensive wall.

Before she could get her bearings or open her mouth to scream, Duarte was on top of her, capturing her wrists in one hand and pinning them into the dirt above her head. He pressed his palm over her ruby-painted lips, fully subjugating her.

Her striking gray eyes flew wide, and she struggled wildly beneath him. He leaned in to whisper in her ear, inhaling her scent like a lover.

"Quiet now, kitten," he purred. "You promised to help my friend Mateo, remember? Tell him where he can find Sofia, and this will all be over soon. I will leave your home, and you won't be harmed tonight."

"I gave you my word," Adrián reminded her, throwing out his arm in front of my chest to hold me back.

I hadn't realized I was advancing on Carmen, impatient to get the information I needed so I could rescue Sofia.

Carmen managed a small, shaky nod. Duarte hummed his approval at her capitulation, dropping a mocking kiss on the tip of her nose.

Her cheeks flushed with rage, but she didn't lash out when he released her and got to his feet. He offered a hand to help her up, but she scowled at him and scrambled upright without his assistance.

She turned sharply, as though exposing her back to Duarte went against all her survival instincts.

"This way," she urged, leading us toward the sprawling mansion, keeping to the shadows cast by the wall that surrounded the property.

We moved far too slowly and quietly, the pace

369

setting my teeth on edge. Adrián's death grip on my upper arm was the only thing tethering me to sanity, a bruising reminder that caution was necessary to ensure Sofia's safe extraction. If it weren't for my friend's punishing, supportive presence at my side, I would have gone out of my mind with feral rage hours ago.

Carmen unlocked a side door to the mansion, admitting us into her home. As we moved through the darkened rooms of the house that weren't currently in use, my pulse pounded through my brain, the hammering of my heart slamming through the silence around us.

When we reached the bottom of a stairwell, Carmen paused, keeping us hidden in the shadows.

"Security is lax this deep into the compound, so you should be able to navigate from here without me," she informed us in an undertone. "The extra manpower we do have posted now is only because of the heightened risks my brother took by allying himself with Caesar."

"And where is Caesar?" Adrián asked, his predator's eyes shining.

"Fighting for his life," she replied. "Pedro stabbed him and only offered medical assistance if Sofia agreed to marry him. Caesar is in our surgeon's care now. He's in the east wing of the house."

"If he lives through the night, he will regret it,"

Adrián vowed.

"Pedro's bedroom is on the third floor." Carmen signed her brother's death warrant. "There will be two guards in the hall. Others will come running if they hear a disturbance."

"Then it's a good thing they'll be distracted by an external assault," Adrián drawled. He offered Carmen a sardonic nod. "Enjoy being Queen of the Ashes."

"What?" she gasped as Duarte snatched his prize, clapping his hand over her mouth and pulling her close to murmur a dark secret in her ear.

"Let's go." Adrián finally released my arm, giving me permission to move freely.

Whatever restraint he'd helped me retain snapped, and I forgot about Carmen and Duarte. Guided by raw, possessive instinct, I ascended the stairs three at a time, closing the distance between me and Sofia.

The two guards in the hall didn't have time to raise their weapons before I flung them out of my way. If the blunt force of my fists didn't kill them, Adrián's knife would. Shots would start firing soon, but hopefully not before I got to Sofia.

I didn't intend to give Ronaldo a warning that I was coming for him. I wouldn't let him put her body between us in an attempt to save himself.

Her harsh sob obliterated my tenuous connection to rational human thought, possessive rage burning through my veins to sear away any civility I possessed. I slammed my shoulder into the door that separated me from her, and the wood splintered around the hinges.

I continued with my forward momentum, barreling straight into my enemy, the man who dared to touch what was mine.

I ripped Ronaldo away from her, lifting him off the bed and tackling him to the floor. He attempted to struggle beneath me, so I shattered his jaw with one brutal punch. His head snapped to the side, and blood sprayed from his lips, leaving dark drops on the polished wooden floorboards.

Sofia's soft shriek clawed for my attention. I wrapped my hand around Ronaldo's neck to keep him down, so I could turn away from him long enough to check on her safety.

Her emerald eyes were wide, her lush lips parted. Tears glistened on her cheeks, and her glossy curls were broken and tangled.

Her harrowed appearance would have been enough to stoke my ire, but my fury consumed me when I noted her shredded dress pooled around her willowy body, leaving her exposed in her sheer, white lace lingerie. She appeared more fragile than ever, shivering on the ivory sheets.

The knife Ronaldo had used to cut her clothes from her body lay on the mattress beside her.

A savage roar echoed through the room, but it ended abruptly in response to her soft whimper.

My attention fixed on her lovely, emerald eyes again. They were dark with horror, my sweet Sofia's mind overwhelmed by the violence she'd been subjected to.

Despite my incendiary fury, a sense of calm purpose settled over me. Protecting Sofia was the only thing in my world that mattered.

That meant shielding her from more bloody nightmares.

"Close your eyes, *florecita*," I commanded gently. "I'll make this quick."

My good girl did as she was told, trusting me to take care of her.

When I was certain she wouldn't witness what I planned to do to Ronaldo, I lifted my weight off him just long enough to grab the knife he'd used to cut away her clothes.

He moaned, but whatever protest or pleading he might have offered was garbled by his ruined jaw.

I wouldn't allow him to make any more sounds of distress that might disturb my sweet Sofia.

I slammed the blunt handle of the blade into the center of his throat, crushing the soft tissue that allowed him to speak and breathe. His gray eyes rolled with terror, and he reached between us to try to wrest the knife away from me. I gave him a few seconds to try, watching his panic cause his pupils to dilate as his weaker body gave way to my strength.

I slowly lowered the wicked tip of the blade to his solar plexus, allowing him to continue to push against me frantically. He jerked beneath me when the knife sank into his flesh, but I'd silenced him effectively, and the sound of his agony wouldn't haunt Sofia after we left this place.

Once the hilt of the blade kissed his torn flesh, I jerked the knife in a downward arc, shifting off him to allow his guts to spill onto the floor and not on me.

I didn't bother to wait to watch the light leave his eyes. He hadn't suffered nearly enough, but he was no longer a threat to Sofia.

I dropped the knife, pushed to my feet, and went to her. She lay curled up on her side, her eyes squeezed shut and her hands clapped tightly over her ears.

I reached for her, but I stopped short when I noted the crimson liquid glistening on my fists.

Fuck.

Moving quickly, I wiped my hands on the white sheets. The fresh blood smeared onto the expensive cotton, but the gore that had caked on earlier during my rampage through her father's house clung stubbornly to my skin.

I frowned down at my blood-soaked clothes. I

didn't want her to see me like this.

The first gunshots rang out, automatic weapons peppering the night with sharp reports. Sofia cringed, her delicate body shaking violently.

I didn't want her to see any of this.

Coming to a decision, I ripped at the white sheet, tearing off a strip of soft cotton. I pressed it against her eyes, and she jolted. I didn't flinch from my plan, wrapping the makeshift blindfold firmly around her head and urging her to drop her hands from her ears so I could tie it in place.

"Good girl," I approved when she didn't fight me. "I'm going to get you out of here."

I pressed a kiss against her tear-stained cheek, leaving a streak of blood behind. Irritated by the sight, I gently wiped it away, resolving to wash every inch of her as soon as I got her home.

I bundled her up in the rest of the ruined sheet, hiding her body that Ronaldo had so cruelly exposed.

Despite the horrors she'd faced tonight, Sofia tucked herself close to me. Her dainty fingers clutched at my bloody t-shirt, and I was relieved that I'd blindfolded her. I doubted she'd be clinging on so tight if she could see what she was holding onto.

As violence erupted around the perimeter, I rushed Sofia out of the mansion. This entire estate would be ashes by morning, but I intended to have her back home and in our bed before then.

CHAPTER 25

MATEO

Sofia had fallen asleep in my arms an hour ago, but I hadn't removed the blindfold. I didn't want to risk her waking up and seeing the blood that painted my body.

Some of it was smeared on her luminous skin, and the white sheet I'd wrapped her in had soaked up the crimson stains on my shirt where I'd held her against my chest.

I frowned at the sight. I didn't like it one bit, and I definitely didn't want to trouble her with the memory of it forever.

The SUV that Adrián had ordered to pick us up at the airport slowed to a stop in front of my house. Before I could shift Sofia to maneuver her out of the car, my phone buzzed in my pocket.

I fished it out to find a text from Adrián.

Caesar will survive. I've decided to let him live in the humiliation of exile. You're welcome.

I closed my eyes against a surge of emotion. A swell of rage told me I wanted Caesar dead even more fiercely than Adrián did.

But relief was stronger. Sofia would find it difficult if her father had been killed tonight. Even if the piece of shit was responsible for her trauma, she would struggle with his death.

She had complicated feelings surrounding her father, and she deserved as much time as she needed to sort through them all. If he died now, she might grieve him forever and never find any peace.

Thank you. I owe you one, boss. I texted my reply.

You owe me several. Remind me not to pay you for a few years.

I smiled and slipped my phone back into my pocket. Adrián didn't mean that. The vicious drug lord was a cold-hearted bastard, but he'd proven the depth of his loyalty to me tonight.

Retaliation against Caesar and Ronaldo had been inevitable, once Caesar had chosen to take Sofia and openly move against Adrián.

But my friend could have arranged a dozen different countermoves that didn't involve him personally aiding in an assault on enemy territory.

His decision to spare Caesar so that I could more

easily comfort Sofia was such a kind gesture that it almost humanized my sadistic boss.

Almost.

I'd also witnessed him having a lot of bloody fun at Ronaldo's estate. Another nightmare scene I was glad I'd hidden from Sofia.

She stirred in my arms as I shifted her, so I could get us both out of the SUV and into the house.

"We're home, *dulzura*," I murmured, shutting the front door behind us.

She reached up to remove the blindfold.

"No."

She responded instantly to my stern tone, her hand dropping to my chest instead.

I dropped a kiss on her forehead. "Good girl. I want to get us both cleaned up before we take that off."

"Okay," she agreed, turning her cheek into my bloodstained shirt. "Mateo?" she asked, hesitant. "Is Daddy... Is he safe?"

My arms stiffened around her, my anger at the mention of her father reflexive. I took a breath and forced myself to relax. She didn't need my anger right now.

"Caesar survived," I informed her. "Adrián is going to allow him to live in exile."

"What does that mean?"

"It means he won't be in LA. He is no longer part

of our organization, or any other like it. Where he ends up is his choice, as long as Adrián approves. He and your mother will be fine."

She was silent for a moment, absorbing the information. "That's good," she finally said. "I know Adrián didn't have to do that. And I...I don't want to see Daddy anytime soon, anyway."

"You never have to see him again, if you don't want to," I promised her.

I would prefer it that way, but she would have to work through this in her own time. It might take a few years for her to fully accept that Caesar was a fuck up of a father, but I wouldn't force that realization on her. My delicate little flower had suffered enough anguish on that motherfucker's account. I wouldn't allow him to inflict any more pain on her life, directly or indirectly.

We arrived in our master bathroom, and I carefully set her down onto her feet, holding her steady while I turned on the shower with one hand. As the water warmed, I gave her hip a little squeeze before releasing her.

"I'm getting rid of these clothes," I told her. "I'll burn them later, but for now, they're going in the laundry hamper. Don't look in there under any circumstances until I tell you it's been handled. Are we clear?"

"Clear," she agreed easily.

Sofia didn't want to see the evidence of her bloody ordeal, either. She'd chosen to be mine, and that meant she knew she was choosing a life in which the man she loved hurt people.

Sofia understood where I came from and why I lived this life. Even though she didn't like it, she accepted me for who I was.

That didn't mean she wanted to see all the gory evidence.

I quickly stripped out of my ruined clothes, tossing them in the laundry hamper to hide them from Sofia's sight.

Once I was naked, I unwound the white sheet I'd wrapped her in when I'd taken her from Ronaldo's estate. She still wore her white lace bra and panty set underneath. The lingerie was pure, completely untouched by a single drop of blood.

I removed the garments carefully, setting them on the sink counter. Later, I would fuck her while she wore them, re-staking my claim over what Ronaldo had tried to take from me.

Steam billowed from the shower stall by the time we were both bare. I grasped her waist and guided her into the spray, which cascaded from four separate showerheads. The cloth around her eyes soaked up water, but she didn't try to remove it. My good girl waited for me to finish a quick scrub-down of my body.

The soap suds on my hands turned pink, and I didn't stop scrubbing until the water circling the drain ran clear.

"I'm going to take off the blindfold now," I told her as I tugged at the knot.

I peeled the sodden cloth from her face and tossed it aside, so I could capture her face in both my hands and look into her eyes when she finally opened them.

She squinted and blinked, taking time to adjust to the light. When her emerald eyes focused on me, my lungs started working properly for the first time since I'd realized she'd been taken from me.

"*Florecita*," I sighed, rubbing my thumb over her petal-soft lips. "I was so worried about you."

Her lower lip quivered beneath my touch. "I was too," she whispered. "Is Ronaldo..."

"You don't have to worry about Ronaldo ever again," I promised, stroking her trembling body. "All of that is over now. Adrián still controls the Rodríguez Cartel's American territory, and your father is in exile. No one will ever threaten you again, Sofia. I'll protect you."

"I know you will." She leaned into me. "Does this mean I'm not your hostage anymore?"

I tucked a wet curl behind her ear. "You're still not allowed to try to run away," I replied, not at all joking.

I'd warned Sofia that there was no going back once she promised that she was mine, and I meant it. I couldn't let her go now any more than I could survive a bullet to the brain.

"I don't want to run away," she reassured me. "But I figure this means you'll have to go back to guarding Adrián now. I can go to my classes on my own."

She pouted slightly around the words. Sofia didn't want to be free of me at all.

I smiled down at her. "I'll see if I can negotiate cutting my hours back for Adrián. He was already threatening to withhold pay, so I'll play hardball."

"Good. I know you can't be with me all the time, but I don't want you to be with Adrián every day, either."

She wrapped her small hand around the back of my neck, pulling me toward her to whisper low in my ear. "You're *mine*, Mateo."

She sealed her claim with a fierce, possessive kiss. Sofia owned me, body and soul, and I reveled in my captivity.

EPILOGUE

Sofia

Five Days Later

"I got you a present, *florecita*," Mateo murmured in my ear, dropping a doting kiss on my neck.

I flushed with pleasure and tilted my head to the side, welcoming more. "You didn't have to get me anything," I protested, even though excitement fizzed through my veins. "You've gotten me too many presents already."

"I don't want to hear you say that ever again," he rebuked, nipping at my shoulder. "I like buying you presents, and you like receiving them. From now on, you accept what I give you, and you will accept that you deserve it. Buying you pretty things makes me happy." His fingers sank into my hair, tugging my head back, so I was trapped beneath his stern, black stare. "And you want to please me, don't you, *dulzura*?"

"Yes," I agreed on a sigh, relieved to let go of the slight tension that gripped my body. Mateo wouldn't take my presents away if I disappointed him. He just wanted me to be happy.

I wanted him to be happy, too.

"Good girl." His low praise rumbled against my lips before he claimed them in a tender kiss, rewarding me for my acquiescence.

"Come," he urged when he finally allowed me space to breathe. "Your present is outside. It was delivered while you were practicing."

He took my hand, guiding me away from my piano, where I'd been working on new song arrangements. Mateo had rescheduled my gig, and I wanted to prepare for my performance next weekend.

He'd sworn he wouldn't leave my side until I stepped on stage. I suspected he'd never let me out of his sight again, if that were an option.

But he was deeply loyal to Adrián, especially after his friend had helped him rescue me. Mateo would have to go back to his duties guarding his boss tomorrow. Neither of us was looking forward to being separated, not even while I was on campus for the day.

I followed where he led, walking through our house toward the front door.

Our house.

All notions of returning to my apartment had been forgotten; my home was with Mateo now. He'd already started talking about buying a bigger place for us, but I'd dismissed the idea. Four thousand square feet was already way more space than two people could possibly need. And I wanted to stay in the house where Mateo and I had fallen in love. I wasn't going anywhere.

He opened the front door for me, ushering me outside. A sleek, white Audi was parked in the driveway, with a huge red bow on the hood.

"It's an automatic," he told me on a low chuckle, ruffling my hair. "Until I can teach you to drive stick, you can take this to campus. But we're going to the track next weekend for your first lesson."

"Thank you!" I flung my arms around him, squeezing him tight to convey my gratitude. "If you teach me to drive stick, does that mean I'll get to drive the Batmobile?" I asked, giggling.

"Maybe one day," he mused. His grin hit me square in the chest, his pure joy knocking the air from my lungs. "If you're very good for me and take your lessons seriously."

I pressed myself closer to his big body, rubbing up against him like a needy kitten. "You know I'll be good for you. I promise."

He hummed his approval, the sound thrumming low in my belly. I shivered in his arms, my nipples pebbling to tight peaks.

"Can I take the Audi for a test drive?" I asked, not putting an inch of space between us. I didn't really want to let him go yet, but I loved my present, and he needed to know how excited I was to receive it.

"Later," he promised, his voice dropping low and rough. "There's something else I need to do with you first."

His huge hands bracketed my waist, and the world tilted in a way that was becoming thrillingly familiar. I let out a happy sigh, relaxing over Mateo's shoulder as he carried me back into the house. He cupped my ass, caressing what was his.

I would never tire of his possessive behavior. Picking me up and carrying me wherever he wanted seemed to have developed into a compulsion for him, as though it brought him deep satisfaction to have me in his arms and thoroughly under his control.

I loved it, too.

When we reached our bed, he set me down on my feet, catching me up in a fierce kiss that stole my breath and captivated all my senses. He began stripping me at his leisure, unzipping my dress and deftly unhooking my bra at my back.

I fumbled at his clothes, my efforts to get him naked considerably less smooth. My fingers shook with a rush of heady anticipation, and I jerked at his cotton t-shirt and jeans.

I was fully bared before he was, and his low laugh rumbled into my mouth as he helped me finish removing his clothes.

Raw hunger overwhelmed my brain, and I started licking at the stark, swirling lines of the tattoo that covered his right pec. I pressed a kiss just over his heart, feeling the strong, steady beat beneath my lips. I lavished extra, special attention upon my mark; the delicate flower tattoo he'd ordered designed just for me.

I relished seeing my possessive brand inked into his skin. Mateo had made me *his*, but he was mine, too.

He cradled the back of my head, inhaling deeply as he held me in place for a few seconds longer, reveling in the feel of me worshipping his body with my mouth.

I shifted, preparing to drop to my knees so that I could worship him more thoroughly. His fist caught in my hair before I could ease down his rippling abs.

"Not now, *dulzura*." His voice took on the slow,

almost drunk quality that let me know he was just as intoxicated by me as I was by him.

He bracketed my hips, turning my body so that I was facing away from him.

My gut knotted when I saw what he'd laid out on the bed: the set of white, lacy lingerie I'd been wearing when Pedro had abducted me.

I shuddered and pressed back against Mateo, leaning on him for support.

His palm settled at the front of my throat, his thumb stroking the line of my artery in a soothing rhythm.

"I want you to wear this for me," he rumbled, nuzzling my hair.

"Why?" I asked, my voice small. Just looking at the scraps of lace made my stomach turn. I felt the phantom scrape of Pedro's knife against my skin as he cut away my dress, laying me bare for his lascivious gaze. A chill raced over my skin, and sweat beaded on the back of my neck.

"I need to see you wearing it while I fuck you," he responded, the words roughened by his own memories of that awful night. His fingers flexed around my neck. "You're *mine*."

I reached up and pressed my hand atop his, welcoming his hold on my neck. "Yes," I promised. "I'm yours."

"I'm going to make the nightmares stop," he

vowed, petting me with his free hand, rubbing his warmth all over my pebbled flesh.

I trembled and pressed deeper into him. He'd woken me up from the grips of three nightmares since he'd rescued me from Pedro. I was blissfully happy with Mateo, but I was still deeply disturbed by what had happened on the Ronaldo family's estate.

"I don't know..." I whispered, eyeing the pure, clean lingerie with trepidation. I worried that putting it on would take me right back to that horrific place.

"Trust me," he cajoled, palming my breasts.

Despite my fear, my body reacted to him, my nipples aching as he tweaked them and toyed with me, drawing out my arousal with a practiced hand.

"I do." I released a shaky breath, melting into him. "Always."

He continued to play with me, lavishing me with praise and affection. He retrieved the lingerie from the bed and eased it onto my body, all the while telling me how proud he was.

By the time the white lace covered my breasts and pussy, most of the chill had faded from my flesh. I snuggled as close to my huge protector as possible, seeking his heat and strength.

As soon as I relaxed into his hold, his demeanor shifted. The gentle giant who had caressed me with such tender care was suddenly replaced by the ruthless, demanding lover who reveled in tormenting my body for his pleasure, pushing my limits and delighting in my submission to his most deviant demands.

I gasped when his fingers sank into my waist, and he pinned me down on the bed, settling his massive weight over my much smaller frame.

Fear flickered through my mind, even as a rush of slick arousal soaked my panties. He'd conditioned me to respond to his aggression with lust, and my body helplessly surrendered to his harsh treatment.

"You belong to me, Sofia," he growled, his black eyes glinting with the same feral light I'd glimpsed when he'd torn Pedro off my body. He'd been terrifying to behold on that night, my personal dark god transformed into a vengeful demon.

Now, the beast was hungry to stake his claim, to erase the taint of Ronaldo's violation. Even though this wild, brutal side of the man I loved caused my belly to quiver with fear, I recognized that he needed to symbolically declare his ownership of my body.

Maybe I wasn't the only one who'd been having nightmares about Pedro's hands on me.

Mateo pinched my nipples, commanding my full attention. The flimsy lace barrier of my bra abraded my tender buds. "No one else touches you," he snarled. "Only me."

He pinched my clit hard, sending a shockwave of pleasure and pain through my body. I shrieked out his name, bucking beneath him. More of his weight fell on me, trapping me for his branding touch.

"Tell me," he demanded. "You're mine."

"I'm yours, Mateo," I swore on a harsh cry. "I'm yours."

He lowered his mouth to my bra, catching the lacy material in his teeth. He ripped at the delicate fabric like a wild, ravenous animal, tearing the flimsy barrier that separated his hands from my most vulnerable flesh.

He kissed and nipped his way down my belly, destroying my panties with the same savagery. As he ripped away the lingerie, I felt the oppressive, lingering horror from the night of my abduction being torn from my psyche. My vicious, possessive protector would never allow anyone to take me from him. He would never allow anyone to hurt me.

His hot tongue lapped at my arousal-soaked folds, his rumble of approval vibrating against my swollen pussy lips.

I cried out at the shock of pleasure, and my fingers tangled in his hair to draw him closer to my aching core.

He grabbed my wrists, settling his body atop mine and pinning my arms above my head with one of his massive hands.

"*Mine!*" he ground out, driving his huge cock into my tight channel in one swift, brutal thrust.

I choked on a sob at the sudden, shocking claim. My inner muscles clenched around him, rippling with little twinges of pain at the rough penetration.

He played with my nipples, mercilessly pinching and tugging, tormenting me in the way I liked best. A fresh wash of arousal eased his jarring thrusts, and my sex relaxed to accommodate his demanding rhythm.

"Good girl," he praised, his voice gravelly with dark pleasure. "Take all of me. Take everything I give you."

I whimpered, writhing beneath him. The burning discomfort in my pussy morphed into white-hot pleasure as his cockhead dragged against my g-spot over and over again, driving me toward bliss with ruthless intent.

I could feel him inside me, skin-to-skin. He'd never taken me without a condom before, but I'd recently gotten the birth control shot. It seemed he didn't want to wait another day to lay claim to me fully.

"I'm going to mark you deep inside." His words were rough, his black eyes sparkling with maddened desire. "And you're going to come when I do."

"Yes," I gasped, rocking my hips to meet his punishing thrusts. I craved everything he offered: the pleasure, the possession. "Please…"

His fingers tightened around my wrists, and he

tormented my nipples as he slammed into me with enough force to rock my entire body.

Pleasure gathered at my core, all my muscles drawing tight in anticipation of ecstatic release. My inner walls squeezed his rock-hard shaft, drawing out his orgasm.

He threw his head back on a roar, his teeth flashing like a triumphant predator. His hot seed lashed inside me, filling me up and branding me as his.

His release triggered my own, and stars burst across my vision as I screamed out his name. His cruel lips crashed down on mine, tasting my absolute surrender. He rode me through my orgasm, both of us greedy to prolong our mutual pleasure.

When he'd released every last drop of his cum inside me, he kept his cock buried deep. He shuddered as the aftershocks of my orgasm caused my inner walls to dance around his shaft, but he didn't withdraw from me.

His kiss softened, the gentle, doting man returning to praise me and tell me how perfect I was. Although I loved when he treated me like this, the vicious, demanding side of him didn't scare me anymore. Mateo possessed the capacity for ruthlessness and brutality, but that didn't make me love him any less. He was my fierce protector as well as my tender boyfriend.

Well, *boyfriend* would never be a suitable term for Mateo, even though that's how I referred to him around my college friends now.

We belonged to each other, our bond essential and irrevocable. Mateo was mine, and I was his. I wouldn't have it any other way.

The End

ALSO BY JULIA SYKES

The Captive Series

Sweet Captivity

Claiming My Sweet Captive

Stealing Beauty

Captive Ever After

Pretty Hostage

Wicked King

Ruthless Savior

Eternally His

The Impossible Series

Impossible

Savior

Rogue

Knight

Mentor

Master

King

A Decadent Christmas (An Impossible Series Christmas Special)

Czar

Crusader

Prey (An Impossible Series Short Story)

Highlander

Decadent Knights (An Impossible Series Short Story)

Centurion

Dex

Hero

Wedding Knight (An Impossible Series Short Story)

Valentines at Dusk (An Impossible Series Short Story)

Nice & Naughty (An Impossible Series Christmas Special)

Dark Lessons

Mafia Ménage Trilogy

Mafia Captive

The Daddy and The Dom

Theirs to Protect

RENEGADE: The Complete Series

The Dark Grove Plantation Series

Holden

Brandon

Damien

Printed in Great Britain
by Amazon